THE HANGING CAPTAIN
by Henry Wade

"One of Wade's triumphs.... Admirably detailed treatment of clues."
— Jacques Barzun and Wendell Hertig Taylor,
A Catalogue of Crime

"One of the greatest English writers of detective stories."
— *Times Literary Supplement*

"You can be sure of Henry Wade."
— *Manchester Guardian*

Henry Wade

The Hanging Captain

PERENNIAL LIBRARY
Harper & Row, Publishers
New York, Cambridge, Philadelphia, San Francisco
London, Mexico City, São Paulo, Sydney

CONTENTS

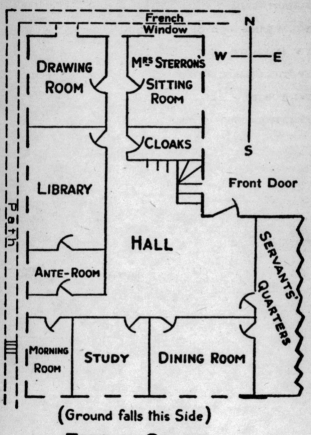

DRAWING ROOM

MRS STERRON'S SITTING ROOM

French Window

N
W — E
S

CLOAKS

Front Door

LIBRARY

HALL

SERVANTS' QUARTERS

ANTE-ROOM

Path

MORNING ROOM

STUDY

DINING ROOM

(Ground falls this Side)

FERRIS COURT

THE HANGING CAPTAIN

I. THE FORTUNATE DRAGOON

A HANDSOME couple, don't you think?"

Sir James Hamsted appeared to give the matter careful consideration before replying solemnly:

"They are, indeed. Mrs. Sterron, if I may be allowed to say so, possesses a genuine beauty which one sees too seldom in these days. Your brother is indeed a fortunate man."

Gerald Sterron smiled. His companion was a casual visitor, otherwise he might have hesitated before venturing upon that particular assertion.

The two men were standing upon a sloping lawn which ran down to the grass tennis-court on which a man and woman, unconscious of the admiration they had evoked, were engaged in a hard-fought game, in which skill was nicely tempered with recklessness. Base-line rallies of immaculate length generally ended in one or other of the players trying to hit the cover off the ball and sending it crashing into the net-cord or soaring over the stop-nets at the end into the shrubbery beyond. The latter was generally the fate of Griselda Sterron's attempted "winners," whilst her opponent's tactful efforts to prolong the set generally found a more controlled ending in the center.

"Oh, heavens, there goes another! Gerald, would you be a dear?"

Griselda's laugh was infectious and, though her brother-in-law might have been regarded as immune from

3

the attraction of her flushed face, there was a smile of
genuine pleasure on his own as he pursued the soaring
Slazenger into a clump of tangled weigela.

His companion, Sir James Hamsted, too old and stiff
now to take part in either game or pursuit, remained
watching the flying figures of the players, as they dashed
from side to side of the court or darted up to the net for
the final smash. They were certainly an attractive pair
to watch: Griselda Sterron, tall, well made, graceful as
a professional dancer, her short chestnut hair curling
back from a high forehead to cling lovingly round the
slender nape of a neck now delicately flushed, brown
eyes flashing with joy of the game, red lips slightly
parted over even white teeth, arms, bare to the shoulder, dazzlingly lovely against the apple-green of her
tennis frock, was a picture fair enough to hold the eye
of any man; it was impossible to believe, now, that she
was in her fortieth year, though when Sir James had
first seen her on the previous evening he had thought
her ill and tired. Then the disparity between her age
and her husband's had not been too apparent; now it
must have been very noticeable if Herbert Sterron had
been present.

But it was not with her husband that Griselda was
playing. Her opponent, hardly less striking in appearance than herself, was a tall, broad-shouldered man of
forty-five. Black hair, close-cropped to hide a natural
curl, framed a face of striking character. The short, bat-
tered nose of the fighter was in itself anything but beautiful, but taken with the square jaw, the straight brows,
and the hard, blue eyes, it formed a picture of manly
attraction that women had found difficult to resist. And
opportunities of resistance had not been infrequent.

"Quick on his feet for his size, isn't he?" said Gerald Sterron, returned, somewhat disheveled, from his successful search.

"Who exactly is he?"

"Carle Venning; Sir Carle Venning to be up to date; he only succeeded last year."

"A neighbor?"

"He is now. He's been everybody's neighbor in his time—a rolling stone, if ever there was one. But he's rolled to some purpose—left his mark wherever he went."

"He sounds a young man of character."

Sir James's prim phrases were in keeping with his appearance.

"Oh, yes, plenty of character," returned Sterron. "He's had every chance to develop it. He was at some public school, but his father, who was a bit of a character himself, took him away early because he thought he was getting stereotyped and sent him round the world—on his own legs, not with a Cook's courier. He crossed the Atlantic before the mast, I believe, sold papers in Chicago, got smashed up by a bronch in the West, found his way to Australia and dug for gold, made a small fortune before he was twenty-five and was robbed of it in a night on his way down to the coast. Then the War came and he stowed away on some boat to get back to England, got held up at Suez but managed to tack on to Lawrence, quarreled with him and made his way through Persia into Georgia, where the Reds caught him and tried three times to shoot him. He escaped each time and eventually joined Kolchak or Denikin—I forget which—and commanded a crowd of international scalliwags, soldiers of fortune like himself. When Kolchak failed he disappeared but turned up a year later in London. Nobody knows to this day what he did in that year, but he's led a comparatively quiet life since then, hunting big game in different parts of the world."

"It seems curious to find such a man in your quiet part of the English countryside," said Sir James.

"Oh, he's still hunting," replied Sterron with a short laugh.

Sir James threw a quick glance at his companion, but remained silent.

"The joke is," continued Sterron, "they've taken the opportunity of his coming home on his father's death to make him High Sheriff of the county! A sense of humor that one hardly expects from the county bumpkins."

Sir James raised his eyebrows.

"County bumpkins? The expression is strange to me."

Sterron shrugged his shoulders.

"A combination of county big-wig and country bumpkin, I suppose. Much the same thing, anyhow."

"You are not yourself a—county bumpkin?"

"I? Oh, no, far from it. I'm a merchant—or was till a year or two ago. Shanghai. But I saw what was coming just before the others did and sold out while there was still something to sell—and Americans with dollars to buy it."

"But you live in England now? In town, perhaps?"

"No, small house at Hindhead—next door to L.G., nearly. We aren't either of us bumpkins—whatever else we may be."

Sterron laughed, but his companion appeared unamused.

"But this appointment of Sir Carle Venning's," he

persisted. "Why do you describe it as a joke? The office, surely, is a sinecure. Some money and two or three Assizes a year?"

"Yes, but nominally responsible for the administration of law and order! A man like that!"

"Is he disorderly? A law-breaker?"

Sterron opened his mouth to reply, but paused. After a time he went on:

"I don't know the details of his career sufficiently well to say, but he is certainly without fear and—I suspect—without scruple. What he wants he will get."

Sir James nodded.

"Yes, his physiognomy suggests that," he replied.

The set had ended and the two players, talking eagerly and intimately, strolled across to a bench beside which was a table with a tray of iced drinks. Sir James Hamsted, feeling perhaps that, while a game might be watched, a *tête-à-tête* conversation might not, turned away up the lawn towards the carriage drive.

"I have some letters to post," he said. "I will stroll down to the village."

"The box in the hall is cleared in time for the next post," said Sterron.

"A walk will be not unwelcome; the afternoon is cooler now."

With an imperceptible shrug Gerald Sterron let him go; the man, however distinguished his career, was an old-fashioned bore. He himself lit a cigarette and strolled up the garden towards the house. As he walked, his mind followed a chain of thought which had been started by his late companion's remark about his brother's good fortune. It was, perhaps, a natural, if rather rash, assumption. To be the husband of so lovely a creature as Griselda and the owner of the historic Ferris Court were foundations enough upon which to build a fairy-tale of good fortune.

Twenty years ago there was no one in his world who would not have envied young Herbert Sterron. At the age of thirty-three, the dashing Dragoon captain, rich, popular, already the owner of Ferris, but well launched on a successful military career, had captured beautiful Griselda Hewth in the height of her first, victorious London season, sweeping her away from under the guns of rival dukes and diamond merchants. For three years the young couple—for Herbert Sterron was still young, though fifteen years older than his wife—had followed in the full tide of pre-War social life, ideally happy, popular, with all the world before them. Then suddenly he had resigned his commission, carried Griselda off to Ferris and buried himself and her in the inaccessible country in which his family home lay. There were rumors of illness, of money troubles, even of marital quarrels, but nobody knew anything—only that the pair had disappeared. The one known cause of possible unhappiness was their childlessness (in those days people expected and wished to have children), but this seemed hardly reason enough for voluntary banishment.

The War came and Herbert Sterron rejoined his regiment, but almost before his old comrades had had time to notice the change in him he had been passed unfit for active service and drafted to a remount depot on the French coast. There or thereabouts he had remained until the Armistice sent him back to Ferris Court—and his young wife. For Griselda had remained with him through whatever tribulations had caused his disappearance from their world, though after the War it soon became apparent to their old friends that she remained with him on principle rather than by inclination. For, though she had not lost her beauty, Griselda was a changed woman; her friendships and affections had taken on an unstable—almost a fickle—quality, while her natural high spirits had developed into something very like hysteria.

Until two years ago, Gerald Sterron had hardly seen his brother and sister-in-law since their marriage. His business, prosperous until after the War, had kept him closely tied to China and, owing to the prior claims of the senior partner, his share in that conflict had been limited to a nominal defense of the Shanghai Bund. Their letters had been few and guarded, so that it had been a severe shock to him, when he had returned to England two years previously, to find his brother (senior by little more than a year) an old and haggard man, sullen in spirit, violent in temper, and utterly changed from the care-free, high-spirited dragoon whom he had seen marry lovely Griselda Hewth.

As for Ferris Court, the Tudor home of twelve generations of Sterrons, that second pillar upon which the good fortune of Herbert Sterron had appeared to rest, a glance at the garden was sufficient hint of the shadow which overhung the fine old house. Weed-encumbered beds and paths, untrimmed edges, overgrown shrubberies, told their tale of straitened means—or neglect sprung from a broken spirit.

His mind, full of memories of his childhood, when these lawns and flowerbeds were weedless and immaculate, when sleek gardeners jostled each other at every turn and glasshouses gave forth their rich crops of fruit in season and out, Gerald walked disconsolately along the reproachful paths. The garden had been laid out in terraces, cleverly divided by borders of flowering shrubs which yet disclosed vistas of view from end to end. Now the shrubs had shot up in search of a sun which the crowding of their neighbors denied them, so that each part of the garden was shut completely from the rest—except at one spot on a higher terrace from which a view of the tennis-court below was still obtainable, and here Gerald Sterron found his brother.

Herbert Sterron had always been a big man, perfect specimen of a Heavy Dragoon; now, the muscle which had kept him fit and active had changed to fat, his shoulders drooped, the flesh of his face hung in pouches from eyes and jowl. He still wore the pre-War cavalry-man's heavy mustache, but it failed to hide the deep lines which dragged down the corners of his mouth and gave his once handsome face a morose expression. Just now, when his brother joined him, there was a flash of anger in his dark eyes that rather improved than marred his appearance.

Captain Sterron was standing on the neglected ter-race, looking down through a gap in the shrubs at the figures of his wife and her companion, sitting on the small bench in intimate conversation. He hardly noticed his brother's approach.

"Shrubberies want thinning out a bit, Herbert," said Gerald, brushing from his gray flannel trousers some traces of his late explorations.

Herbert shot his brother a quick look, then turned his eyes back to the court as if a magnet were drawing them.

"Damned swash-buckler!" he muttered angrily.

The object and the intensity of his feelings were too obvious to be ignored, even if Gerald had felt inclined to be tactful.

"Venning? Fine figure of a man, isn't he?"

"Fine . . . ! My God, he'll look fine before I've finished with him!"

Gerald laughed.

"I should leave him alone if I were you," he said. "He'd break you up in about thirty seconds."

Herbert Sterron turned his gaze back upon his brother, a crafty gleam replacing, and not improving, the previous look of anger.

"Oh, I shan't play into his hands," he said. "I'll break him without touching him!"

Gerald carefully filled and lit his pipe, watching the expressions on his brother's face with detached interest as he did so.

"Very laudable—perhaps desirable. But how are you going to set about it?"

Herbert eyed his brother cautiously, as if balancing the pros and cons of confidence; apparently the pros had it, aided, no doubt, by the natural pride of creation.

"Two ways," he said; "either would do, but one might suit me better than the other."

"Let's hear it then." Gerald stifled a yawn—perhaps a tactical yawn.

"Divorce! He's trying to become respectable—county gentleman, High Sheriff, perhaps Lord Lieutenant some day. Divorce'll smash all that!"

"It certainly would, but . . ."

Herbert Sterron broke in, not listening to him:

"He'd have to marry her. He likes her hanging round his neck for an hour or two now, I don't doubt, but how'll he like it for a lifetime, eh? How'll he like that?"

His brother eyed him distastefully.

"It's difficult to believe you were once an officer and . . . a gentleman, Herbert," he said coolly. "In any case, you'll never divorce her. You couldn't live here alone and you wouldn't get any other woman to marry you, let alone live with you."

Herbert flinched as if his brother had struck him. His face whitened, but the color quickly flooded back into it.

"Wouldn't I?" he exclaimed. "Wouldn't I? You wait. I . . ." he broke off, as if he regretted having said so much.

"And what's your alternative plan?" asked Gerald. "A bit more effective than the other, I hope."

A grin of almost malignant enjoyment spread over Herbert Sterron's lined face.

"So effective that I might positively not enjoy it myself," he said, then turned on his heel and slouched away.

Gerald Sterron watched his brother's retreating form till it disappeared round a corner, then turned himself and strolled towards the house, frowning as if in disapproval of the malicious imaginings to which he had been treated. Almost mechanically he mounted the shallow stone steps of each familiar terrace and picked his way through the rose garden towards the side door of the old house. In the dark passage—dark by contrast with the sun outside—he almost collided with a young woman carrying a handful of papers.

"Oh, Mr. Sterron, I'm so sorry!" exclaimed the girl,

"I'm trying to find Captain Sterron to sign some letters before the post goes."

"He went towards the west walk; you'll probably find him in the pigeon house, Miss Nawten."

"Thank you so much. I must fly if I'm to get these done in time."

The girl—she was barely thirty—flew, with a grace of movement that even the unsusceptible Shanghai merchant could not fail to notice.

For a moment Gerald watched her with an unconscious smile, but the pleasure soon faded from his expression, leaving his face set in a frown of concentrated thought. Crossing the hall he entered the library, a long room which occupied a large part of the west wing of Ferris. Although faded and cracked the quiet, green paint with which the room was decorated had a restful effect upon the eye—especially on such a glaring day as this; the handsome bookcases, too, filled with their treasures in dull brown and faded gold, were well calculated to have a soothing effect upon a troubled mind. Gerald Sterron, however, appeared immune from these influences; he wandered restlessly from bookcase to bookcase, took out a volume or two, pushed them back into place, flung himself into a chair and picked up a newspaper which lay on the floor beside it. For a time he appeared to read, then the paper subsided gradually into his lap, while his eyes remained fixed steadily on the door straight in front of him.

For a long time there was silence in the room, then a bumble-bee blundered in at the open window and, after a noisy circuit, tried to go out again, but only succeeded in banging himself heavily against all the windows that were closed. The sound seemed to disturb

Gerald's train of thought; he frowned, dragged himself out of his chair, captured and released the intruder, and went out again into the hall. Here there was even more complete silence than in the library, a silence with a peculiar quality of depression rather than of peace. Standing in the middle of the hall, Gerald looked about him, as if in search of occupation or companion, took a step or two towards the door of the study, changed his mind and mounted slowly to his bedroom on the first floor. Here he seemed no better at ease but wandered aimlessly about the room, fiddling with first one thing and then another, lighting a cigarette and throwing it out of the window. Then, his attention attracted by something outside, he picked up a pair of field-glasses that lay on the sill and leveled them at a square brick building that peeped from among the trees at the far end of the large garden. For more than a minute he gazed, then lowered the glasses slowly to their former resting-place. His face was almost expressionless, save that the mouth pursed into a silent whistle.

"So that's where the wind lies," he murmured.

II. AFTER DINNER

WHEN he saw his hostess again at dinner, Sir James Hamsted was once more struck by the change in her appearance. The flush and sparkle of the afternoon had given place to pallor and an expression of weary boredom. Perhaps the vigor and speed of the game had been too great; the body no longer equal to the demands of the spirit—Mrs. Sterron was, after all, no longer a young woman. In these days of rush and worry people exhausted themselves easily; they had no reserves of strength to fall back upon. It was regrettable, thought Sir James, to see that lovely face marred by lines of fatigue, though the brown eyes seemed even larger by reason of the dark shadows beneath them.

Mrs. Sterron's clothes, too, had changed their character. The sleeveless, apple-green tennis frock had given place to a high, black evening dress of almost nun-like simplicity. A fichu of old lace at the neck alone relieved the somber effect, though Sir James was struck by the beauty of the slim white hands emerging from the close-fitting sleeves. Even her hair seemed changed, for Mrs. Sterron had pressed the chestnut curls closely against her head with a fillet of black velvet. Her lips seemed colorless by comparison with the afternoon, though a woman would have realized that a stick of lighter shade had emphasized the beauty of their shape.

But there was no other woman present in the dining-room at Ferris Court and Sir James Hamsted alone

seemed conscious of the change, though once he caught
Herbert Sterron looking at his wife with a half-smile
that was uncomfortably suggestive of a sneer. Conversation took the form of reminiscences exchanged between
Sir James and Gerald Sterron, chiefly on the subject
of commerce and diplomacy in the East. Gerald Sterron,
though his style was dry and unemotional, talked well;
this was his subject and he did not often get the chance
to ventilate it; Sir James Hamsted, though speaking as
an observer rather than an expert, evidently knew what
he was talking about and had formed opinions of his
own on the subject. Probably, thought Gerald—who
knew nothing about his fellow-guest—Sir James was the
sort of man who read extensively, talked freely with
members of clubs like the Athenæum and the Royal,
and was prepared to lay down the law on any topic from
the depth of an armchair. It was a useful accomplish-
ment, at least on an occasion like the present, for Captain Sterron was silent and morose, and his wife, though
a conscientious hostess, became *distraite* as soon as her
guests were comfortably launched upon their discussion.

Dessert had hardly been put upon the table when
Mrs. Sterron rose. She smiled at Sir James, who opened
the door for her, and held out a slender hand.

"I will say good night, Sir James, if you will excuse
me," she said. "I have a couple of long letters to write,
and then I shall go to bed with a book. A solitary woman
is an encumbrance, I know, among a number of men."

Sir James tried to murmur an adequate denial, but
his hostess passed on into the hall without waiting for
him to frame his words.

The three men sat on for a time, talking and enjoying the fine port which the Ferris Court cellars could

still produce. At least, two of them enjoyed it; Herbert Sterron had touched no wine during dinner and now sat nibbling at a rather unexpected chocolate. To remain silent and sober while other men talk and drink is an indifferent pastime, but Gerald Sterron paid no heed to his brother's obvious impatience and saw to it that the decanter circulated between Sir James and himself until it was empty. As Sir James tilted his glass for the last time, Herbert pushed back his chair.

"Come and smoke your cigar in my study, Hamsted," he said. "I should be glad of a word with you."

This obviously was no invitation to his brother and Gerald, with a smile, stayed behind to blow out the candles which alone now lit the darkly-gleaming table.

Herbert led his guest into the adjoining room and closed the door. Pulling forward a comfortable chair next to the writing-table for Sir James he pushed a box of cigars across to him. Drawing a bunch of keys from his pocket, he walked across to a tall cupboard and fitted a key into one of its drawers. Possibly it was the wrong key, or else he was nervous, as the drawer for a time resisted his efforts; at last he got it open and drew out a large portfolio, which he carried across to the writing-table.

In the meantime Sir James had been placidly smoking his cigar, watching the blue smoke curl upwards till it turned to brown against a lamp-lit patch of ceiling. He appeared quite uninterested in the occupation of his host.

Herbert cleared his throat.

"These are the drawings," he said, fumbling with the strap of the portfolio. "Of course, I'm no expert myself, but I believe they're . . . that's to say, I've always understood that they were first rate . . . unique, you know. My father collected them."

Sir James Hamsted released a cloud of smoke through his nostrils. He was doing, if Sterron could have known it, exactly what a fighting ship may do in war.

"Very interesting. Very interesting," he said languidly.

The portfolio was open at last and Herbert pushed it across the table towards his companion.

"There's a list, you'll see," he said. "Michael Angelo, Titian, Rubens, Reynolds, Constable, Sargent. All seem to be well-known names," he added, with a nervous laugh.

With careful fingers Sir James turned over the sheets of paper, some mere scraps, on which appeared the lovely charcoal and pencil drawings, the sepia and color washes, of the masters.

A trickle of smoke issuing from his nose veiled the glitter of excitement in the old man's eyes.

"Yes," he said, "here are the notes, the sketches . . . the hints of what is to come. Now show me the drawings themselves."

Herbert's jaw dropped.

"But . . . but . . ." he stammered. "These are the things . . . aren't they?"

Sir James stared at him, his eyebrows raised.

"I see," he said at last. "I see. I thought . . . I understood that you had got something good."

"But aren't these good? My father, I'm sure, thought they were."

Hamsted shrugged his shoulders.

"Oh, they're interesting little things, certainly. To a beginner—your father, I believe, only began to collect towards the end of his life—a beginner would set great store by them. I should have realized that. Well, well, one has these little disappointments."

"Then you don't . . . you are not prepared to make me an offer for them?"

Sir James laughed indulgently.

"Oh, well," he said, "if you want to part with them, I daresay I can make you an offer, but you will understand that it will be quite unimportant."

Herbert Sterron's lined face showed a bitter disappointment that was almost pathetic.

"What have you got in mind?" he asked gloomily.

Sir James pursed up his lips and gazed at the glowing end of his cigar.

"Well . . . ll," he said. "I'll have another look at them, in case I've missed anything. I should like to find something worth while. . . . You are sure this is really all? . . . Well, it's a pity to disappoint you."

He shuffled casually through the sheets of paper.

"No, I'm afraid they're really not worth much to you, Sterron. Still, try, by all means. Some of the dealers, perhaps, or another beginner might be interested."

"Do you mean you're not going to make an offer at all?"

"Oh, I don't say that. I meant that you might do better somewhere else. Still, if you like, I'll give you a couple of hundred for them."

A look almost of despair spread over Sterron's face. Slowly he refastened the portfolio.

"I see," he said. "Thanks. It's good of you to make an offer. I must think it over. I can't deny that this is a blow. I had expected something quite different."

"Very sorry, my dear fellow, but there it is . . .

take it or leave it. You're sure there's nothing else?"

"Nothing like this. There are some miniatures, but they're a bit more ris . . . difficult."

"Oh, well, let's have a look at them. One never knows. We might yet find some mutual cause for satisfaction."

Going once more to the cupboard, Herbert put away the portfolio and returned with a mahogany box. In it lay a number of small flat objects wrapped in tissue paper. He unfolded one and laid it on the table—an exquisite miniature by Samuel Cooper of a Cavalier Sterron, framed in flat gold.

"Ah," said Sir James. "Yes. That's a very charming piece of work, very charming indeed. I feel sure you have something here, Sterron, which you should be able to realize with advantage. I myself am not particularly interested in this particular branch of art, but there is certainly a market for . . ."

The door opened and Gerald Sterron walked into the room. Herbert dropped a sheet of foolscap over the miniature and crumpled the tissue paper in his hand.

"Come on, Sir James," said Gerald. "You promised me my revenge. The board is put out in the library, where we played last night. I'm sure Herbert will spare you to me now."

Hamsted rose to his feet.

"Certainly," he exclaimed. "I shall be delighted to have another game with you. Your brother and I are well matched, Sterron; I thought he was going to give me a beating last night, but he made a slip and I was able to exploit it."

He chuckled with pleasure at the memory.

"We'll have a chance to finish our talk another time,

no doubt. I'll come along now; mustn't leave it too late or you'll keep me up till breakfast, eh?"

"Needn't worry about that, Sir James. Willing has put out some sandwiches for us in case we sit late . . . and a decanter. I'll follow in a minute; I just want a word with Herbert about a car for me tomorrow. Oh, and I found that back number of the *Nineteenth Century*, with the article on Li Hung Chang we were talking about. It's in the library. You know the way. Through the little ante-room."

Gerald opened the door for his prospective opponent and, shutting it after him, returned to where his brother still stood by the writing-table.

"Who, by the way, is that chap, Herbert?" he asked.

"Hamsted? A friend of mine," replied Herbert curtly.

"So I gathered. I wondered in what connection; I don't remember him in our young days. He's not local, I gather?"

"No. He's a member of my club."

"The Cavalry?"

Herbert glowered.

"I don't belong to the Cavalry any longer. A pot-house in King Street is all I can afford now."

"I see. He hardly strikes me as the 'pot-house' type. What does he do?"

"Why not ask him? I'm not his keeper." Herbert sat heavily down in an armchair and picked up *The Times*. His ill-temper was unmistakable, but Gerald ignored it. Choosing a cigarette from the box on the writing-table, he lit it and took two or three appreciative breaths while he contemplated how best to frame the question he had come to ask.

"You said something about divorce this afternoon," he said at last. "You're not really serious, I take it?"

Herbert shot him a quick glance, then returned to perusal of the paper.

"Why shouldn't I be?"

"There seem to me any number of reasons why you shouldn't be, but for one, it seems desperately hard on Griselda. She stuck to you all these years; she can't have had a particularly amusing life, buried down here. You know that better than I do."

"Stuck to me?" Herbert glared at his brother. "Do you call it 'sticking to me' to behave as she is doing with this man Venning?"

"Oh, come, my dear fellow. That's nothing but a mild flirtation. She must have some amusement. An attractive woman fifteen years younger than her husband can hardly be expected to walk through life with her eyes on the ground. Be reasonable."

Herbert rose to his feet and strode impatiently up and down the room. Then flung himself down in his chair again.

"Your ideas of reason and mine don't agree," he said. "Perhaps I'm old-fashioned. I want a wife who is faithful to me in every way, who thinks of me and not of her own amusement. Besides, this isn't a flirtation. Do you suppose a womanizer like Venning is satisfied with that? If she's not his lover now, she soon will be. And I shall have proof. Don't make any mistake about that; I shall have the proof."

"You can't have proof if the thing doesn't exist; and personally I'm quite convinced that it doesn't. I hope you haven't let this mischievous nonsense go any farther.

You haven't talked or written to any one else about it, have you?"

"I've taken steps to see that whatever happens that cad Venning will be marked for life. Whatever happens!"

Gerald looked at his brother through narrowed eyelids, as if trying to judge how much weight to attach to the other's rather melodramatic speech.

"I think you'd better tell me what these steps that you have taken are," he said.

Herbert jerked over a page of *The Times* angrily.

"I see no necessity to do anything of the kind," he said. "You needn't trouble to interfere. . . . I've made up my mind."

Gerald shrugged his shoulders and, taking a fresh cigarette from the box, tapped it carefully upon the surface of the table. He glanced at the clock; it was just on ten.

"Well, I must go and amuse your pot-house friend," he said, rising.

Walking to the door, he opened it.

"See you in the morning."

Herbert grunted.

Outside, Gerald paused for a moment in thought, drawing deeply at his cigarette, then walked slowly across the hall towards the door of the ante-room which led into the library. Immersed in thought, he did not see a door at the other end of the hall swing softly open.

III. OFFICIALS

THE morning of Sunday, 28th August, was clear and sunny, the sort of morning on which it was a crime to lie in bed. That view of the matter, however, did not appear to strike Gerald Sterron when he was roused from his slumbers shortly before seven o'clock by the firm hand of Willing, the butler, gripping his shoulder.

"I'm very sorry to disturb you, sir, but I'm worried about the Captain. He's still in the study, I think, sir . . . the door's locked . . . but he doesn't answer."

Willing's voice was less firm than his grip on Gerald's shoulder had been; his eyes, too, had lost something of their customary benignity.

Gerald stared at him, only half-awake and struggling to disentangle reality from the dream from which he had been wakened. The dream had been an unpleasant one, but reality, it seemed, might be worse.

"In the study?" he murmured. "Got up early? What time is it?"

"Seven o'clock, sir, just on. No, sir, the Captain's not been to bed. His bed's not been slept in nor his pyjamas moved from where I laid them last night. I think he must be in the study, sir; the door's locked . . . on the inside. One of the girls told Henry, sir, and he came to fetch me from my house. I was just rising, sir," added the butler, apologetically fingering his unshaven chin.

Gerald Sterron sat up and slipped his legs out of bed.

He was a small man, six inches shorter and several stone lighter than his brother, but he looked hard and fit and for all his fifty-four years there was hardly a line on his face or a gray hair on his head. With his thin black mustache he looked more like a middle-aged cinema star than a retired Shanghai merchant. Slipping on an embroidered silk dressing-gown and pushing his feet into his discarded evening shoes, he followed Willing out into the passage and down into the big hall. Outside the study door a little group of housemaids and footman was standing, whispering nervously together.

"They'd better get on with their work, Willing," said Gerald calmly. "We can ring if we want any one."

The group hurriedly dispersed. Gerald knelt down before the door and peered into the keyhole.

"Can't see anything," he said; "key must be there."

Then, putting his mouth to the keyhole, he called sharply:

"Herbert! . . . Herbert!"

There was no reply.

Gerald rose to his feet.

"Seems odd," he said. "What about the windows? Have you tried them?"

"I haven't tried them, sir, but they're shut and the curtain's drawn. The ground falls away on that side of the house, you'll remember, sir; one can't get at the windows without a ladder."

"No, of course not. Well, we must force the door, then, Willing; I don't suppose it's very strong."

Gerald drew back a pace and, measuring his distance carefully, raised his right foot and drove the heel with a crash against the keyhole. The door cracked ominously.

"Lucky I didn't put on bedroom slippers," said Gerald calmly. "I'm afraid this'll wake the house. Mrs. Sterron, by the way; where is she?"

"Mrs. Sterron has not been wakened, sir. Turton—her maid—did ask me, but I said not."

"Quite right. No need to alarm her unnecessarily. I think one more'll do it."

Again he drove his heel with astonishing force against the keyhole. There was a splintering of wood and a crack appeared above and below the lock.

"Shoulders, now."

The two men put their shoulders to the door and gave a sudden heave. With a crash the door swung open. The room was in darkness, save for a small reading-lamp which cast a dull-red glow upon the writing-table. Gerald switched on the chandelier light—then stepped back with a gasp, almost upsetting the butler, who, with dropped jaw, stared over Sterron's shoulder. The eyes of both men were fixed in stupefied horror upon a body which hung against the curtain of the farther window—the body of Herbert Sterron. The sight was a terrible one and for several seconds the two men seemed rooted to the spot where they stood. Gerald was the first to recover himself; hurrying across the room, he seized the hanging legs and tried to raise the body. The weight seemed tremendous.

"Pick up that chair, Willing," he gasped. "Get up on it and cut him down. Have you got . . . ?"

"Stop a minute!"

Both men turned towards the door, where stood Sir James Hamsted, clad in trousers and a thick dressing-gown. Willing had checked in the act of stooping to pick up the chair which lay on its side close to the dangling feet of his dead master.

"You had better not touch anything more than you can help," said Sir James. Crossing the room, he felt the dead man's hand. "He is quite dead; has been dead for hours. It will be wiser to leave him until the police come . . . and a doctor."

Gerald Sterron seemed on the point of resisting the suggestion, but there was something about the newcomer's manner that took him by surprise. On the previous day, Sir James had seemed to him a harmless old creature of no particular character; now he had an air of authority that claimed command of the situation. Still, Gerald made an effort to carry out his first intention.

"Surely we must cut him down?" he exclaimed. "How can one be certain he is dead? It's impossible to see in this light. Willing, draw those other curtains."

"No!" said Sir James. "Do not touch anything. We can do no good and it is essential that the police should see things as they are."

Reluctantly Gerald let go of the body which he had been trying to raise. His efforts had been sufficient to take some of the weight off the cord by which it hung from the curtain pole and the head had rolled slightly over on to one shoulder. Now it straightened up again with a lifelike movement most horrible to see. Willing hurried from the room, murmuring something about brandy.

"We had better leave the room now and close the door," said Sir James. "I see that there is a telephone instrument upon the table, but it would be wiser not to touch it if there is another upon the premises. We must summon the police."

Gerald, irritated though he was by the older man's prim phraseology, no less than by his assumption of command, still felt that it might be wiser to follow his advice. With a last anxious look at his unfortunate brother he left the room, Sir James following and closing the door. In the hall they found Willing with a decanter of brandy and some glasses; it was evident that he had already followed his own prescription.

Sir James waved away the proffered pick-me-up.

"More use if you produced some coffee—and some breakfast," he said curtly. "But first of all get me some tape and sealing-wax; I must seal this door. Perhaps you would telephone for the police and a doctor in the meantime, Mr. Sterron?"

Instinctively Gerald found himself carrying out the other's instructions, rather glad to leave the control of a trying situation in some one else's hands. When he came back to report that police and doctor were on their way he found Sir James carefully applying sealing-wax to strips of tape across the broken door. Unconsciously Gerald smiled at the sight of this sedate old man applying himself so seriously to a task that he must have learnt from the pages of detective fiction. He found himself studying his companion with renewed interest.

Sir James Hamsted was a man of, he guessed, rather more than sixty, but definitely more old-fashioned than most men of his age. He wore a rather full, gray beard and gold-rimmed spectacles, both of which added to the impression of age, whilst the stoop of his thin shoulders spoilt the effect of an otherwise well-kept figure. His eyes behind the thick glasses appeared weak and inclined to water, but the set of his mouth, though partly concealed by the beard, was firm. The long, sinuous fingers, as they manipulated the tape and wax, gave a greater impression of strength and character than the rest of his make-up.

Sealing the last gobbet of wax with his signet-ring, Sir James turned to his companion.

"Where are they coming from—the police and the doctor?" he asked. "Hylam?"

"Yes—the Superintendent's coming out himself; Rawle, or some name like that. He's collecting the doctor—Tanwort; I believe he looks after Herbert."

"Police surgeon, too?"

"So I gathered."

"When do they expect to be here?"

"Oh, it's about five miles from Hylam—won't take long, though the doctor may have to dress; it's still pretty early for a Sunday morning; 'long lie' for professional men."

"Then it may be half an hour or more before they arrive. I think I shall mount guard outside the windows. I gather from the butler that they are well above ground-level on that side of the house, but it will be as well to be on the safe side. In the meantime, Mr. Sterron, there is your sister-in-law to be informed."

Gerald's face fell. He had for the moment forgotten all about Griselda. Breaking the news to her would be a distressing business, but it was difficult to see on who else's shoulders he could put it. Reluctantly he turned to mount the broad staircase.

"I will see that you are informed when the police arrive," said Sir James.

"Officious old bore," thought Gerald, rather unjustly.

Upon the first landing he found another meeting of housemaids in full whisper. Mrs. Sterron's maid, Turton, was among them. The meeting broke up at Gerald's approach, but Turton, too dignified to scurry with the others, held her ground. She was a middle-aged woman, calm and placid.

"Is Mrs. Sterron awake yet?"

"Not yet, sir, I believe. I do not call Mrs. Sterron on a Sunday until half-past eight, but I looked in just now and she seemed to be sleeping."

Gerald pondered a moment; would it not be kinder to let her sleep on while she could? But a little reflection caused him to change his mind.

"I think you had better wake her, Turton," he said. "The doctor will be here soon and may want to see her. Just ask her if I may have a word with her."

"Very good, sir."

Turton disappeared down the passage and was absent for at least ten minutes. At last she reappeared and led the way to Mrs. Sterron's door.

The room which Gerald entered was still in semi-darkness. Heavy curtains, only one of which was half-drawn, shrouded the windows, and the great four-post bed was still in shadow. In it lay Griselda Sterron, propped up upon pillows, some light-colored wrap round her shoulders and a lace cap on her head. In the half-darkness her face looked dull and heavy. With a slight movement of her hand she signaled her brother-in-law to sit by the bed.

"What is it, Gerald?" she asked in a drowsy voice. "You wanted to see me."

Gerald found himself fidgeting like a nervous school-boy. Pulling himself together he cleared his throat.

"I am afraid you must prepare yourself for bad news, my dear," he said. Then, as she did not speak, but only stared drowsily at him, he added more sharply: "Herbert is dead."

"Dead?"

Griselda hardly seemed to grasp the significance of the word. She still stared dully at her brother-in-law, who felt a surge of annoyance at her insensibility.

"Yes, dead. He has killed himself," he said brusquely.

At last intelligence dawned in the big brown eyes, which widened into a look of horror. Her hand flew to her mouth as if to check a scream. Then, suddenly, the blood drained from her face, leaving it a ghastly white, her eyes turned up, and her head rolled heavily on to her shoulder.

"Good Lord!" exclaimed Gerald, springing up. "I didn't know women could do that in these days."

He dashed to the door and flung it open. Turton was standing correctly a few paces down the passage.

"Mrs. Sterron has fainted!"

Instantly Turton came to life. Walking quickly into her mistress's room she firmly shut the door. Gerald walked slowly down the passage, feeling ashamed of the abrupt—even ill-tempered—fashion of his news-breaking.

Evidently the "professional men" had not taken long to emerge from their Sunday morning "long lie," for, as Gerald descended the staircase, he heard a car pull up outside the front door. Willing had been waiting in the hall and at once admitted the little group of officials.

Dr. Tanwort, police surgeon to the Hylam division, led the way. He was followed by a uniformed police superintendent, a short, stocky man, of heavy countenance, whom he introduced to Gerald as Superintendent Dawle. A sergeant, also in uniform, followed, whilst two constables could be seen standing by the car —the long-suffering police car which was expected to carry its full quota of outsize passengers (and sometimes one or two extra) month in, month out, without complaining—or breaking down, as a private car would have done.

Dr. Tanwort was a small, normally boisterous and confident little man, but in the presence of the rich and great, he tended to a nervous hush or diffident garrulity according to the circumstances which he thought demanded the one or the other. The Sterrons were no longer rich, but the family was one of the oldest pillars of the county and the present occasion pointed unmistakably to "hush."

"I have responded as quickly as possible to your melancholy summons, Mr. Sterron," he murmured. "Your poor brother; may I . . . will you lead me to him?"

Superintendent Dawle, cap in hand, stood silently in the background, his eyes quickly taking in the details of a house which he had not previously had occasion to enter.

Before Gerald could lead the way to the study—just across the hall—Sir James appeared through the front door.

"I am Sir James Hamsted," he said, addressing the Superintendent; "I have sealed the door which was broken in, but you will probably wish to place one of your constables outside the windows, where I have myself been on guard until your arrival. If you will follow me, I will lead the way."

Without waiting to see whether his suggestion was approved or not, he walked out of the house. Superintendent Dawle followed imperturbably, signing to his sergeant to remain. In a minute they were back.

"Now here is the study door which was broken open by Mr. Gerald Sterron and the butler when no response was received from Captain Sterron. So far as I know, nothing has been touched in the room itself, with the exception that Mr. Gerald Sterron slightly lifted the body until I intervened. On that point you will, of course, be informed by Mr. Sterron and the butler; I myself touched nothing inside the room and only so much of the outside of the door as was necessary for the affixing of the seals."

Sir James spoke in the careful monotone of the Civil Servant. As he finished, he bent down to examine the seals.

"That is the imprint of my signet," he said. "The seals are intact. I now hand over responsibility to you gentlemen and shall retire to the library. Should you require any information from me, I shall, of course, be happy to give it."

Without waiting for comment, Sir James turned on his heel and walked down the short passage to the ante-room. The others watched him go in a silence that was almost awed.

Superintendent Dawle was the first to break it.

"Well, Doctor, we'd better get in," he said, carefully detaching the sealed tape from the door jamb.

As the door swung open on the still darkened room —dark by contrast with the sunny hall in spite of the electric light—the Superintendent turned to Gerald.

"Was this how you found it, sir? The light, I mean."

"No, there was only that lamp on the table burning. We switched on the other when we came in."

"And nothing else has been touched? I think that was what the other gentleman said."

"I tried to lift my brother's body; I don't think I touched anything else. Certainly I didn't move anything. Did you, Willing?"

The butler, who had been hovering in the background, stepped forward.

"Nothing, sir, unless maybe I pushed a chair aside on my way in."

"All right; we'll ask you later about that," said Dawle. "No doubt I shall be able to have a word with you presently, sir, when Dr. Tanwort has examined the body." This to Gerald.

Dr. Tanwort coughed nervously.

"There would be no objection, of course, to Mr. Sterron being present during my examination should he wish it," he murmured.

"I make no doubt Mr. Sterron'll be more comfortable having his breakfast, Doctor," the Superintendent interposed blandly. "Now, I'll follow you in."

The door closed upon the two officials, leaving Gerald Sterron and Willing outside. Almost at once, however, it opened again and Superintendent Dawle walked across to the front door. Returning with a constable, he posted him in the hall outside the study door, while he himself reëntered the room. The sergeant had disappeared on some errand of his own.

Gerald watched these maneuvers from the landing above; then, with a shrug of the shoulders, went off to enquire after his sister-in-law.

IV. THE POLICE AT WORK

INSIDE the study, Superintendent Dawle and Dr. Tanwort stood looking up at the dead man.

"Not the way I'd choose to do away with myself," said Tanwort, who, in the absence of any one whom he considered his superior, quickly regained buoyancy. "I shouldn't like any one to see me looking like that, let alone my own wife."

"You think he did away with himself, Doctor?"

"Not a doubt of it, I should say. No murderer that ever I heard of chose hanging as a method; too difficult —and too damn suggestive, eh?"

"Well, sir, that's a point on which we shall have to satisfy ourselves. Hadn't we better cut him down?"

"Yes, if you've seen all you want to, Superintendent. I'll take the weight if you'll get on that chair and cut the cord."

"I think we'll leave that particular chair where it is for the moment, sir."

Dawle crossed the room and fetched a chair from beside the door. Climbing on to it, he carefully examined the cord by which the dead man was hanging. It was evidently a piece of the cord used for pulling the heavy curtains to and fro; thick as it was, however, it seemed extraordinary that it could bear the weight of so heavy a man as Herbert Sterron. It had been passed over the wooden curtain pole, one end fastened to the man's neck and the other to a radiator which stood in the window.

Superintendent Dawle got down from his chair again and, taking a two-foot rule from his pocket, measured the height of the chair which lay on its side close by. Then he measured the distance between the dead man's feet and the floor.

"Evidently stood on tip-toe while he tied the noose round his neck and then kicked the chair over," he said.

"Yes. Death by strangulation; not neck-breaking, the crude way you fellows do it," said the doctor. "Come on; let's have him down."

Remounting his chair, Dawle put one arm round the body, whilst with the other hand he cut the cord. Even with Dr. Tanwort supporting the weight below, Dawle was nearly pulled off his balance as the cord parted.

"My God, he's a weight," exclaimed the little doctor, staggering to retain his feet.

Carefully Dawle, with both hands now under the dead man's arms, descended from the chair. Together they carried Herbert Sterron's body to the leather sofa by the farther window and laid it carefully down.

"Phew!" Dr. Tanwort straightened his back. "Any objection to drawing those curtains, Dawle? I can see better by daylight."

The Superintendent took hold of the cord which corresponded to the one he had cut; it required a strong tug to draw back the curtains. Dr. Tanwort bent over the prostrate figure and gently fingered the livid mark round the neck.

"Buried very deep," he said. "If this cord hadn't been so thick it would probably have cut right through the flesh—if it hadn't broken first."

Burrowing into the flesh with his finger, he at last brought a section of the cord to light.

"I'll cut this here," he said, "then you can examine the knot if it interests you."

"What causes all that discoloration, sir?" asked Dawle, pointing to the bluish-red zone above the constriction mark.

"Ecchymosis—bruising—rupture of small blood vessels."

"No doubt death was due to strangulation?"

"None at all. Look at his bluish appearance, blue lips, the blood-stained froth, the protruding tongue—sure sign of strangulation. Of course I'll hunt him over for bullet holes and corrosive poisons if you like," added Tanwort facetiously, "but I *fancy* my certificate will be for strangulation."

"What about time of death, sir?"

Dr. Tanwort lifted the dead man's arm, which was quite stiff.

"As you see, rigor is pretty complete, though the body is not yet quite cold. If you want to be as exact as possible, I must take the temperature, but an ordinary clinical thermometer won't do—it doesn't register low enough. See if they've got a bath thermometer, Superintendent—one not in a case."

Dawle left the room and presently returned with the required instrument. After some five minutes, the doctor gave his verdict.

"Let's see, it's about eight now. I should put death at eight to twelve hours ago, probably somewhere halfway between the two. Wait a minute, though; rigor is accelerated by heat; it was a hot night last night, so I should say not much more than eight to ten hours ago."

"Thank you, sir. Then I'll arrange for the body to be

taken to the mortuary. You'll see the Coroner, sir, or shall I?"

"I'll see him in the first place. No doubt he'll want to have a word with you as well. I don't want the inquest before three tomorrow; I've got a Harley Street man coming down for a consultation and I want to give him lunch—pick his brains, you know; one never can tell when it'll come in useful. Well, if you don't want me any more, I'll be off. Devilish hungry, I'm getting. Good Lord, it's not eight yet; feels more like lunchtime. Your car run me back, Dawle? Thanks, so long."

The little doctor strutted out through the door which the Superintendent had opened for him. Dawle beckoned to the policeman in the hall.

"Drive Dr. Tanwort back to his house, Moler," he said. "But bring me my bag first, and if you see Sergeant Gable, send him along. Oh, and ask that butler for a pair of steps. Sorry, Doctor, he won't keep you long."

Shutting the door, Dawle walked back to the sofa and gazed down upon its tragic burden. Bending down he closely examined the blue lips and swollen tongue, and the angry mark round the neck.

"Wish I knew more about doctoring," he muttered. "Might tell you a lot, all this sort of thing. Doctors know, but they don't always know what to look for."

Picking up the end of the cord which had been embedded in the neck, Dawle examined the knot.

"H'm. Running noose. Nothing strange about that."

There was a knock at the door. Dawle strode across and opened it slightly. Outside stood Sergeant Gable with a tall pair of steps in one hand and a tray in the other. Dawle beckoned him in.

"I took the liberty of bringing you something to eat, sir," he said, depositing the tray on a table.

Dawle looked gratefully at the steaming cup of coffee and plateful of thick bacon sandwiches.

"Thoughtful of you," he said. "Had anything yourself?"

Sergeant Gable, a good-looking young man, smiled.

"Yes, thank you, sir. I've done nicely and the footman was seeing to Coggs and Moler."

"Get anything out of them?" asked Dawle, munching at a sandwich.

"Just a bit, sir."

"Well, I'll hear about that later. Set those steps up by the drawn curtain. Careful you don't touch anything, especially that chair."

Opening the large bag which P.C. Moler had brought in from the car, the Superintendent extracted an electric torch. Climbing to the top of the steps, he flashed the light on to the top of the curtain pole.

"Plenty of dust here," he said. "And finger-marks, but I'm afraid the dust'll blurr any prints. If his were on it that'd settle it. Hallo, what's this?"

Scratching his chin, Dawle closely examined an abrasion on the varnish of the pole. Descending the steps he handed the torch to Sergeant Gable.

"Go up and tell me what you see there," he said. "Don't touch it."

Gable obeyed.

"Looks as if some one had been fingering the pole, sir," he said.

"Yes, I know that, but what else?"

"There's a mark on the varnish as if something had rubbed it off, sir."

"That suggest anything to you?"

"Well, sir, I don't rightly know what's been happening in here, but they told me outside the gentleman had hanged himself and I'd make a guess that this mark is where the rope went."

The Superintendent looked questioningly at his junior, as if expecting more, but Sergeant Gable was not qualifying for the rôle of Watson.

"All right. Come down."

Taking care not to disturb the curtain rings on the finger-marked pole, Superintendent Dawle parted the curtains and looked at the big sash window behind them. It was shut but not latched. Crossing to the other window, from which the curtains had been already drawn, he examined it carefully. The latch in this case was fastened.

"One or two points here want clearing up, Gable," he said. "Finger-prints, in the first place. You can get to work on them at once. I want that fallen chair done very carefully and the pole, of course, and both window-sashes and the door—the handles are bound to have been touched by two or three people this morning, but the panels might show something—perhaps the jambs, too. We'll do the outside of it, too, if we can keep people out of the way. No good starting talk if we can avoid it. This is a suicide case so far, and if it turns out not to be, the longer somebody thinks we think it's suicide the better."

Sergeant Gable nodded, his eyes glistening with interest.

"Now you get ahead with those prints while I talk to some of these people. I'll leave Moler outside the door, so you won't be disturbed."

The young sergeant, who had recently been through a finger-print course at Scotland Yard, lost no time in getting to work. The Superintendent's capacious bag contained a powder-blowing outfit and a formidable camera; both of these were quickly in operation.

Superintendent Dawle unearthed Willing and was shown the telephone instrument outside the pantry, by means of which he summoned an ambulance to remove the body. He ought, he knew, to notify the Chief Constable, but it was still early and he decided to risk leaving it a bit longer. Another hour to himself would be worth a lot to him.

Having asked for an empty room in which he could interview people, he was shown into the ante-room which led through into the library.* The rooms on the ground floor, apart from the servants' quarters, consisted of dining-room, study, and small morning-room on the south side, ante-room, library, and drawing-room on the west, and Mrs. Sterron's sitting-room at the north-east corner. The small morning-room was closed and used as a dump.

"I'll start with you, Mr. Willing," said the Superintendent, taking a chair at the table in the center of the room and pulling out a note-book. "Now, in the first place, how long have you been with Captain Sterron?"

"Close on ten years, sir. I came to the Captain in January, 1923."

"Ah, that's long service in these days. You'll be able to help me a lot, Mr. Willing. . . . Now, I understand you were the first to give the alarm."

*See floor plan on page ix.

"Not quite that, sir." In grave tones the butler described the course of the morning's events, up to the arrival of the police.

"Do you remember whether you touched or disturbed anything when you went into the study?"

"I don't think so, sir. I was going to pick up a chair that had fallen down, but Sir James Hamsted told me not to."

"And you saw your master alive last . . . when?"

"Last night, sir, at ten o'clock. I take in the whisky and receive orders at ten o'clock every night."

"And was he then in his usual spirits?"

"Oh, yes . . . if you can call them spirits."

"Ah. You wouldn't describe him as a high-spirited . . . a cheerful man?"

"Far from it, sir. Very far from it."

"Well, I'll leave that point for the moment, though I may want to know more later on. Just at the moment I'd like to know something about your master's routine habits. Did he, for instance, always give you his orders at ten o'clock every night?"

"Pretty nearly always, sir. He was very regular in his habits."

"And did he, then, go to bed . . . after he'd had a drink?"

"Oh, no, not at once. He'd generally sit up an hour or so, I believe, though, of course, I'd not be in the house myself."

"Ah, you don't live in the house?"

"I have a cottage down by the drive gates, sir."

"I think I saw it. Very nice house, Mr. Willing."

The butler inclined his head; the movement suggested that while he acknowledged the compliment he did not need it.

"So the Captain usually sat up till eleven or thereabouts and then went to bed? What about the windows? Who shut them?"

"I shut one, sir, if both were open, at ten o'clock. The other was always open if the Captain was in there. He would shut it himself when he went to bed."

"He always did shut it?"

"Pretty nearly always, sir. Once in a way he'd forget, but not often. It's not as dangerous as you might think, because on that side of the house the ground falls away; you'd need a ladder to get in at that window, even if it was open."

"Yes, I've noticed that. Have you ever known your master shut the window but not latch it?"

"I can't say I have, sir, but then I don't open the room in the mornings myself. Ethel, the second housemaid, does that. She's once or twice told me that the window had been left open all night and I've mentioned it to the Captain, but I don't recollect her ever saying it was shut but not latched. I could make enquiries if you think it important."

"Oh, don't trouble," replied Dawle, who had no wish to start the household talking. He would have a chance to question Ethel himself. "Ethel, perhaps, will be the maid who found the study locked this morning?"

"That is so, sir."

"Now, just a word more about your master. I'm sure you don't want to talk about him to us outsiders, Mr. Willing, but the Coroner'll be bound to ask these questions and it's a help to know beforehand. You said he wasn't a cheerful sort; would you say he was downright depressed? The kind that might take his own life?"

The butler considered carefully before replying.

"I certainly never anticipated this happening, sir," he said at last. "But the Captain was certainly very much under the weather at times; very much under the weather."

"Anything to account for it?"

This, Dawle realized, was the crucial question. He had no doubt that Willing, who had been ten years in Captain Sterron's service, could make a pretty shrewd guess at, if he did not actually know, the cause of the dead man's depression; but would he pass on his knowledge to the police?

"That's a very difficult thing to say, sir." (Ah, he was going to hedge.) "The master never talked about his troubles. I fancy he suffered from ill-health, though he didn't often see a doctor—not here, anyhow. Dr. Tanwort has been here occasionally; he might be able to inform you on that point."

"I'll ask him. And was he happy . . . I'm afraid this is a delicate point, Mr. Willing, but it's bound to come . . . was he happy in his married life?"

"I've no reason to suppose anything else, sir. The Captain and Mrs. Sterron have lived together—not in the same room, I don't mean—ever since I've known them. Not always going off in different directions like many do in these days."

"No cause for jealousy on either side?"

"As to that, I couldn't say," replied Willing firmly.

"He knows something but won't tell," thought the Superintendent; "better leave it for the moment."

"But you had no immediate cause to anticipate anything of this kind?" he continued aloud.

"Oh, no, sir; certainly not."

"Thank you, Mr. Willing. I don't think I need trouble you any more just now. D'you think I might have a word with Mr. Sterron or Sir James Hamsted?"

"I will endeavor to find one or other of them, sir."

Left alone, Superintendent Dawle looked round the little ante-room. It was a small, featureless place, that looked as if it was never used except as a passage-room; probably it had been originally designed as a waiting-room for suppliants to some influential Sterron of old days, holding audience in the big library next door. A number of chairs and a cabinet or two round the walls, with the table at which he was sitting, were the only furniture. An ash-tray in the form of a copper bowl reminded Dawle that he was dying for a smoke, but it would hardly do to indulge his craving just yet. In the bowl, he noticed, was the stump of a cigarette and a fair quantity of ash. Idly picking up the stump, Dawle saw that it bore the name "Pertari," which was strange to him—but he was no expert on cigarettes.

Willing reappeared to report that Mr. Sterron was not at the moment to be found, but that Sir James Hamsted was in the library next door and would be glad to receive the Superintendent there.

The library was a long, well-proportioned room, with a fireplace at the far end and a second door leading out into the hall. Sir James Hamsted was standing looking out of one of the three windows.

"Come in, Superintendent," he said. "If you will sit down, I will give you such information as is in my power."

He waved Dawle to a chair, but himself remained standing. The statement which followed was precise and exact, given forth in a monotonous tone, as if it were being read.

"I am Sir James Hamsted. I am Chief Inspector of Factories under the Home Office. I have known Captain Sterron, not very intimately, for a number of years, and recently he invited me to spend a week-end with him here. I am interested, among other subjects, in architecture, and as I had always heard that Ferris was a fine example of the Tudor period, I decided to accept. I came down on Friday evening and had intended to stay until tomorrow, Monday morning; I should naturally wish now to relieve Mrs. Sterron of the burden of entertaining a comparative stranger at such a time, but it is, of course, for you to say whether I am at liberty to depart."

Sir James paused, evidently expecting this point to be cleared up.

"As soon as we've had this little talk, Sir James, which I am sure will clear up any points there may be, I shall have no objection to your leaving. Unless, that is, the Chief Constable thinks differently."

"Ah, yes, the Chief Constable; he has been notified?"

"Not yet, Sir James."

"He should be notified at once. Do so now, Superintendent; I will await your return."

Dawle was not a little taken aback at being ordered about in this peremptory fashion, but as he had been feeling rather guilty he complied. Returning from the telephone, he found Sir James where he had left him. The "statement" was taken up as if there had been no interruption.

"I had not previously met either Mrs. Sterron or Mr. Gerald Sterron. Relations between Captain and Mrs. Sterron appeared to me to be courteous but not intimate, certainly not affectionate. Those between Captain Sterron and his brother less courteous but possibly more affectionate; on the latter point I am uncertain. I have always known Captain Sterron to be of a silent disposition, but the last thirty-six hours have shown me that he was more than that—he was definitely morose. I had no reason to suppose that he would take his own life, neither do I know of any reason why any one else should take it. It is true that yesterday Mrs. Sterron was playing lawn tennis with a gentleman of the name —I am given to understand—of Sir Carle Venning, and that the two appeared to take more than a little pleasure in each other's company, but that is hardly evidence of a desire or intention to do bodily violence."

Superintendent Dawle had pricked up his ears at this last piece of information, but he only murmured: "Quite so, sir," to the final remark.

"Now as to this morning. I usually wake early and read or write for some hours before breakfast. I was doing so this morning—writing—dressed in trousers and a dressing-gown, when I became conscious of some commotion in the house. Footsteps were hurrying down the passage, voices were audible in subdued but urgent tones. I did not feel it within my province to intervene, but when I heard the sound of heavy blows upon wood I decided that the time had come to do so. Leaving my bedroom, I descended the main staircase and was in time to see Mr. Sterron and the butler, Willing, burst open the door of the study and, after a pause, rush into the room. I followed with all possible haste and was in time to prevent the butler from picking up a chair which lay on its side near the feet of the corpse. I also restrained him from drawing, at Mr. Sterron's request, the curtains of the other window—the one not behind Captain Sterron's body. I should say that I saw at a glance that Captain Sterron was dead—had been dead for many hours. In order to prevent any further disturbance of the room, I closed the door and sealed it; my seals were intact when I handed them over to you."

Superintendent Dawle, who had been taking rapid shorthand notes, looked up with respectful admiration.

"A very clear and complete statement, sir, if I may be allowed to say so," he said. "The Coroner himself could not ask for anything better."

The shadow of a smile hovered across Sir James's rigid mouth.

"Thank you, Superintendent. I shall, of course, be prepared to repeat it at the inquest. I do not think I can amplify it."

"There's just one point I should like to ask you about, sir—a purely formal enquiry. Did you, by any chance, notice when you got into the study whether the key was in the lock on the inside of the door?"

A quick frown crossed Sir James's face.

"I had intended to refer to that point," he said. "I did notice that the key was in the lock on the inside of the door; I made a point of looking for it."

"Would there have been any possibility, sir, of the key being placed there by either of the two persons who broke open the door—after they got into the room?"

Sir James carefully scrutinized the impassive, almost heavy face of the Superintendent.

"In my opinion, Superintendent," he said weightily, "there is not the slightest chance of that having been done, except by an expert in sleight-of-hand. I was not actually on their heels when they opened the door, but I was in sight of them and I saw them disappear into the interior of the room. They were by the body when I reached the door."

V. "I AM RESPONSIBLE"

MAJOR GEORGE THRENGOOD, Chief Constable of the county, was the younger son of a second cousin of the Lord Lieutenant. He had served for twenty years in one of the less spectacular cavalry regiments and, when an officer from another regiment was brought in to command over his head, he realized that the time had come to seek a livelihood elsewhere. Having no qualifications for civilian employment, other than the somewhat vague phrase "experience of administration and control of men," he naturally thought of the police—the county police—the county of which Cousin Frederick . . . A fortunate vacancy and an amenable Standing Joint Committee (it was a very rural county) completed the chain of happy circumstance, and at the age of forty-five George Threngood found himself a Chief Constable standing in the hall of Ferris Court, waiting rather nervously to do his first really difficult job.

Herbert Sterron he had known slightly and disliked considerably; Griselda Sterron he had met and admired at various county functions and entertainments—had even gone so far as to feel slightly romantic about her, without being able to persuade himself that she reciprocated the sentiment. Gerald Sterron he knew not at all.

Willing, who had admitted the Chief Constable, was now on his way to discover whether Mrs. Sterron would receive him—George Threngood fondly hoped that she would not. In that hope he was disappointed, but his heart quickened a pace when he learnt that he was to be received in Mrs. Sterron's bedroom.

Mrs. Sterron, however, was not in bed; dressed in a black chiffon wrap, she lay upon a Madame Recamier sofa; nor was she alone. On a low stool beside her sat a priest, dressed in a cassock, who rose to his feet as Threngood entered. For a second the two men exchanged glances of mutual embarrassment; then the Chief Constable remembered his duty.

"Mrs. Sterron, I'm so terribly distressed to hear of this tragedy. Please accept my most sincere sympathy."

Griselda, who had recovered much of her natural color since her brother-in-law's visit, though her face was whitened with powder, gave a wan smile.

"Thank you, Major Threngood," she said in a low voice. "I can hardly realize yet what has happened. It is all too terrible."

"Of course, yes, the shock. . . ." Threngood found himself stammering. "I am afraid that in the course of our duties, Mrs. Sterron, we shall have to ask you some questions, though we will try to cause you as little distress as possible."

The priest took a step or two towards the door.

"Don't go, Father!" exclaimed Griselda in a more robust voice. "Major Threngood, this is Father Speyd; I don't know whether you have met."

The two men exchanged stiff bows.

"He is helping me so much. Surely it is not necessary to put me through a cross-examination just now . . . so soon. . . ." Her voice trailed away into silence, her large eyes filled with tears.

Threngood cursed under his breath.

"Of course there's no immediate hurry," he mumbled, ". . . in half an hour or so, perhaps. . . ."

Griselda nodded from behind her lace handkerchief. "I'll try," she whispered.

Sadly doubtful about the manner in which his "duty" was being done, the Chief Constable retired, leaving the priest in sole, though apparently not triumphant, possession of the field. Descending the stairs with the intention of finding his Superintendent, Threngood encountered Gerald Sterron in the hall and, explaining his identity, was drawn off into the library, which was now empty, Dawle thereby receiving a further respite in which to carry on his enquiries undisturbed.

At the moment he was engaged in questioning the housemaid, Ethel, in the ante-room. She repeated what Willing had already told him, both about the events of the morning and about the study window—"the Captain" sometimes forgot to shut it; she did not remember ever having found it shut but not latched; if he remembered to shut it, she thought he would remember to latch it. Dawle assured her that the point was of no importance.

"There's just one point about cigarette and cigar ash in the study," he said; "those things sometimes help one to trace people's movements—even what the state of their minds has been."

Ethel stared at him in awe-struck admiration; there was no fathoming the cleverness of the police.

"Would the ash-trays in the study be cleared every day?"

"Oh, yes, sir; first thing every morning when the windows are opened. They make the room smell so stale."

"I see. So any ash I find about in the study will have been made yesterday? They've not, of course, been cleared this morning, because you couldn't get in."

"No, sir. I haven't been in since just before dinner yesterday; I cleared them then."

"Ah, that fines it down. And the same applies to the rest of the house? This tray, for instance," he pointed to the copper bowl, "would that be last night's ash or this morning's?"

The girl blushed.

"Oh, dear!" she exclaimed. "I'm that forgetful! But there, we're all in a to-do this morning; I've forgotten half my duties."

Dawle smiled.

"Well, well, this isn't a very serious matter, anyhow. You can run along now, Ethel; I don't think I've any more to ask you."

Ethel disappeared, carrying the offending bowl.

Having heard his Chief's voice in the adjoining room, Superintendent Dawle tapped at the door and entered. Major Threngood greeted his subordinate with a friendly smile—his best feature.

"Ah, there you are, Dawle," he said. "Mr. Sterron is just telling me about this unhappy business."

"I haven't had a chance of a word with Mr. Sterron yet," said the Superintendent. "May I be allowed to listen, sir?"

"Of course. Go on, Mr. Sterron. You were telling me how you and the butler burst the door open."

Gerald Sterron took up his tale.

"As soon as the door burst open, I switched on the electric light. Then we saw my brother's body hanging against the curtains of the window. It was a pretty ghastly shock—rather stunned me for a second. Then I got across the room quickly and tried to take the weight off the rope. I told Willing to get up on a chair to cut the cord, but at that moment Sir James Hamsted called to him from the doorway to leave things alone. I didn't know he was there. He came across and had a look at the body and said that Herbert was certainly dead. He . . . he rather took command of the situation; I think I was a bit stunned by the shock, or I don't know that I should have given in as easily as I did. It was rather feeble of me. But I daresay he was quite right."

Gerald gave a deprecating smile as he lit a cigarette, after offering his case to Threngood and the Superintendent, both of whom, on principle, declined.

"Can you tell me anything about Sir James Hamsted, sir?" asked Dawle. "I can't quite place him."

Gerald smiled.

"Nor can I," he said; "he seems rather out of the picture here, doesn't he? I never met him before this week-end. My brother told me he was a club friend. He's quite an interesting man, I should think, though rather old-fashioned in his way of talking. He's a good chess player."

"You played chess last night, sir?"

"Yes, we had a long game."

"What time would that be, sir?"

"I don't know what time we started, but we went on till after two o'clock. The deuce of a game the old man gave me."

"When did you last see your brother, sir?"

"I saw him not long after dinner. He and Hamsted went into the study directly after dinner and stayed there some time. I wanted to have my revenge on Sir

James—he'd beaten me the night before—so I went in and dug him out at last. I stayed talking to him—to Herbert—for a bit and then came along in here and we had our game."

"Sir James came along before you, sir?"

"Yes, he did." Gerald's voice assumed a graver note. "I suppose I was the last person to see poor Herbert alive," he said.

"You don't know what time it was you left the study?"

"I don't think I do."

"Was it before or after the butler came in for orders?"

"I don't know that either; he didn't come while I was there."

"I'm sorry to be persistent, sir, but it's rather important to fix the moment when he was last seen alive. Did you notice whether the curtains were drawn or open when you were there?"

Gerald pondered.

"They were open, I think," he said; "yes, I'm sure of it, and the windows, too. It was a warm night."

"Both of them?"

"Yes, both."

"Thank you, sir; that fixes it to a certain extent. It must have been before Willing went in."

"Oh? He saw him after I did?"

"Undoubtedly, sir. And then you were in here till two o'clock, playing chess with Sir James?"

"Yes, that's right. Willing had put us some sandwiches. I felt sure we were in for a long sitting; I wasn't going to be beaten again."

"And you heard nothing . . . unusual . . . all that time?"

"Nothing. At least, I didn't."

"Not the sound of a chair falling over, for instance?"

Gerald Sterron stared at the Superintendent.

"I see," he said. "You mean when he kicked the chair away! How horrible! If we'd heard that we might have been able to save him."

He paused for a moment, his face troubled.

"No. We—I—didn't hear anything. It's a fairly thick carpet in that room, I think."

"Yes, sir, I noticed that. No doubt that accounts for it."

There was an appreciable pause while Superintendent Dawle ran his eye over his notes. At last he looked up.

"I think that's all I have to ask Mr. Sterron about events, sir," he said to his Chief. "But, of course, there's the bigger question to go into. Perhaps you will wish to do that yourself."

Major Threngood shook his head.

"You'd better carry on, Dawle," he said. "Of course we want to save Mr. Sterron and the family from any unavoidable distress, but I suppose you will need to ask something about . . . motive, eh?"

"That's what was in my mind, sir." The Superintendent turned to Gerald. "If you wouldn't mind telling me, sir, if you know of any reason why your brother should have taken his life."

Gerald Sterron's face clouded. He walked across to the window and looked out upon the sunny landscape, but it appeared to bring no relief to his troubled mind.

"I find it very difficult to answer that question," he said, turning back into the room. "I have been away from England for more than twenty years, with occasional visits on leave. During that time I've seen hardly anything of my brother and heard little more. During the last two years, since I have been back in England, I have seen rather more of him, but not enough to recover the intimacy of our boyhood—we were very close friends then."

Gerald lit a cigarette and inhaled deep breaths of smoke.

"There's no concealing the fact," he said, "that my brother's life has been a bit of a mystery. When he married, twenty years ago, he had a promising career in the army in front of him, besides being popular in society and pretty well off. Then, all of a sudden he retired and buried himself down here. I've never discovered why, though as he was passed unfit for active service it may have been something to do with his health. Or it may have been money. He seems to have made a complete mess of things financially. My father was pretty well off when he died. There was a small mortgage on the estate, but nothing cumbersome. Now I believe everything is tied up in mortgages and—as you'll see if you look round the place—there's no money to keep things up. He must have gambled or speculated; he can hardly have spent it living down here. Whether you think there's enough there to account for his killing himself, I don't know. Possibly a combination of the two causes is the explanation."

"You don't know of anything else, sir? No family trouble?"

Gerald raised the Sterron eyebrow.

"Family trouble? Of what sort?"

"No grounds for jealousy, sir, where Mrs. Sterron is concerned?"

"Good heavens, no; certainly not. Where did you get that idea from?"

Threngood stepped into the opening breach.

"Of course not, Mr. Sterron," he said. "We don't expect that for a moment. My own . . . that is . . . we all know that Mrs. Sterron has been the most devoted wife. You can put that out of your head, Superintendent."

Dawle closed his note-book.

"Very good, sir," he said.

An uncomfortable pause followed, Gerald Sterron making no attempt to help the police out of their embarrassment. It was ended by the Chief Constable.

"As a matter of form," he said nervously, "I think we should ask Mrs. Sterron one or two questions. Of course, not," he added hurriedly, "anything of a nature to upset her. I will put the questions myself."

He glanced nervously from Sterron to the Superintendent, whose face was a complete blank.

"I have already offered my condolences to Mrs. Sterron, but she was not prepared at that time to . . ."

The door swung open and the somber figure of Father Speyd appeared in the doorway. Seeing the three men, he closed the door and strode into the room. He was a striking figure. The tight-fitting cassock accentuated the length and thinness of his body, which none the less had an appearance of sinuous strength. His face, too, was thin and drawn to the point of emaciation, but dark, deep-set eyes and thin aquiline nose gave it a look of almost romantic beauty. The eyes now showed a bright gleam of excitement; on the thin cheeks glowed two patches of vivid color.

"Major Threngood," he said. "I believe you are the Chief Constable. I have a statement that I wish to make at once. *I* am responsible for this man's death!"

VI. FATHER SPEYD

THE three previous occupants of the library stared at the newcomer in blank astonishment. Superintendent Dawle was the first to recover himself. He cleared his throat noisily.

"It is my duty to warn you . . ." he began, but the priest cut him short.

"Oh, I don't mean with my hands," he said coldly. "I warned him of the wrath that would strike him if he persisted in his vile treatment of this poor child. I spoke—perhaps more strongly than I should—but with all the force of which I am capable I adjured him to mend his evil ways. He has chosen the path which is forbidden to us, but at least those ways are ended. I am, as I have said, responsible."

Melodramatic as his words were, they none the less were in keeping with his appearance and did not sound incongruous.

"What on earth are you talking about?" exclaimed Sterron angrily. "And who are you?"

"I am Father Speyd. I am well known in Hylam."

Superintendent Dawle nodded.

"I cannot speak in greater detail; what I know has been told me in . . . in confidence. Perhaps I should not have said so much, but I feared that a wrong construction—a wrong interpretation might be made of this act of self-destruction. I fear, Mr. Sterron, that I have grieved you. Your brother . . . Forgive my impetuosity if you can."

The eager light had died out of Father Speyd's eyes, leaving them tired and anxious. His voice was low and penitent. Evidently he was a man of quick emotions.

Sterron continued to glare at him, but in silence. Major Threngood attempted to ease the awkward situation.

"I'm sure we are all upset," he said. "Captain Sterron's death has been a terrible shock to every one. Mrs. Sterron was perhaps a member of your—er—flock, Father Speyd?"

"She worships with us," said Speyd simply.

"Quite. And no doubt she confides in you—in the—er—usual manner. We mustn't attempt to abuse that confidence. Now, Mr. Sterron, if I may have a word or two with your sister-in-law. . . ."

He walked out of the room, compelling Gerald to follow him. Superintendent Dawle looked at the priest quizzically.

"You wouldn't like to tell *me* a bit more, padre, I suppose?"

Speyd's face relaxed.

"I'd tell you, Dawle, if I could tell any one. I really have said more than I ought to have. My feelings carry me away at times—as I daresay you've noticed before now. Don't make me repeat in public what I've said to you today; it would do no good. So long as you realize that this is the cause of Captain Sterron's action." Dawle looked thoughtfully at Father Speyd.

"I see, padre," he said. "I don't suppose there'll be any need to call on you at the inquest. But you might tell me when you said all this to Captain Sterron."

"Yesterday morning. I made up my mind that I must speak to him. He has never received me here; I came once, just after my arrival in Hylam, but he was most offensive to me and I could not come again. I met him yesterday morning outside Hylam; I knew that he always came in on Saturday morning, so I waited for him outside the town."

"How did he take it—your telling him off?"

"He was shaken—really shaken, I felt. He did not answer me, but drove away hurriedly."

"I see, padre. Well, thanks very much. And if I were you, I'd keep even that much to yourself."

"I shall, Dawle; I shall. Well, I must get back to my people. Mrs. Sterron sent her car to fetch me this morning. She was in deep distress."

Shaking his head sadly, he left the room.

Superintendent Dawle knew Father Speyd a great deal better than did most people in Hylam. During the War, he had been on the headquarters of the same brigade as that in which Speyd was a chaplain, and had formed a great attachment for the hot-headed but warm-hearted young priest.

It was only since the War that Speyd had taken to calling himself "Father." After leaving the army, he had tended rapidly to the higher extremity of church-manship until he attained definitely to what Dawle described as "fancy dress." Now he was a member of a small community known as the "Hylam Fathers," who were descended from the Oxford Movement of Manning's day, and had split off from an older foundation to form one of even more extreme views. Dawle thought that the change, so far as Speyd was concerned, had not been for the better. The army chaplain whom he had known had always been erratic, even emotional; now he had become (Dawle thought) hysterical—almost unbalanced. He did not attach a great deal of value to the outburst to which he and the others had just listened.

He had been amused at the way in which the Chief Constable had side-tracked him when it came to the point of questioning Mrs. Sterron. Evidently his Chief though him too deficient in tact for such a delicate task. He himself had always thought that Chief Constables were much too frightened of hurting people's feelings—especially people of "county" standing. He could see already the end towards which Major Threngood was working—a "hush-hush" inquest with a shelving of all awkward enquiries and a verdict of "unsound mind." Well, that was for other people to decide; for himself, he would go on, with an open mind, collecting such evidence as he could find.

His next step, he thought, must be to examine the outside of the study windows, and the ground below them. Leaving the house by the front door, he walked round the north wing, along the west face, and down a flight of steps on to the terrace from which the southern front rose. Here he saw that the study windows were a good twelve feet above ground level, so that, in the absence of any pipes or projections, it would have been impossible for any one to enter through the windows without the help of a ladder. On the other hand, it would have been possible to *leave* that way without any such help; the drop, though a severe one, would not have been impossible for an active man.

There was a stretch of turf below the window, but the ground was so hard that it was doubtful if it would receive any imprint. Still, he set himself to make a thorough examination while P.C. Coggs, who had been on guard, went in search of a short ladder. In one place below the unlatched window a dried worm-cast had been crushed to powder, but there was nothing to show that this had been done on the previous night nor by what agency.

Coggs soon returned with a ten-rung ladder.

"Good lad," said Dawle; "was it difficult to find?"

"Not if you knows where to look for ladders," said the rustic Coggs with a grin. "In the lean-to next the potting-shed."

"These country houses ask to be burgled every night," thought Dawle. "Wonder if I ought to hunt this ladder over for finger-prints."

It seemed a pretty hopeless task, but no doubt the enthusiast, Gable, would be ready to tackle it. Setting the ladder against the house, Dawle mounted till his head was on a level with the window-sill. This he examined with great care, but could see no sign of a scratch, nor anything to suggest that any one had climbed in or out that way. It was, of course, highly improbable that any one could have climbed in, without alarming the occupant of the room, even if the curtains had been shut, but the evidence showed that as long as Captain Sterron was in the room they would have been drawn back. There was, of course, the possibility of exit that way; all that Dawle could say about this as a result of his search was that it remained a possibility.

Returning to the study, he found Sergeant Gable still at work upon his finger-prints, dusting, photographing, numbering and listing. It was a task calling for infinite patience and care, the sort of task upon which the art of criminal investigation in England is based; there was no brainwork in it, only care, thoroughness and method. All these Sergeant Gable was now applying.

"Knock off a minute, Gable, and tell me what you got from the back regions," said Dawle.

Sergeant Gable straightened his aching back with a sigh of relief.

"Not much in the way of fact, sir, but a good deal of talk."

"Anything to hang your hat on?"

"Well, sir, I wouldn't say there wasn't, though it *is* only talk. Cook's been here some time and wasn't saying anything—more respect to her; but some of the girls were ready enough to air their fancies. They think their mistress has been carrying on with the gentleman at High Oaks—Sir Carle Venning."

"Carrying on? What do they mean by that? Flirting? Or more?"

"One or two of them thought it was just for a little fun—the Captain doesn't seem to have been very cheerful company for his lady—but one of the housemaids said she had seen a man's muddy footprint in the lady's sitting-room one morning when she went to do the room—one that hadn't been there the evening before."

"Muddy footprint in the sitting-room! That seems a bit unlikely."

"There's a French window to that room, sir—opens down to the ground. Any one can go in and out that way, without coming in at the front door."

"Ah, I see. But why shouldn't it have been the Captain himself?"

"She said he never went in there. It doesn't seem likely that he'd go in that way at night, with mud about."

"May have been Mr. Sterron, the brother-in-law, or some other gentleman staying in the house."

"She says there was no other gentleman staying in the house at the time."

"You don't seem to have wasted your time, Gable." Superintendent Dawle was never slow to show approval. "Which girl was this? Ethel?"

"I believe she did say that was her name, sir."

"And yours is George, eh?" The Superintendent grinned and Sergeant Gable had the grace to blush.

"Well, it's all in a good cause. I must have a talk with her myself."

"She's disengaged this evening, I understand," said Gable with a blank face.

"Now, then, young fellow, no lip. You get on back to your powder-puff; I must do some work. How much of this room have you still got to do? I don't want to touch anything you haven't photographed."

"I've done the two windows, the writing-table and chair, and the fallen chair, sir. I was just going to start on the inside of the door."

"Right you are. Go ahead."

Dawle went over to a small table by the fireplace on which stood a tray containing whisky decanter and glasses.

"One glass been used, I see," he said. "You must check this up for prints, Gable."

"I shan't forget it, sir."

The Superintendent next turned to the writing-table and started to go through the blotting pad, the correspondence baskets, and—when they had afforded nothing of interest—the drawers. The ambulance had already taken away the body of the unfortunate dragoon, but Superintendent Dawle had possessed himself of the dead man's keys—and everything else that his pockets contained. The second drawer down, when it had been unlocked, quickly attracted his attention. Accounts—other people's accounts—always fascinated Superintendent Dawle. The black account book which he now had in his hands gave promise of intriguing study; it was neatly kept and the most cursory inspection showed that it contained the details of Herbert Sterron's Stock Exchange transactions. Dawle put it aside for more leisured examination.

Other account books lay in the same drawer, most of them dealing with house and estate accounts. The next drawer yielded an index file of letters, mostly of a business, though some of a private, nature. The latter attracted Dawle's closest attention but, in a first run through, he could find nothing which seemed to throw any light on the tragedy.

Completing his search of the drawers he returned to the top of the table. The stationery box was examined and one or two books of reference which lay on the table were shaken, in case they contained any letters or sheets of paper. Nothing of the kind appeared, but Dawle's attention was attracted by a quantity of red ink scattered over the leaves of a *Baronetage and Landed Gentry*. At first the Superintendent thought that the red splashes were the result of an accident; then he saw that they ended abruptly at one place, as if the preceding part of the book had been turned back when the splashes were made. Opening the book at that place, he saw that the page was scored over with red ink. On one margin was drawn the rough figure of a man hanging from a gallows, whilst a long stroke and an arrow attached this grim cartoon to a name in the directory—the name of Sir Carle Venning, fifth baronet.

Dawle whistled.

"Come and look at this, Gable," he said. "What do you make of that?"

Sergeant Gable examined the page with interest.

"He seems to have known as much as the house-maids, sir," he said.

"What does he mean by that gallows, d'you suppose?"

"I doubt if he meant anything except temper and spite. If he knew about this affair, he might have felt a bit . . . primitive."

Gable bent down and examined the page more closely; then he smelt it.

"This ink's quite fresh, sir, I should say. It might be worth while sending it up to the Yard; they've got a chap there who specializes in inks and papers."

"That's not a bad idea, Gable. It'd be interesting to know if he did it last night."

"It might be worth hunting over for prints, too, sir. This paper looks as if it would hold them."

Dawle laughed.

"You and your prints!" he said. "All right; try it."

Gable blew a fine cloud of dark powder over the page, then blew it off again. A few grains adhered to the red ink marks, but there was not a sign of a print.

"That's disappointing, sir. I felt sure it'd take a print of some kind, but there's not a scrap of one."

"Well, it can't be helped. You know, Gable, there's that old proverb about no smoke without fire; we've got no proof that Mrs. Sterron and Sir Carle were . . . more than friends, but I've heard enough to make me want to know more. For instance, I wouldn't mind knowing what they were both doing between nine and twelve last night."

Sergeant Gable eyed his superior officer with interest.

"You don't think, sir, that they . . . ?"

"I haven't got as far as thinking yet, my lad; I merely want to know. Here's a man suddenly found dead by hanging. It's not an accident; it must be either suicide or murder. Suicide looks obvious, but why should he suddenly take his life? To clear the way for another man he evidently don't love?" Dawle pointed to the mutilated directory. "On the other hand, we've a pretty shrewd notion that that man would have liked him out of the way. We've got to satisfy ourselves that he didn't put him out. And the first step t'ards satisfying ourselves is to find out where he was and what he was doing at the time of death. And while we're finding out about him, we may as well find out about her."

There was a tap at the door and P.C. Moler put his head in.

"Beg pardon, sir, but there's a gentleman here wants a word with you."

Superintendent Dawle went out into the hall, where he found Sir James Hamsted, evidently dressed for traveling.

"The Chief Constable has kindly told me that there is no necessity for me to remain any longer, Superintendent. I thought that before leaving I would ascertain whether you had any further questions to ask me."

"That's very good of you, sir. There is just one point I'd like to ask you about. Perhaps you'd be so good as to step in here, sir."

Dawle ushered Sir James into the study and shut the door.

"I'd like to get a little more accurate about the time of things last night, sir. I understand that you and Captain Sterron had a conversation in here after dinner, and that then you left and Mr. Sterron was here for a bit, and then you and he had a game of chess together. Can you confirm that, sir, and tell me anything about times?"

"I can confirm it, certainly, but I am not sure that I can give you the times accurately. For instance, I do not know what time it was that I left this room after my conversation with Captain Sterron. I suppose we rose from dinner at about 9.15 to 9.30 P.M., and that our conversation lasted for some quarter of an hour to twenty minutes, but I am afraid that is very vague. On the other hand, I can tell you that Mr. Sterron rejoined me in the library just before ten, because I remember thinking it was getting late, if we were to play our game of chess, and looking up at the clock. As to the time of our game ending, I think it was either just before or just after two. It was a very long game."

"And you were together all that time from ten to two?"

"Yes, all the time."

"And you heard nothing unusual?"

"Nothing; the house was very silent and I think we should have heard any unusual noise. On the other hand, it is true that we were absorbed in our game."

"Mrs. Sterron, sir; was she in here while you were talking to the Captain, or in the library while you were playing chess?"

"No. She retired immediately after dinner. I understood her to say that she had some letters to write."

"And you saw no one else in the house during the evening? No other visitor?"

"No, none."

"Well, sir, I'm very much obliged to you for this little talk. May I have your address, in case there is anything else I want to ask you?"

"It is in the telephone directory. I shall, of course, come down for the inquest, if you will let me know the time and place."

"Very useful type of witness, that, Gable," said the Superintendent when Sir James had departed. "Knows what he knows—and what he doesn't know. You must get in touch with the girls again, Gable, and find out what my lady was up to last night. Find out, too, about those letters she said she had to write; I don't suppose the post has left here yet, but in any case they should be easy to trace."

A gong—a very subdued gong—sounded through the house.

"Good, they'll be going in to lunch now and we shall be able to move about a bit."

Footsteps sounded in the hall outside and the dining-room door closed.

"Sounded like two of 'em—a man and a woman. Hasn't put her off her grub, then."

"There's a secretary, sir; it may have been her."

"Oh, there is, is there? I haven't heard about her. At least, I suppose I have, but I'd forgotten about it. What's she like, Gable?"

"Youngish, not bad-looking, they tell me. Name of Nawten."

"Ah, you haven't come across her yourself? No, she'd be front regions, I suppose. Well, we mustn't overlook anybody. Now, then, come along and do the outside of this door."

Carefully Sergeant Gable sprayed his cloud of powder over the outside panels of the door, then as carefully blew it off again. A fair amount remained adhering to what were presumably blurred finger-prints. The handle itself was a hopeless muddle and so was the wooden frame just above it, where people were accustomed to take hold of the door to shut it. Carefully Gable ran his eye up and down the surface.

"Here's rather an interesting print, sir," he said, pointing to a mark considerably above the others.

Superintendent Dawle examined it carefully.

"Yes, that's a good print," he said; "seems to have got a scar right across it, unless it's a flaw in the wood."

"It's a scar all right, sir. Right down the ball of the first finger of the right hand. That should be easy enough to trace. But isn't that rather an odd place for a print—so high up?"

"Not necessarily, I don't think. May have been some one pushing the door open. You can see the hand was pointing upwards, from the position of the other fingers. Just get a photograph of that and then we'll make a faint pencil mark so that we shall know the height in case we want it again."

As soon as that job was done, Dawle sent Sergeant Gable off to enquire about Mrs. Sterron's movements on the previous night, and also about her letters. The servants' hall dinner would, of course, be over by now, and with the "dining-room" engaged, it was a good time to question the female servants. Dawle himself crossed the hall and went along the passage beyond the library door. On the left beyond that was the drawing-room, now looking rather dreary with its unchanged flowers. Opposite to it was a room of similar size and shape, the appearance of which at once identified it as Mrs. Sterron's sitting-room. Dawle was not at the moment interested in its contents, though he would dearly have liked to run through the writing-table, but he was interested in the French window at the northern end of the room—a window which opened direct on to the path which ran round the house. Clearly this was a postern by which the lady of the house could admit—and dismiss—any one she liked, without any one else in the house being the wiser.

Dawle examined the floor just inside the window, but in this weather there was little chance of finding any footmarks. The best that he could get out of his search of the room was the fact that the sofa looked as if it had been sat on by two people; he assumed for the moment that no one else had used the room since the previous night and that the maids had been too much agitated to tidy it that morning. He was just ending his search when Sergeant Gable appeared.

"Nobody knows anything about Mrs. Sterron last night, sir, except perhaps her maid, and she won't talk. But Ethel says there were no letters in the basket when she came to open the shutters this morning, and there are none of Mrs. Sterron's in the post-box now."

VII. "LEAVE IT ALONE!"

SUPERINTENDENT DAWLE drove back to Hylam with the Chief Constable, leaving his own car for Sergeant Gable who, with the two constables, would remain in case the news of the tragedy should bring a crowd of Sunday afternoon sensation-seekers out to Ferris Court.

Major Threngood had not, Dawle gathered, been much more successful in getting information out of Mrs. Sterron at his second interview with her than at his first. She was still suffering from shock and seemed to the Chief Constable rather hysterical. She had talked a good deal but conveyed very little; she was completely surprised by what had occurred, the idea of suicide in connection with her husband had never occurred to her, and she knew of no reason why he should make away with himself unless it was something to do with his health. She thought that, in spite of the financial crisis through which the country was passing, her husband had succeeded in saving money recently as he had done for some years past. Certainly he did not seem to be unduly worried about money, though he was always very careful ("mean," the Chief Constable gathered) about it. There was nothing at all enlightening in all that. Nothing was said about Sir Carle Venning and Dawle gathered that his Chief had not asked Mrs. Sterron about him; "tact" had been well to the fore— and information was in the background.

The two officials had a hurried lunch at a wayside

inn on their way to Hylam and then drove straight to Dr. Tanwort's house.

The police surgeon had just finished his Sunday luncheon of roast beef and apple-tart and was smoking his Sunday afternoon cigar. Being now on his own dung-hill he was more than usually buoyant.

"Ah, Major, glad to see you here, melancholy occasion or no melancholy occasion. Have a cigar—my own choosing, not a Christmas present—no? What about you, Superintendent? Well, you'll excuse me if I go on with my own—crime to let a good cigar go out."

He drew slowly at the rather anemic-looking weed.

"Now, then in what way can I help you? I've not tackled the P.M. yet—do that this afternoon. Not that I expect it to reveal anything we don't know already."

"You're satisfied as to the cause of death?"

"Oh, quite, quite. All the evidence of death from asphyxia induced by strangulation—both circumstantial and clinical. I shall make an examination of the stomach and brain as a matter of form, but there can be no doubt about it."

"Do you know of any reason why he should have taken his own life? You were his doctor, weren't you?"

"I was, yes; his local doctor; he went to a man in Harley Street as well. I haven't seen him often—only from time to time. But I know his history. Yes, I think I can account for it, so far as one ever can account for another man's actions. I shouldn't have taken the same way out myself, it's true, but then I flatter myself that I should never have been in the same hole. Captain Sterron suffered—has suffered for many years—you'll understand, gentlemen, that this is strictly confidential —professional secrecy and all that, but as I'm police surgeon, I suppose I must do my best to assist the police, eh?"

Major Threngood did not feel at all so sure about the correctness of the doctor's attitude, but after all it was the business of the police—as it had been of Rikki Tikki—to "run and find out"; other people must look after their own ethics.

"Captain Sterron suffered from a distressing complaint. Yes, very severely, only two or three years after his marriage. Seems very extraordinary to us that a man can't—but there, these big, full-blooded men are often very little more than animals. Complete breakdown of health as a result; left the army and buried himself down here. Frequent repercussions. Wonder she stuck to him myself, but these High Church people are very funny about that."

"But do you mean to tell me that Sterron killed himself because of this . . . complaint?"

"That's what I believe."

"Was it as bad as all that? Would you have said his life was a burden to him?"

Dr. Tanwort considered.

"I shouldn't have put it as high as all that," he said, "but sensitive people get very much upset about that sort of thing. It may have been preying on his mind for years."

"But why—if it's been going on all these years—why should he suddenly take this extreme step now?"

"Ah, why, indeed? That's one of the things one'll never know about one's fellow-men, Major—why they do the things they do when they do them. Probably no two of us, though we might decide to take the same course of action, would ever decide to take it at the same time." Dr. Tanwort prided himself upon being something of a philosopher. "Perhaps some special event, or circumstances, unknown to us, started a train of remorse, or despair . . . which ended in that noose. It's a funny world, but there it is."

The Chief Constable turned to his Superintendent.

"Do you want to ask Dr. Tanwort any questions, Dawle?" he asked.

"Not till after he's made his autopsy, sir, I fancy. But I'd like him to be on a special look-out for bruises or marks of violence of any kind."

"Oh, of course, naturally, Superintendent. As a matter of fact, I've already made a superficial examination to that end—the appearance changes so quickly you know—post-mortem staining is very liable to be mistaken for bruising, if one leaves it too long. But there's nothing of that kind. And a big man like Sterron couldn't have been strangled without a great deal of violence."

"No scalp wound or bump, sir? He couldn't have been stunned?"

"Oh, no, quite impossible."

"What about chloroform?"

"Bound to have smelt it in a room shut up all night."

Superintendent Dawle relapsed into silence. The Chief Constable rose to his feet.

"I'm much obliged to you, Doctor," he said. "You'll let us have your report as soon as possible, I'm sure. I must go and see the Coroner about his inquest."

"I've had a word with him already, Major," said Tanwort, ushering his visitors out into the little hall. "We thought three o'clock tomorrow, if that suited you."

"I see. Well, I'll have a talk to him about it. Good afternoon."

Superintendent Dawle shared his chief's feeling that the police surgeon was inclined to take too much upon himself. The time of the inquest was no business of his, except that he would be called to give evidence at it.

"Let's go along to your office and talk this over, Dawle," said Major Threngood. "Then I'll see Lovejoy."

Within five minutes the two officials were sitting in the Superintendent's bare but spotless room.

"Unless anything unexpected crops up in the post-mortem, I take it that we can go right ahead with this, Dawle? You're satisfied, I suppose?"

The Superintendent remained silent for a full minute, collecting his thoughts.

"I wouldn't like to say that, sir, until after the autopsy," he said at last. "I'd like to be sure there's nothing in the stomach that could have made him unconscious while some one strung him up."

"But what puts that idea in your head?"

"I wouldn't say it was as much as an idea, sir, but I'd just like to be sure. There's that unlatched window; somebody *could* have got out that way."

"But who would want to kill Captain Sterron?"

"Well, sir, as I told you coming over, there's this story about Sir Carle Venning and Mrs. Sterron."

The Chief Constable frowned.

"Mere servants' chatter," he said. "We can't pay any attention to that."

"Sir James Hamsted said he'd noticed something of the kind, sir."

"But he'd only been there twenty-four hours! What could he have seen?"

"Not much, perhaps, sir, but it shows which way the wind was blowing. I think I should go over and see Sir Carle and find out what he was doing last night."

Consternation showed itself unmistakably in the Chief Constable's guileless face.

"Good heavens, man, you can't do that! There'd be a frightful row. Why, he's High Sheriff!"

Lèse-majesté to a High Sheriff! It would be the Lord Lieutenant—Cousin Frederick—next!

Superintendent Dawle's face assumed its most mulish aspect.

"I should consider we were not doing our duty, sir, without we looked into that matter."

"No, no, Dawle, I can't have that. It would create a most unpleasant sensation if it become known—as it very well might—that we were making such an enquiry. I can't see that there's any justification for it, Dawle, I really can't."

"Very well, sir. Of course, it's for you to say."

The significant note in the Superintendent's voice brought home to Threngood the responsibility of his position. For the first time since his appointment he realized that his office was something more than an interesting, well-paid job. It might carry with it the difference between life and death, justice and injustice; it was a terrible responsibility.

For five minutes he sat, his head clasped between his hands. Then abruptly he got up.

"No, Dawle," he said. "Unless something fresh turns up at the inquest, I can't agree to stirring up mud on such flimsy evidence. Leave it alone."

"Does that refer only to Sir Carle Venning, sir, or do you want all police enquiry stopped?"

"Why, what other enquiry can there be?"

"There were other people in the house last night, sir, and there may be other motives. For instance, we don't know what's in the will yet, but, unless Captain Sterron's left everything to his wife, the odds are that Ferris Court will now go to his brother, Mr. Gerald Sterron."

VIII. INQUEST

THE inquest on Captain Herbert Sterron, which after all had been postponed till Tuesday morning, was held in the Board Room of the Hylam Hospital. The room was not a large one and by the time the various officials, witnesses and relatives had been accommodated, there was not much room left for the general public. The case had not aroused as much interest as might have been expected, possibly because there had been no suggestion of foul play and also because Captain Sterron himself had never aroused much interest in the neighborhood.

Superintendent Dawle, who had been careful to take an inconspicuous seat while yet being near the Coroner in case he was needed, looked round at the crowded room. In the front row of seats facing the Coroner sat Mrs. Sterron, with Gerald Sterron on one side of her and on the other a man in London clothes whom Dawle took to be a solicitor. Sir James Hamsted occupied a chair on the other side of Gerald Sterron. Griselda Sterron herself was in black, not yet in the widow's weeds which she would undoubtedly wear as soon as they were ready for her, but in a well-cut coat and skirt and a small black hat that hid the brilliant hair and emphasized the largeness and darkness of her eyes. She sat very quietly with her eyes upon her folded hands, occasionally inclining her head to listen to a whispered word from one of her neighbors. Superintendent Dawle had not yet had an opportunity of talking to her, but had received from the Chief Constable a restrained account of his own two interviews. Rather unjustly Dawle had formed his own opinion of the lady from this and other hearsay evidence; he wondered what sort of pose she would choose to adopt in the witness-box.

The Coroner, Mr. Robert Lovejoy, senior partner of Messrs. Lovejoy, Grone & Lovejoy, Solicitors, Hylam, took his seat punctually at 11 A.M. Having informed the jury that he had himself viewed the body, that they were entitled to do so if they wished but need not, and having received their assurance that they were happy to leave that melancholy privilege to him, he proceeded to call witnesses as to identity in the persons of Mrs. Sterron, widow, and Mr. Gerald Sterron, brother of the deceased.

Dawle saw at once that Griselda Sterron was either genuinely shocked by her husband's death or else had decided that this was an occasion where care was more important than effect. Instead of the dramatic performance which he had expected, she answered the Coroner's sympathetic questions in a quiet, even voice and gave no sign of being aware of the eager interest which her words and her appearance were arousing.

Having given, in reply to the Coroner's questions, her own name and the date of her marriage, she assured the jury that she identified the deceased as the man to whom she had been married. Very shortly she gave her own account of the evening of her husband's death. She had, she said, retired immediately after dinner to write some letters before going early to bed; she had felt over-tired and had taken a sleeping draught in order to ensure a good night's rest. She and her husband occupied separate rooms—had done so for many years.

She had not heard any unusual sound, owing, no doubt, to the effect of the sleeping draught. The Coroner thanked her and asked her to stand down, intimating that he might have some further questions to put to her at a later stage.

Gerald Sterron, looking, in his somber clothes, considerably older than he had done on the previous day, gave formal evidence of identification, the Coroner intimating that, in his case, too, it would probably be more convenient to postpone his further examination until after the medical evidence had been taken.

Ethel Sturt, housemaid, next informed the jury how she had found the study door locked on the inside, why that had surprised her, what time she had made her discovery, and how she had informed "Mr. Willing."

Harold Willing, butler, for his part recounted his own examination of the study door, his awakening of Mr. Gerald Sterron, his participation in the breaking-down of the door, and the discovery of his master's body suspended from the curtain pole. His description of the scene and his own reaction to it were so realistic that the whole audience—those of it, that is, who did not know the story beforehand—were held spellbound. A woman at the back of the court gave a little scream of excited horror, and Mr. Willing, suddenly realizing that he was displaying characteristics which he was not supposed to possess, dried up and answered the remaining formal enquiries in a flat monotone.

The next witness was clearly the star turn, both in his own estimation and that of the public. Dr. Tanwort strode to the chair which constituted the witness-box with firm steps, took the oath with assurance, and gave his name and style with the unmistakable pride of a man who knows that that name and style are respected, and rightly respected, by his fellows.

"Please give us an account of your investigations in your own words, Dr. Tanwort," said the Coroner courteously.

"Certainly, Mr. Coroner. I was called at my house by telephone at about 7 A.M. on Sunday morning by Superintendent Dawle, who informed me shortly of what had occurred and that he would pick me up in his car and take me to Ferris Court. Arrived there, I, in company with Superintendent Dawle, entered the study and at once saw the body of the deceased, whom I identified as Captain Herbert Sterron, suspended by a piece of cord from the pole which carries the curtains. The other end of the cord was fastened, I may say, to a radiator standing in the window.

"I saw at once that the deceased had been dead for some hours. With the help of Superintendent Dawle, I cut the body down and laid it upon a sofa. I then examined it. The ligature was in the form of a running noose and was deeply embedded in the flesh of the neck. The deceased is a heavy man, a good fourteen stone, I should say, and if the cord had not been unusually thick for curtain cord—I should add that it had evidently been cut from the length of cord used for drawing the curtains—it might easily have cut right into the flesh. It might also have broken if there had been anything of a drop, but neither of these things had occurred.

"The appearance of the deceased, the nature of the constriction mark round the neck, the circumstances in which the body was found, and subsequent post-mortem examination of the lungs and chest were all consistent with, and only consistent with, death from asphyxia from strangulation; but to make doubly sure that there can have been no contributory cause of death, I have examined the stomach, which contains nothing at all abnormal—no drug or poison of any kind—and the whole surface of the body, which displays no sign whatever of violence. I have no hesitation in saying that death is due to the cause I have stated—asphyxia arising from strangulation—and that it was self-inflicted."

"Thank you, Dr. Tanwort, that is very clear." Mr. Lovejoy made a pretense of examining his notes, whereas actually he was wondering how best to overcome a rather awkward passage in the enquiry.

"I think, gentlemen," he said, addressing the jury, "that it will be convenient if at this point we ask Mrs. Sterron to return and complete her evidence. I shan't keep you long, Doctor."

Dr. Tanwort, glancing at his watch as if to indicate that his time was indeed precious, returned to his seat and was replaced by Griselda.

"Now, Mrs. Sterron," began the Coroner. "I am anxious to cause you as little distress as possible, but I am bound to ask you one or two questions of a rather personal nature. You have heard the last witness state that, in his opinion, your husband took his own life. Had you any reason to anticipate his doing so?"

Superintendent Dawle, who was watching Griselda very closely, thought that she turned a shade paler at the question, in spite of the fact that she must have anticipated it. Her reply, however, came without hesitation.

"I certainly did not."

"Can you suggest any reason for his doing so?"

For a second the brown eyes lifted, not to the Coroner's face but to the back of the room. It was only a momentary glance and Dawle, following it, could see no one who might have attracted it.

"I really don't know what to suggest," said Mrs. Sterron in a voice that barely carried to the jury. "My husband has been liable to fits of depression for a very long time—since before the War. . . . They were due partly to ill-health and partly to money troubles. I suppose it must have been something to do with one of those."

"You know of no immediate cause? No special trouble arising from one or other of those causes?"

"No, I don't. But my husband did not confide in me very much. He might have had some trouble without telling me."

Mr. Lovejoy shifted his chair and cleared his throat.

"Now, Mrs. Sterron, there's one subject I must touch on which is rather delicate, I'm afraid. You said just now—in your first examination—that you and your husband had for many years occupied separate rooms; was that due to some estrangement between you?"

Griselda raised her eyes and looked the Coroner squarely in the face.

"My husband and I were not estranged, Mr. Lovejoy," she said.

"But you did not admit him to your bedroom?"

A flush spread over Griselda's face, making it suddenly alive and beautiful. There was a note of indignation in her voice as she answered.

"I was my husband's wife . . . always," she said.

"You   mean . . . in   the . . . er . . . technical sense?"

"In every sense."

"Thank you, Mrs. Sterron. I am sure we are very glad to hear it," said Mr. Lovejoy, somewhat taken aback. "And there was no ground for his action so far as you personally were concerned?"

"What do you mean?"

"There was no question of jealousy on his part?"

"Jealousy of what?"

How tiresome women could be, thought Mr. Lovejoy. He had been leading her so gently, so tactfully through the delicate stages—unfortunately inevitable in an enquiry of this character—and here she was insisting on the dotting of i's and crossing of t's.

"Jealous of you, madam—of your affection for some other man," said Mr. Lovejoy testily.

"What other man? Why should you suggest such a thing?"

There was no pale, drooping widow now, but an angry, indignant woman. Had the former quiet manner been deliberately adopted, Dawle wondered, as a background to this righteous wrath? If so, it was admirably done—and effective. The Coroner stammered and withdrew.

"I . . . I have no reason to suppose that such a state of affairs existed. I merely asked—as a matter of form—whether it did."

"It did not!"

"That's the stuff to give 'im," murmured Henry, the footman, into the rosy ear of Ethel.

"Thank you, Mrs. Sterron. I don't think I need detain you any longer. Unless, that is, any member of the jury wishes, through me, to ask you anything."

More than one member of the jury would have liked

to, but Griselda's counter-attack had been too effective; they held their peace.

"I should say, Mrs. Sterron, that if you like to retire now, I see no further necessity to detain you. The jury will in due course wish, I have no doubt, to express their very deep sympathy with you in the grievous loss you have sustained; an expression with which I shall beg to be allowed to associate myself."

"Thank you."

With head erect now, and bright eyes, Griselda Sterron walked out of the room, followed by her brother-in-law. It was an effective exit and there was a regrettably ill-timed attempt at applause, instantly suppressed by the Coroner's officer.

Mr. Lovejoy heaved an inward sigh of relief. Now Mrs. Sterron was out of the way he could more easily handle the remainder of Dr. Tanwort's evidence.

Recalled, the police surgeon attempted a repetition of his former rendering of the part of "expert witness"; somehow it now fell slightly flat, perhaps because of the absence of the "name and style" and of the oath.

"Dr. Tanwort, you were the deceased's medical attendant, were you not?"

"I was, sir."

"Mrs. Sterron has told us that her husband suffered from ill-health which sometimes caused depression. Can you tell us anything about that?"

"I can tell you that he did occasionally suffer from ill-health and that he did have fits of depression. Or rather, I should say, that he suffered a persistent depression of spirits which at times was more pronounced than at others."

"And the nature of that ill-health?"

Dr. Tanwort produced his pocket-book and from the pocket-book a piece of paper.

"Perhaps it would be more convenient, Mr. Coroner, if I gave you that in writing."

He handed the piece of paper to the Coroner's officer, who gave it to the Coroner, who glanced at it and passed it on to the jury.

"I think I may agree to that course," said Mr. Lovejoy.

The piece of paper passed round the jury, to whom, with one or two exceptions, it appeared to convey very little, and was then handed by the Coroner to Captain Sterron's solicitor, who in turn glanced at and returned it.

"Any question which the jury wish to ask . . . through me?"

An elderly, thin-faced man, who was well known to Superintendent Dawle as a rather unsuccessful chemist, rose to his feet.

"D'you mean to tell us," he asked, "that that's enough to make a man hang himself?"

"A sensitive man might do so, certainly," replied Dr. Tanwort warily, scenting a slight.

"Through me, I said, Mr. Leck," said the Coroner.

Mr. Leck sniffed audibly and sat down.

Mr. Lovejoy glanced at the solicitor, who shook his head.

"That is all, then, Dr. Tanwort, thank you. The jury and I are much obliged to you for your evidence."

Mr. Leck sniffed again and Dr. Tanwort, throwing him a glance of indignation, strode out of the room. A youth in the background brought the palms of his hands smartly together and two or three others laughed.

"Silence!" roared the Coroner's officer.

"If there is any further interruption of that nature," said Mr. Lovejoy icily, "I shall clear the court."

"Mr. John Halfcastle."

The London-clad man who had sat next to Griselda advanced and took the oath.

"You are Mr. John Halfcastle?"

"Yes, sir."

"You represent Halfcastle and Blett, solicitors to the late Captain Sterron?"

"That is so."

"You have heard Mrs. Sterron tell us that her late husband was depressed about money troubles. Can you tell us about that?"

Mr. Halfcastle, in whom twenty years of Lincoln's Inn had engendered a gravity and caution beyond his age, took time to think before committing himself to an answer.

"I am in a position to provide information on the subject of the deceased's financial position," he said at last.

Mr. Lovejoy with difficulty repressed a smile; how well he and his witness knew the moves.

"If you will be so good, Mr. Halfcastle. Quite briefly, in the first place. Then if any points occur to the jury or myself upon which we should like further enlightenment, I will frame some questions."

Mr. Halfcastle picked up a sheet of foolscap paper which he had previously taken from his attaché case.

"Captain Sterron inherited the property, including the mansion house of Ferris Court, from his father in 1907. After paying death duties, which at that time were not unduly severe, Captain Sterron was left with a substantial income, derived partly from his agricultural estate, but principally from stocks and from property in Liverpool. Unfortunately, Captain Sterron attempted to increase the income by exchanging his securities of a trustee status for others of a more attractive but less stable nature; he suffered a series of misfortunes and his position became definitely embarrassed. The War improved matters for a time, principally owing to the considerable reduction in expenditure which was effected by the closing of Ferris Court. Since the War, the growing agricultural depression has reduced to a pittance the income previously derived from the agricultural estate and Captain Sterron has had to rely upon a few remaining dividends and the income from property in Liverpool."

"What sort of property?" asked a member of the jury.

"House property in Everdale."

"Slum landlord," interjected the juryman.

"Mr. Leck, please!" exclaimed the Coroner sharply. "I must ask you to control yourself. I am sorry, Mr. Halfcastle; please continue."

"Captain Sterron has for some years been attempting to restore the financial stability of the estate which had been destroyed by his unfortunate . . . er . . ."

"Speculations," from among the jury.

The Coroner glared.

"The word, I think, effectively describes the transactions in question," said Mr. Halfcastle with a slight smile. "By a deed, executed in 1924, he assigned to trustees the income from his Liverpool property for a period of twenty-one years, such income to be accumulated and reinvested in the form of a sinking-fund. In the meantime, Captain Sterron has reduced his expenditure at Ferris to the lowest possible point consistent with maintaining the structure and contents in adequate repair. It is hoped that by the time the trust expires, that is to say, in 1945, a sufficient sum will have been accumulated to provide an income adequate to the maintenance of such a property as Ferris Court."

Mr. Lovejoy waited a moment for the witness to continue, but as Mr. Halfcastle had apparently said all he proposed to say, the Coroner took up the running.

"That is all very clear, I think, Mr. Halfcastle. Can you now tell us whether Captain Sterron was unduly depressed by his financial position?"

"He was worried by it and, I think, deeply remorseful at his own share of responsibility in the misfortunes that had befallen the estate."

"Was all this preying on his mind?"

"That I am not in a position to say."

"Was the financial situation so serious as, in your opinion, to drive a sensitive man to self-destruction?"

"That, again, sir, I cannot answer. I have no criterion upon which to base an opinion."

"Let me put it this way: did you expect Captain Sterron to commit suicide?"

"Certainly not."

"Were you surprised to learn that he had?"

Mr. Halfcastle raised his eyebrows.

"I was not aware, sir, that it had yet been established that he had."

The Coroner blushed.

"I must apologize, Mr. Halfcastle," he said. "I fully accept your correction. I should say: 'Would it surprise you to hear that it had been suggested that he had taken his own life?'"

Again the shadow of a smile flickered across Mr. Halfcastle's full lips.

"It would never surprise me to hear anything suggested," he said.

Mr. Lovejoy frowned. Was this London solicitor having the impertinence to play with him?

"I am afraid I do not make myself clear to you, sir," he said sharply, "though my meaning must surely be plain. You say that you did not expect Captain Sterron to commit suicide; I ask you now: does the idea of suicide by Captain Sterron surprise you? Or not?"

"It does surprise me."

"Thank you. Now, gentlemen, have you any further questions which you would like put to Mr. Halfcastle?"

Mr. Leck rose to his feet again.

"If he was so hard up, why didn't he sell the place and let a better man have it?"

"That question is not in any way relevant to the enquiry. I shall not put it to the witness," said the Coroner acidly.

"If you will permit me, sir," said Mr. Halfcastle, "I should like none the less to answer it. My client would have considered it the deepest disgrace for any individual Sterron to sell a property which had been in the family for no fewer than four hundred years."

"A very proper answer. Thank you, Mr. Halfcastle." The Coroner consulted his watch.

"Gentlemen, it is now 1.15 and we have still three or four more witnesses to hear. We will adjourn until 2

P.M. You will be conducted by my officer to a room in which lunch will be provided for you. I must caution you not to hold any communication with any member of the outside public and especially not to discuss the case other than among yourselves."

IX. ADJOURNMENT

THE court cleared slowly of all save those who had either brought their lunch with them or preferred to go without it rather than run the risk of losing their seats. The Coroner remained at his table writing up his notes, but looked up as a precise voice addressed him.

"Mr. Coroner, I shall have to return to town directly after giving my evidence. Have I your permission to pay my last respects to my old friend now? I am Sir James Hamsted."

Mr. Lovejoy rose to his feet.

"I am very pleased to meet you, Sir James," he said. "Of course I know you well by name. I am very sorry not to have been able to call you sooner, but it seemed to me essential to get Mrs. Sterron out of the way first and then call the two witnesses as to causes of depression. I gathered that your evidence was purely corroboratory of that given by Mr. Gerald Sterron."

"Up to a point, yes. Your conduct of the case so far, if I may be allowed to say so, sir, appears to me exemplary."

Mr. Lovejoy bowed.

"Very good of you, Sir James. Now, you want to see the body? Certainly. A little unusual perhaps, but I shall be very happy to take you over to the mortuary myself. Then there can be no ground for criticism."

He led the way down a long corridor, up some steps, round a corner and out through a side door. A long incline took them on to the gravel sweep at the back of the hospital, where ambulances discharged their loads on to the wheeled trollies that could run up the incline. Across the gravel sweep stood a squat brick building, into the door of which Mr. Lovejoy now fitted a key.

"Chapel on the right, mortuary on the left," he said, fitting a small key into the inner door.

Footsteps sounded on the gravel outside and Dr. Tanwort appeared.

"Going in, Mr. Lovejoy? I thought I'd just come and see that all was ship-shape. They'll be taking the body back to Ferris after you've recorded your finding, I understand."

"So I am told," replied the Coroner. "You know Sir James Hamsted? This is Dr. Tanwort, Sir James; the police surgeon."

Sir James nodded. Dr. Tanwort bowed.

"I had the pleasure . . . er . . . er . . . the somewhat melancholy pleasure under the circumstances . . . of meeting you at Ferris Court on Sunday, Sir James. A very sad business. An old friend of yours, I understand."

Sir James nodded again and Mr. Lovejoy, seeing that his companion was not interested in Dr. Tanwort, pushed open the door and went in.

The low, white-tiled room was lit by two frosted windows, which, in spite of the sunshine without, admitted only a dull, greenish light. On a slab in the center of the room lay a still, shrouded figure. Mr. Lovejoy turned back the thick cotton sheet and the three men looked down upon the mortal remains of Herbert Sterron. The body had not yet been finally draped for burial as the jury had the technical right to make a complete inspection of it should they wish; it was, however, heavily bandaged to cover the wounds of the post-mortem examination of chest and abdomen and brain. The features had almost lost the contorted look which Sir James Hamsted had last seen on them; even the constriction mark had become less terrible.

Sir James bent down and stared closely at the dead features—a stare which Mr. Lovejoy found disconcerting. Dr. Tanwort, accustomed to such sights and less impressed by the great in death than in their living dignity, fussed about the room, tidying up bandages and appliances that he had forgotten previously to remove. Presently he rejoined the others, carrying a kidney-dish containing a set of dentures.

"What are we to do with these, Mr. Coroner?" he asked. "Seems a pity to bury 'em. Good work here—expensive work. A dental hospital would be only too thankful for them."

Mr. Lovejoy looked pained.

"Surely they should be left . . . er . . . *in situ*, unless the relatives direct otherwise," he said.

"Easier said than done, as a matter of fact," replied Tanwort lightly, "I can't make the damn things fit."

"What's that?" exclaimed Sir James sharply.

"I can't make them fit, Sir James. I tried this morning."

"Which, the lower plate?"

"Yes."

"Let me look at it."

The air of authority, which had had such a powerful effect upon Gerald Sterron, had returned. Dr. Tanwort instinctively held out the dish. Sir James picked up the lower plate and examined it carefully.

"Open the mouth," he said shortly.

Obediently Dr. Tanwort complied and Sir James, his long, slim fingers moving carefully from side to side, inserted the plate and attempted to fit it into position. Mr. Lovejoy watched with mingled astonishment and interest.

"Torch," snapped Sir James.

Dr. Tanwort extracted a thin electric torch from his waistcoat pocket and flashed it into the mouth. Sir James's head bent closer as he patiently manipulated the obstinate denture. At last he pulled it out and again closely examined it.

"This has been bent," he said. "By whom?"

"Not by me," said Dr. Tanwort indignantly. "It was loose in the mouth when I made my examination."

"What! Loose in the mouth; and you have not reported the fact?"

He glared at the unfortunate doctor, who in turn stared and stammered.

"W-why should I? W-what's the significance?"

"Significance? Good heavens, man; where are your wits?" Sir James turned to Lovejoy. "Mr. Coroner, this is a most serious matter. It runs entirely counter to the suggestion of suicide. You must surely see that for yourself."

The Coroner looked slightly bewildered.

"Er . . . not altogether. You mean that force . . ."

"I mean that, unless I am much mistaken, this man did not die of strangulation at all."

Turning down the dead man's lower lip he took the torch from Dr. Tanwort's nerveless hand and switched on the light.

"Look," he said. "As I thought—bruised and swollen

—even now. What have you been about, Dr. Tanwort? Of what has your examination consisted? You have not, I see, made any microscopic section of the constriction mark; how could you be sure that the discoloration was due to ecchymosis and not to hypostasis?"

Dr. Tanwort rallied in his own defense.

"By what right, sir, may I ask, do you question me? This is a professional matter. No layman has any right to speak to me in such a way." The blustering tone barely concealed the underlying anxiety. It was a last effort.

"I am not a layman, Dr. Tanwort, as you should know if you kept up to date with your work. I was a doctor in general practice for twenty years before I was appointed Inspector of Factories under the Home Office. I have written many articles upon medical jurisprudence arising out of experience gained during my service as coroner to the South-Western district of London. It has seldom been my lot to see such a slip-shod piece of work as this."

Dr. Tanwort's wind-blown buoyancy collapsed. Mr. Lovejoy was in little better case. He knew the name of Hamsted vaguely in connection with Government work, but had entirely failed to associate it with the almost forgotten London holder of his own honorable office.

Having made his effect, Sir James spoke more quietly.

"There is very little doubt that this man was first suffocated and then hanged after death to simulate suicide," he said. "It is an old trick and one that should not in these days have passed a detailed examination, though I admit that it was cleverly faked. No doubt, Mr. Coroner, you will now think it advisable to adjourn your enquiry until the police have had time to look more closely into the matter."

And so it came about that when the court was re-opened, the public were astonished to hear that, owing to the appearance of fresh evidence of an important character, the enquiry would stand adjourned until that day fortnight.

X. GRACE NAWTEN

SUPERINTENDENT DAWLE listened in respectful but complacent silence while his Chief and the Coroner discussed the startling discovery made by Sir James Hamsted. Dawle was in the comfortable position of having urged further investigation, of having expressed suspicions—indefinite, it was true, but still, suspicions. The Chief Constable, on the other hand, had insisted on a "hush-hush" policy, on leaving mud unstirred, and the mud, in the pleasant way it has, had of its own accord given forth a stench sufficient to attract attention.

It was most fortunate—for the Chief Constable—that the new discovery had been made before the verdict of the Coroner's jury had been given; the public would now think that the new discovery was due to the "tireless assiduity" of the police; whereas if the latter had sat still and allowed a verdict of "suicide" to be given without raising the slightest question of doubt, it would have looked very much as if they had been caught napping. Which would have been unfair to Superintendent Dawle, who, though the particular evidence had escaped him—after all, his expert witness had made a glaring blunder—had none the less been full of suspicion.

He was, then, in the happy position of being able to say "I told you so" to his Chief, though, of course, wild horses would not have induced him to say it. But he could, and did, with all possible respect, look it.

"Of course, we shall have to get a second post-mortem examination made now," Mr. Lovejoy was saying. "I gather from Sir James that Tanwort's was a most superficial affair. There should have been a section taken from the neck so that a microscopic examination of the constriction mark could be made. Apparently the only way you can really tell whether the hanging was done before or after death is to see whether there is bruising—ecchymosis, they call it—about the mark of the ligature, or on the larynx. The discoloration which is visible to the eye may simply be due to post-mortem staining—and that's what seems to have happened in this case. Examination of the tissues under the microscope will tell at once which it is; Tanwort seems to have taken it for granted."

"Well, he'll lose his police job, anyway," growled Major Threngood. "Who are we going to get to do it, then? Hamsted?"

"Oh, no, he's not practicing now and his position in any case puts that quite out of the question. No, we had better get the Home Office to send somebody down. Lemuel, or Pryde. Tanwort will probably have to be present. Doctors are very careful of each other's feelings."

"Damn the fellow; I wouldn't bother about his feelings—letting us down like that."

The Chief Constable turned to Superintendent Dawle.

"If we're going to have the Home Office shoving its oar in we shall have to have the Yard," he said crossly.

Dawle's expression changed in a flash from complacence to consternation.

"Of course, it's as you decide, sir," he managed to get out.

"Technically, yes, but you know what it'll be. If we don't call them in the Home Office'll be badgering us every day about the progress we're making and are we sure we hadn't better let the Yard send a man down, etc., etc. We'd better face up to it and have him down straight away. It'll be an unpleasant business anyway; we'd better let them pull the chestnuts out of the fire—not that there'll be any chestnuts."

Dawle's gloomy silence can hardly have been taken for consent, but the Chief Constable did not bother about that. After Mr. Lovejoy had spoken to the Home Office Major Threngood took over the telephone and in a few minutes announced that Scotland Yard were sending a man down that evening.

"You'd better start getting on to the job straight away, Dawle," said Major Threngood; "then you can have something to start him on when he comes."

"I beg your pardon, sir, but what exactly is the position? I've never had experience of working with Scotland Yard before. Does he work direct under the Yard or under us?"

"Technically, I believe, he's lent to us and so, nominally, at any rate, works under my orders. But he certainly reports to the Yard as well, and, in practice, I think it means working together—tact, and all that sort of thing. I expect you'll find he knows how to behave himself. It's an inspector they're sending, so he'll be junior to you, Dawle, but I should go easy with him."

Superintendent Dawle thought that the relationship sounded rather vague and unsatisfactory, but he could do no more than acquiesce, with a mental reservation.

"Shall I get away out and have a talk with Sir Carle Venning, now, sir?" he asked.

Major Threngood shifted uneasily in his chair.

"No, dammit," he said, "let the Yard do that. It's a bit too awkward. High Sheriff, you know. No, you get along up to Ferris and put through some routine enquiries with the staff. Now we know there's something wrong, you'll probably stumble on something."

Superintendent Dawle was not sure that the last expression was altogether flattering to his detective powers, but he could only do as he was told. In any case, he thought it possible that the Sterrons' solicitor would still be at Ferris and he wanted a word or two with that gentleman. He did not intend to hand the whole case over to the Scotland Yard man without a struggle. No doubt Scotland Yard would take any credit that might accrue, but he himself intended to get some fun out of it.

Superintendent Dawle, however, did not get much fun out of Mr. John Halfcastle that afternoon. As he drove up to Ferris Court he saw the solicitor leaving the front door preparatory to entering the Sterrons' car. Hurriedly jumping from his own, he was just in time to stop the other car from moving off.

"Just a minute, sir, please," he said, putting his head in at the window. "I'd be glad to have a word with you before you go."

"It must be only a word, then," said Mr. Halfcastle, looking at his watch. "I've got a train to catch."

"I just want to know about the deceased's will, sir. No doubt you can tell me about the disposal of his property?"

The solicitor looked keenly at Dawle.

"Not now," he said. "You'll have to wait till the will's read, after the funeral, and we don't know when that'll be, now. I understand that the Coroner has not yet given his certificate for burial."

Superintendent Dawle had had little experience of cases of major importance. Probably he overestimated the powers of the police; certainly he underestimated the difficulty of getting information out of a London solicitor who did not want to part with it.

"That won't do, sir," he said sharply. "I've got my investigation to make and I can't wait indefinitely. I want that information now."

"Well, you won't get it before then without my clients' consent, and certainly not if you speak to me in that tone of voice, my friend. Drive on, Hayman; I shall miss the train."

Not averse from getting a rise out of the police, the chauffeur let his clutch in with a jerk, and Superintendent Dawle had to jump back to avoid being knocked over. Red with anger, he watched the car disappear down the drive; then, turning sharply, he saw the grinning face of Henry, the footman, framed in the doorway.

"Tell your mistress I'd be glad of a word with her," he said sharply.

Henry looked perplexed.

"I don't think Mrs. Sterron can see you, sir. She's gone to bed."

Dawle glowered. There was a conspiracy to annoy him this afternoon.

"Can I do anything for you, Superintendent?" asked a pleasant voice. "I'm so sorry you can't see Mrs. Sterron, but you'll understand that she's had a very trying day. She's asleep now, I think."

Dawle gazed at the attractive figure that had appeared behind him in the drive and felt mollified. Grace Nawten was certainly a refreshing sight on this summer's afternoon after the stuffy squalor of the Coroner's court. Dressed in a gray muslin frock, with short sleeves, she looked, with her slim figure and clear complexion, even younger than her twenty-nine years. Her fair, unshortened hair was uncovered, and her blue eyes looked with a friendly smile at the hot and angry policeman. A critical observer might have found fault with her mouth, which was too thin for beauty. But Superintendent Dawle was not now inclined to be critical; his good temper returned as quickly as it had flown. He returned the smile with one which, if not so attractive, was certainly not less friendly.

"I wanted a word with Mr. Halfcastle in the first place, miss," he said, "but he disappeared. Then I asked for Mrs. Sterron and I'm told I can't see her either. I'm afraid I was a bit put out. I wanted a special bit of information rather badly."

"Perhaps I can give it you. I'm Captain Sterron's secretary," said the girl. "What is the information you want?"

Dawle glanced over his shoulder to see whether Henry was listening, but the front door was closed now.

"I want to know," he said, instinctively dropping his voice, "who inherits Ferris Court."

Grace Nawten looked at him thoughtfully.

"Perhaps I can tell you," she said. "Just wait a second while I put these roses in water, and we'll go for a stroll in the garden."

She slipped in through the front door, which was evidently not kept locked. The second had not stretched itself into more than seven minutes before she was back, carrying a piece of folded paper.

"Come along," she said. "We'll go down to the pigeon-house at the end of the garden. It's quiet there."

The pigeon-house proved to be a brick building, originally intended, no doubt, for the habitation of pigeons, but now converted into a summer-house. It could only be approached by the broad terrace which it ended, so that it was a good place in which to talk without fear of being overheard.

Grace Nawten waved to her companion to share the wooden bench which the house contained, and at once handed him the piece of paper which she was carrying. It was a foolscap sheet bearing a number of typewritten sentences and figures.

"Those are the notes of Captain Sterron's instructions for a new will which he had prepared about six months ago," she said. "I don't know whether he ever signed it, but I know those notes and a covering letter were sent to Halfcastle and Blett, and Mr. Halfcastle came down about a fortnight later. I assumed that he brought the will to be signed."

"You didn't witness it, then, miss?"

"No, but then I couldn't. As you'll see, if you look at the notes, I am a beneficiary."

With considerable interest Superintendent Dawle studied the document in his hand. It was simple and easy to understand. In default of sons of his own, Captain Sterron left Ferris Court and the Liverpool property, subject to the accumulation settlement, together with the residue of the estate, to his brother, Gerald Heathcote Sterron, his heirs and assigns. A jointure of two thousand pounds, together with a life interest in

Ferris Lodge, the dower house, were left to his wife Griselda Sterron, with the proviso that the dower house and half the jointure should be forfeited in the event of her remarriage. Substantial legacies were provided for employees, including £200 a year for his secretary, Miss Grace Nawten, and £100 a year each for his butler, Harold Willing, and his cook, Mary Sone.

"Very generous provisions, miss, if I may be allowed to say so," ventured Superintendent Dawle.

"He was a very generous man, within the limitations of the task he had set himself—to put the estate on its legs again," answered Miss Nawten quietly.

"Ah, that's interesting," said Dawle reflectively.

"Yes. It isn't what everybody will tell you, Superintendent." There was an unmistakable significance in the girl's voice. "But ask any of the people who have worked for him a long time."

"Have you been with him long yourself, miss?"

"Only two years. I was astonished when he told me what he was going to put in his will. I hardly knew whether I ought to allow him to, but I won't deny that it means a tremendous lot to me. I don't believe it would have made any difference even if I had tried to stop him."

"Perhaps not, miss. And so Mr. Gerald, the brother, gets the property?"

"Yes," said Grace shortly.

Superintendent Dawle looked at his watch.

"I really ought to be getting back, miss," he said. "I've got to meet a train. I suppose you wouldn't allow me to keep this paper, eh?"

Grace Nawten hesitated.

"I don't know that I ought to," she said. "I daresay

I oughtn't to have shown it to you, but I want you to find out who killed Captain Sterron."

Dawle looked searchingly at his companion.

"What makes you say that, miss?" he asked. "There's been nothing said about killing."

The girl smiled.

"You must think us all very simple," she answered. "In any case, I never had any doubt that Captain Sterron had been murdered."

XI. SIR CARLE VENNING

THE third-class passengers who traveled down to Hylam by the 4.30 from St. Pancras on Tuesday afternoon would have been greatly surprised to learn that the fresh-complexioned, clerkly young man in pince-nez who journeyed with them was a well-known Scotland Yard detective.

Detective-Inspector Lott was actually in his fortieth year, but that, as inspectors go, is definitely young. He sedulously cultivated the appearance both of youth and clerkliness and with his well-cared-for clothes and the golden chain to his pince-nez would have passed anywhere for the holder of some well-paid clerical post in a Government office. His record at the Yard was exceptional; apart from a slight check two years previously, when he had allowed the man whom he was arresting for the murder of a Queenborough Alderman to commit suicide under his nose, he had gone from success to success, until now it was generally said that in five or six years' time he and his slightly younger rival, Inspector John Poole, would be running neck-and-neck to the post of a Chief-Inspectorship.

If Lott had a weakness it was a somewhat over-developed sense of humor which found particular delight in twitting those members of his profession whom he considered less gifted than himself—irrespective of their rank. This idiosyncrasy had earned him more than one official reprimand, but Lott was well aware of his own value and knew that he could afford to indulge his hobby without serious risk.

As the train drew up at Hylam he wondered what sort of colleague he would find waiting to welcome him with anything but open arms. His experience with county constabularies had led him to expect a fair amount of stupidity, not unmixed with deliberate obstruction, but he trusted to his own brain to help him over both these obstacles. The uniformed Superintendent, stocky and somewhat bucolic in appearance, who was waiting beside a car outside the station, seemed a fair specimen of what he had expected to find. He approached the officer and raised his hat.

"I am Detective-Inspector Lott, New Scotland Yard, sir," he said. "I daresay you are expecting me."

Superintendent Dawle examined the newcomer with evident surprise.

"Are you?" he said. "Well, I'm pleased to meet you. I'm Superintendent Dawle." He held out his hand. Lott shook it gently.

"I am looking forward to my visit to your beautiful town, sir," he said, in a deliberately prim voice.

Dawle stared. Hylam was one of the least attractive towns in the Midlands.

"Well, jump in, anyway," he said. "We'll get along to the Station."

It was not far to go and Dawle did not attempt to begin his story during the short journey. Once settled in his office, however, he wasted no time, and Lott was bound to admit that the local man knew how to outline a case. He listened in silence till the other had finished.

"Is there any particular difficulty that I ought to know about, Superintendent?" he asked. "I mean, I wondered why you had thought it necessary to call us in."

Superintendent Dawle looked down his nose.

"That's for the Chief Constable to say," he answered. "There's no special difficulty that I know of."

"Had you any suspicion yourself that it was murder —not suicide?" asked Lott.

Dawle rubbed his chin.

"Not quite so much as a suspicion," he said after a pause. "But there were one or two little things that pointed that way—the unlatched window, for instance, and the mark on the curtain pole."

"Curtain pole? What mark was that? You haven't mentioned that, Mr. Dawle."

"Ah, no, p'raps I haven't. Well, it was like this; I got a ladder to look for finger-prints on the pole, where the cord had been put over it. There were plenty of marks, but they were in the dust and when we tried to get prints there was nothing. But there was a mark where the cord had chafed the polish off the pole. That did just strike me as a bit odd."

"Ah, you mean odd that there should be friction?"

"Yes. You see, one end of the cord was tied to the radiator; after going over the pole the other end was tied in a noose round his neck. He just kicked the chair over—or so we thought—and strangled; there was no drop, and there didn't seem any reason for *friction*— not enough to rub the varnish away. Of course, this explains it."

"You mean that the body was *pulled* up by the cord running over the pole and then tied?"

"Yes. I expect the chap took the weight of the body on one arm while he pulled the head up by the cord with the other. That would be enough to cause friction without the weight breaking the cord. It's easy to be wise after the event, but I suppose I ought to have taken more notice of it."

Lott had been so much interested in the little point that he had forgotten to pull the Superintendent's leg.

"Most people wouldn't have spotted it at all, sir," he said, in a tone of admiration that was almost sincere.

"Oh, I expect you'll find a good deal that I've overlooked," replied Dawle with becoming modesty.

"Well, I shall certainly try to," said Lott with a laugh. "Now, tell me this, sir; now that you know it's murder, have you any idea who did it?"

Dawle thought for a time before answering.

"All I can say is," he replied, "that there are two people with good reasons for doing it; one was on the spot and the other wasn't so far away."

"That sounds promising. Who are they?"

"There's the brother for one. He inherits the property—at least, I believe he does—I haven't got it officially yet. He was in the house and in the room, too, within a short time of when it must have been done."

"Why d'you want to look any farther?"

"I don't know that we need, but we've hardly thought about it yet. He's got a sort of half-alibi that'll want looking into."

"And the other fellow?"

"Chap who's running after the wife—widow. rather. Well, there you are; now he can have her."

"He wasn't in the house?"

"No, but he was there in the afternoon, and he only lives a few miles away. Sir Carle Venning. He's the High Sheriff." Dawle gave a sudden laugh. "Matter of fact, that's probably why you're here; the Chief didn't fancy us pulling in our own High Sheriff. Might make a mistake, too; then we should look bloody silly."

Lott stared, his eyes unnaturally large behind the convex glasses.

"I see," he said slowly. "I'm to make the bloomers and look 'bloody silly.' I don't know that I fancy being a cat's-paw."

Dawle laughed.

"You can't help yourself, young man. We called on Scotland Yard and they've sent you."

Lott realized that for a change it was the local police force who might be going to get some fun out of *him*.

"I'll have to watch my step," he said.

For some time the two police officers continued to discuss the case. Dawle showed the C.I.D. man the notes of Herbert Sterron's will and also the ink-stained directory which he had impounded, and it was eventually agreed that as there were two promising lines of enquiry, Lott should take one—the awkward line of tackling the High Sheriff—while Dawle took the other represented by Gerald Sterron. The Superintendent thought that it was too late to do any more that day, but the C.I.D. man believed in striking while the iron was hot. After his dinner, especially if he took a liberal quantity of wine or spirits with it, he thought that Sir Carle Venning might not have such a close guard on his tongue as at other times. In any case, he borrowed a car and drove out to the baronet's house.

High Oaks was not a family seat of the caliber of Ferris Court. It had only been built in the reign of George IV., and indeed, the Venning family was not traceable to a much earlier age. Still, it had three times passed from father to son, was comfortable, reasonably well furnished, and to a Venning it was something more than home.

A hard-faced manservant, neither butler nor footman, opened the door.

"Is Sir Carle Venning at home?" asked Lott with an ingratiating smile. The smile cut no ice; perhaps Stainer's heart was made of a less soluble material. He deliberately looked the detective up and down, decided that he was a lawyer's clerk, and adjusted his tone accordingly.

"Sir Carle is at home but he doesn't see any one at this time of night."

"Is he alone?"

"That's neither here nor there," was the curt reply.

"Well, perhaps it is a little bit. I don't want to disturb him if he's really engaged. Perhaps you would tell him that Detective-Inspector Lott, of New Scotland Yard, would be glad if he could spare him a few minutes' conversation."

The man's face fell. Lott almost laughed aloud at the instantaneous dropping of the discourteous manner.

"Certainly, sir; will you step inside into the hall," he said. "I will let Sir Carle know you are here."

"That chap's been in trouble at some time," thought Lott as the manservant hurried away. In a minute he was back and, beckoning Lott to follow, showed him into a comfortable sitting-room, in which, in spite of the time of year, a bright fire was burning. Sir Carle Venning, in evening dress but an old smoking jacket, was standing with his back to the fire, busily engaged in lighting a large cigar. As the flame of the match burnt up, Lott got a good impression of the striking features which had so much interested Sir James Hamsted a few days previously.

"Good evening, Inspector," said Sir Carle, waving his cigar towards a chair on one side of the fireplace. "I hope you won't find it too hot in here; I'm so accustomed to the tropics that I find the evenings very chilly. Will you have a cigar?"

"Thank you, sir, I don't smoke," replied Lott untruthfully.

"A drink, then?"

"No, thank you, sir. I've only just finished my dinner."

"Ah, so have I. I hope you aren't going to upset my digestion. What have I done? Overshot the speed limit or something?"

Sir Carle laughed heartily, but Lott's quick ear detected—or though it detected—the slightest note of nervousness in both laugh and voice. He instantly decided to work on that note.

"I'm sorry to disturb you at so late an hour, sir," he said, "but I've only just been called in in connection with the death of Captain Sterron, and I don't want to waste any time. There is reason to believe that Captain Sterron considered himself to have grounds for jealousy in connection with yourself and Mrs. Sterron; would you care to make a statement on the subject?"

Sir Carle's jaw had dropped. He was not a man who was ever likely to look frightened, but he did appear to be definitely uncomfortable.

"Where on earth do you get that idea from?" he asked. "And what has it got to do with Sterron's death, anyway?"

Lott ignored the first part of the question.

"It may have to do with it in more than one way, sir. For instance, there has been a suggestion of suicide; if it was suicide there must be a reason for it; jealousy of that kind might be the reason."

"But good heavens, man, why rake up muck of that kind? Nothing of the sort was suggested at the inquest?"

"You were there, sir?" asked Lott suavely.

"Well, I just looked in in case . . . that's to say, he was a friend of mine; I thought I ought to put in an appearance."

Now Superintendent Dawle had told Lott that Sir Carle had *not* been at the inquest; he must have kept well in the background. The detective continued in an even tone.

"And then there are other possibilities, sir. In connection with them I have to enquire as to the whereabouts of every one in any way closely connected with Captain Sterron at the time that his death occurred."

Sir Carle rose quickly from his chair and flicked into the fire an ash from his cigar that did not need flicking.

"Look here, Inspector," he said; "this is a very extraordinary line you're taking. Do you know who I am?"

"High Sheriff of the County, sir? Oh, yes, I know that, but if you were the Lord Lieutenant it would not stop me from doing my duty."

Sir Carle stared at his visitor, but his thoughts were evidently elsewhere. Presently he tapped his coat pockets.

"You want to know where I was on Saturday night?" he asked. "It was Saturday night, wasn't it? I must get my diary. I haven't got a very good memory. Excuse me a minute."

He walked quickly to the door and disappeared.

"Now, what's he gone for?" wondered Lott.

His eyes ran round the room. It was furnished in no particular style, but the chairs were comfortable, the bookshelves well lined with readable books, the walls hung mostly with enlarged photographs of scenes in different parts of the world. A signed photograph of a Russian general in Cossack uniform stood on the mantelpiece, side by side with a signed photograph of a celebrated French actress, less comprehensively attired. The room was untidy but fairly clean; unquestionably a man's room. Just as Lott was beginning to wonder whether Sir Carle had sought the better part of valor in flight, the baronet returned, carrying a Badminton diary.

"Couldn't find the damn thing," he said. "Now, here we are: 'Saturday, 27th, tennis, Ferris Court' . . . I was there that afternoon . . . 'dinner and play, Birmingham, Frank Bowys.' That's a friend, Captain Bowys; we ran into Birmingham, dined at the 'Herring Bone' and went on to see that revue of Jack Hallibut's that's been running in London all the year; he's just taking it on tour. *Tickle My Ankle*, that's the thing."

"What time did you get home then, sir, please?"

Venning considered.

"Well, the show was over about eleven, I suppose. We had to get the car off the park; say we started about ten-past. It's forty miles; we should have been back here at about half-past twelve."

"And Captain Bowys was with you all the time?"

"Yes, practically."

"What do you mean by 'practically,' sir?"

"Well, we weren't hanging round each other's necks all the time. We each met a friend or two, both at the 'Herring Bone' and at the show, but to all intents and purposes we were together all the time."

"I see, sir. That seems quite satisfactory. There's really only one thing more I need trouble you with at the moment."

Venning had quite recovered his composure—if, indeed, he had ever lost it other than in the detective's imagination.

"And what's that?" he asked.

Lott bent forward.

"Are you going to let me have that statement, sir? About your relations with Mrs. Sterron?"

Sir Carle's face flushed with anger.

"Certainly I'm not!" he exclaimed. "There are no relations. We're friends; that's all. As I was with her husband."

"Really friends were you, sir? Good friends?"

"Certainly."

"Then how do you account, sir, for the fact that, on the day of his death, Captain Sterron scored your name in the directory through and through with red ink and drew a picture of you hanging from a gallows beside it?"

As Lott spoke, in his calm, precise voice, he watched the baronet's face. His quick flush of anger had quickly yielded to returning complacence; now, as the detective spoke, his mouth drew together in a grim line, his eyes hardened, his whole face set in a look that must have come to it many times in his adventurous life, the look that meant—"Danger!"

XII. FOOTSTEPS

SUPERINTENDENT DAWLE did not follow Lott's example in getting out on his trail that night. He had had a long and tiring day and had only returned from Ferris Court an hour or two ago; he thought he might leave the unhappy household in peace for that night. Instead, he spent an hour with Sergeant Gable, going through the latter's carefully tabulated finger-print notes and photographs. With the exception of the scarred finger-mark on the outside of the study door, nothing of startling significance had so far emerged from the search, though a number of prints were still unidentified. The glass from which whisky had been drunk showed, as was only to be expected, prints of Captain Sterron's fingers and thumb, as well as a fainter set, near the bottom, which Sergeant Gable was able to identify as belonging to the butler. Both Willing and Henry, the footman, had unconsciously supplied the delighted Gable with excellent prints with which to compare his photographs.

Dawle wished that he had taken photographs of the ash-tray in the ante-room, but Ethel, in her belated burst of duty, had not only emptied but polished it. No recognizable prints had been found on the curtain pole, nor on the overturned chair. Prints of both Herbert Sterron's and Willing's hands were identifiable in several places on furniture and door, and there were other prints which must now be identified. This meant obtaining prints from everybody in the household of

Ferris Court as well as, if possible, people outside it who might conceivably be connected with the crime; a task which, if it was to be done without the subject's knowledge, was much easier to achieve in theory than in practice. Having discussed the problem with his subordinate, Superintendent Dawle took himself off to bed.

By half-past nine on the following morning he was out at Ferris. He had made up his mind that frankness —or at least, apparent frankness—was his best course of action, and with this in mind he at once asked to see Mr. Gerald Sterron.

The ex-merchant received him in the library. He was dressed in a gray flannel suit, but wore a black tie. His manner was frank—as frank as the Superintendent's.

"Have you come to tell us what this new piece of evidence is, Superintendent?" he asked. "The adjournment was rather a surprise . . . a dramatic surprise, the papers call it. What's it all about?"

"Well, sir," replied Dawle; "I'm not at liberty to tell you the exact nature of the evidence, but it's only fair that you should know—in the strictest confidence, if you please, sir—that it appears to throw some doubt upon the theory of suicide."

Gerald Sterron frowned slightly.

"Not suicide?" he queried. "Do you mean that you suspect murder?"

"I wouldn't go so far as to say that we suspect anything, sir," replied the Superintendent cautiously, "but we shall have to make further enquiries before we can be satisfied that it really was suicide."

"That's very . . . upsetting, Superintendent. And have I got to keep it to myself?"

"I leave it to you to decide whether Mrs. Sterron

should be told—in confidence—sir. Of course, you are at liberty to tell your legal adviser—on the same understanding."

"Thanks; I think I must do that. It would probably be a mistake to worry Mrs. Sterron with it just yet, in case it turns out to be a mare's nest, as I hope it will. What can I do to help you in the way of further enquiries, Superintendent?"

Dawle took his plunge.

"In the first place, sir, I want everybody's finger-prints in the house, so that we can identify what we've found. As we don't want to excite talk, we shall have to get the prints without people realizing it; that will probably be easy enough where the domestics are concerned, but I shall have to ask your help to get Mrs. Sterron's, and perhaps you'll be good enough to let me have your own."

Gerald made a slight grimace but raised no objection. His own prints were soon taken on the pieces of shiny paste-board which Dawle produced, and the Superintendent explained what he wanted done about Mrs. Sterron.

Now for the second plunge.

"There's just one thing more, sir," he said. "On the same lines, we want to find out about everybody's movements that night. You've already given me a pretty full account of your own, but I wanted to ask you again whether you could fix the time you left Captain Sterron?"

Gerald shook his head.

"I can't, Superintendent. I've been thinking it over, but I've got nothing to fix it by. If I made a guess it would only be a guess, and I don't suppose you want that."

"No, sir; that might be worse than no help. Well, if you can't, of course you can't. Now, is there absolutely nothing you can think of that can help us? Nothing unusual or suspicious? No sounds? Nobody doing anything out of the ordinary? Sometimes, when one knows that something was wrong and casts one's mind back, one does remember something unusual."

Gerald smiled.

"You've only just told me that something *was* wrong —and you haven't told me *what* was. You must give me time to cast my mind back."

"Of course, sir. Then, if I may, I'll just have a word with your butler."

Dawle's interview with Willing yielded one piece of evidence of some importance. When the butler brought the whisky to his master in the study at ten o'clock on Saturday night, he had seen Mr. Gerald just quitting the study; that was important as affording a second check on the time of Gerald leaving the study; Sir James Hamsted had already told Dawle that Gerald had rejoined him in the library at, or just before, ten.

"Why didn't you tell me this when I questioned you before, Willing?" asked the Superintendent sternly.

"You didn't ask me if I'd seen any one, sir. You asked me what time I'd last seen my master alive. I told you at ten o'clock, sir, when I took in the whisky."

"Ah, yes; well, it doesn't really matter," said Dawle, remembering that he did not want yet to arouse undue excitement. "And after you'd seen Mr. Gerald . . . by the way, did he see you?"

"I don't think so, sir. He was walking towards the ante-room; he had his back to me."

"Ah, then, he wouldn't. And after you'd seen him, you went into the study and got your orders from Captain Sterron?"

"That is quite correct, sir."

"What was he doing at the time?"

"He was sitting in the armchair near the window, reading *The Times*, sir."

"And he gave you orders?"

"Yes, sir; the suit he would wear in the morning and about wanting the car in the afternoon."

"Oh, he said that? Did he say where he was going?"

"No, sir; just that he would want the car, but not Hayman with it."

"I see, and then you shut the far window and left?"

"That is so, sir."

And that was all; no other variation from the previous story. Dawle felt unmistakable disappointment at the alibi that was materializing for Gerald Sterron; an alibi not offered by himself (he had said he did not know what time he left his brother) but emerging from the evidence of others. Sterron had such an obvious motive for getting rid of his brother, the simplest of all motives, since the days of Cain and Abel: so that he might possess what the other had—in this case, Ferris Court and nearly all that went with it. Of course, Sir Carle Venning had a good, primary motive, too—to possess, in his case, Griselda Sterron; but now that the C.I.D. man had taken up that line, Dawle felt the natural hope that his own line would prove to be the right one.

Still, he was not going to give up because of an early

check. With a bit of thinking he might see his way round the difficulty. He would just complete what had to be done at Ferris and then get back to Hylam to do this thinking in his own quarters—he found that thinking came more easily to him there.

What had to be done at Ferris Court consisted of getting the finger-prints of its inmates and this, with the help of Gerald Sterron, Dawle was able to do in about an hour. He toyed with the idea of interviewing Mrs. Sterron, but came to the conclusion that he would get no change out of that clever lady and might put her on her guard; she really belonged to Inspector Lott and his Venning trail. By midday Dawle was back in Hylam, where he spent half an hour with Sergeant Gable going through the finger-prints. As a result of their checking it was possible to say that all the prints obtained by Gable had been made by people who naturally would leave prints in the place where these were found—Captain Sterron, Willing, a couple of housemaids, and one or two prints, especially on the study door, made by Gerald Sterron. The only unidentifiable print was the one on the outside of the door, the print of a scarred fore-finger; that would probably prove to belong to Sir James Hamsted.

The need for getting a copy of Sir James's prints, combined with a desire to test still further Gerald Sterron's alibi, decided Dawle to run up to London. There was a fast train at two and that would just give him time to get some lunch and to have that half-hour of quiet thinking—he was never able to concentrate in a train—which he so much needed. To lunch, then, he betook himself and, having demolished half a loaf and a slightly smaller quantity of cheese, washed down by a pint of mild and bitter, he lit his pipe and settled down to his problem.

Dr. Tanwort had given it as his opinion that Captain Sterron had died between ten and twelve o'clock on Saturday night. That meant that he died while Gerald Sterron and Sir James Hamsted were playing chess. Even if Dr. Tanwort's opinion was unreliable—and Dawle had naturally not much faith in him after Sir James's revelation—he could hardly be wrong by as much as two hours, and even that margin was covered by Sterron's alibi, for the Captain was undoubtedly alive at ten (unless the butler was lying) and the game of chess had gone on till 2 A.M. Could that alibi have been cooked? Only, it seemed, if *two* people were lying. The 10 P.M. margin was confirmed by both Hamsted and Willing (it was not Gerald's statement at all); the 2 A.M. margin was given by Hamsted and Gerald himself. Of course, it was possible that there was collusion somewhere but collusion in murder was a terrible risk and therefore unlikely; for the moment Dawle decided to ignore that possibility.

How else, then? Could Gerald Sterron have deceived either of the other two? He could hardly have deceived Willing, for Willing was working to a routine time-table, and at ten o'clock had seen him leaving the study in which immediately afterwards Willing found his master still alive. Gerald had gone straight on into the library and remained there till 2 A.M. But had he? Had he gone straight into the library? Willing had only seen him going towards the ante-room which led into the library; could he have waited in the ante-room and gone back into the study after Willing had left it and killed his brother then? That ash-tray in the ante-room;

it had contained not only a cigarette end, but a quantity of ash, as if some one had been smoking there for an appreciable time—and it was hardly a room in which any one would choose to stay and smoke—it was only a passage-room. But if Gerald were waiting for Willing to leave the study, what more likely than that he would wait in that ante-room and smoke to keep his nerves quiet? Had he been smoking when he left the study? Willing had not said so, but then he had not asked Willing and the butler was clearly not a man who volunteered information.

Dawle sprang to his feet. That was a point that could be settled at once. He did not like using the telephone on a confidential enquiry, but he was so eager to know that he decided to risk it. He soon heard the Ferris Court butler's voice on the other end of the line.

"Willing," he said, "there's a small point about some cigarette ash in the study that I want to clear up. Did you happen to notice whether Mr. Gerald Sterron was smoking a cigarette when you saw him leave the study?"

"Yes, sir. I noticed that he was. Mr. Gerald smokes a great many cigarettes, sir."

"Does he smoke 'Pertaris'?"

"Those are the cigarettes Captain Sterron has for his guests, sir. Mr. Gerald often smoked them. Captain Sterron did not smoke at all, but there was a box in the study, and he always carried a case."

"Thank you, Willing." The Superintendent could hardly keep the gratification out of his voice. "That clears that up. I thought that must be the explanation."

Dawle hung up the receiver and returned to his chair, refilling his pipe with eager fingers. That was definite support of his theory—that Gerald had waited in the ante-room and gone back to the study after Willing had left. But how about the time of his joining Sir James in the library; surely the old man had been pretty definite about that?

Dawle reached for his note-book and flicked over the pages. Yes, here it was: "Mr. Sterron rejoined me in the library just before ten. I remember thinking it was getting late and looking at the clock." The clock? Could that be the explanation? Had the clock been wrong? Had it been deliberately put back so as to deceive Sir James? Here was another point that must be checked. Perhaps a housemaid would have noticed if the clock were slow the following morning. He must find out, but not over the telephone; it would not do to trust to that medium of communication a second time, especially if it meant talking to a girl. Besides, it was time to catch his train.

The journey from Hylam to London is a tedious one, even in an express, but Superintendent Dawle found it passed quickly enough. Contrary to his usual experience he had no difficulty in concentrating his thoughts on this occasion, and by the time he reached the metropolis he was more convinced than ever that he was on the right trail and had found the chink in Gerald Sterron's alibi.

He had taken the precaution before leaving Hylam to telephone to Sir James's house to announce his visit, and he found the ex-coroner awaiting him.

"Your visit is not unexpected, Superintendent," said Sir James. "Now that the fact of murder has been established you will naturally wish to go more closely over the ground. Except in one particular, I do not think that I can add to the statement which I have already made, but I shall be happy to answer any questions which you may choose to put to me."

The two men were sitting in the study of Sir James's gloomy Cromwell Road house. Portentous tomes filled the heavy bookcases and piles of Blue Books and official reports were heaped upon every available space.

"In the first place, Sir James," began Dawle, "I'd like to go closely into the question of times on Saturday night. You told me, I think, that you couldn't fix the time of your leaving the study after your talk with Captain Sterron, but that you went straight to the library and that Mr. Gerald Sterron joined you there at ten o'clock. That's right, isn't it, sir?"

"A little before ten, I think I said, Superintendent."

Dawle looked at his notes.

"I beg your pardon, sir; that's quite right. You're sure on that point? Because some one else tells me they saw Mr. Sterron leaving the study at ten o'clock."

"That may well be. Clocks are not always exact to a minute. It was certainly a few minutes to ten by the clock in the library when Mr. Sterron joined me. It may have been slow."

"That's an interesting point, sir. Do you think it possible that that clock was really a good deal slower even than that? That it was really, say, a quarter-past ten when Mr. Sterron joined you?"

Sir James studied his visitor with interest and took time before he answered.

"I had not considered the possibility," he said. "I suppose it *is* a possibility. I did not check the time with any other clock. I do not carry a watch in evening dress."

"Did Mr. Sterron call your attention to the time when he came in?"

"I think he said he was sorry to keep me waiting; nothing more than that. The remark would tend to make me note the time."

"And the time your game stopped; you said 'just before or just after two'; how do you come to know that?"

"I think we both automatically talked about the length of the game and so noted the time. I just do not happen to remember whether it was just before or just after two; it was one or the other, a few minutes either way."

"I see, sir; and, of course, if the clock had been put back it would affect that time, too."

"Of course."

"Did you happen to notice anything peculiar about Mr. Sterron's manner when he came in, Sir James?"

"No, nothing; he was quite calm. He played well, though perhaps rather slowly."

"Thank you, Sir James; I don't think I have any more to ask. Of course, you will appreciate that what we have discussed is strictly confidential."

"Of course. Now, I have . . ."

The door opened and Sir James's parlormaid appeared, carrying a tray.

"Ah, here is tea. You will join me in a cup, I hope, Superintendent."

The tea, a delicious China, and the thin savory sandwiches were a surprise, as well as a delight, to Dawle. He had not expected anything so feminine in this austere house. Sir James talked pleasantly upon topics of the day and it was not until he had rung and the tray had been removed that he returned to his unfinished sentence.

"I have," he said, "one addition to make to my previous statement, an addition which may or may not be of interest to you. Like you, when the fact of murder was established, I cast my mind back over the ground again to see if I could not recollect anything which might have a bearing on this new development. You will remember that you asked me whether I had heard anything unusual and I replied that I had not. I was thinking then of some noise inside the house. But it has since come back to me that, at some time after our game had started, I *did* hear a sound outside the house; the sound of footsteps upon a gravel path."

XIII. BIRMINGHAM

INSPECTOR LOTT had been considerably impressed by the appearance and manner of Sir Carle Venning. The baronet did not strike him as being the sort of man who would be likely to commit a cold-blooded murder, but if he had decided upon a course of action he would not be deterred from it by fear of the consequences. And he had certainly not been at his ease during the examination which Lott had put him through; at the last he had even given the strong impression of being conscious that he was in danger.

What danger? To the detective, his mind centered upon the case which he was investigating, there appeared to be but one answer. So that it was with the thrilling sensation of being upon a hot scent that he left High Oaks and motored back to Hylam. On the way he considered his next course of action and eventually decided that, before taking up the Ferris Court end of the thread, he would check Sir Carle's Birmingham alibi. Leaving word to that effect at the Police Station, he turned in for the night.

The following morning Lott reconsidered his plan of action. He realized that it was no good going to Birmingham to check a dinner and theatre alibi before evening—the staff would not all be at work. But there was Captain Bowys to be questioned and, as that gentleman lived in Derby, there would be plenty of time to have a talk with him in the morning and get back to Birmingham in the afternoon. Having discovered the gallant captain in the telephone directory, Lott rang him up. He had forgotten, however, that retired army officers are not usually such early risers as they were when the bugle called; the captain was still in bed and it took an appreciable amount of message sending and "holding on" before Lott learnt that Captain Bowys had an engagement in the morning but would see him at three o'clock in the afternoon.

That seemed to indicate a wasted morning, but Detective-Inspector Lott was not a man to kick his heels about when engaged on a case. Although he did not intend to pay a formal call at Ferris Court yet there was no reason why he should not carry out that preliminary reconnaissance which, in detection as in tactics, is time so seldom wasted. Borrowing a bicycle and "countrifying" himself to the extent of exchanging his billycock for a cap, Lott set out. Those five miles on a scorching August day to a man accustomed to the passive transportation of London might have been expected to find out the detective's weak spots, but Lott did not turn a hair. He took his time, walked up hills, stopped for a breather at the top of them, and arrived at Ferris feeling, if anything, the fresher for the exercise.

The grounds of Ferris Court were fairly extensive and were surrounded, on the one side by the main road which had already run through the village of Ferris, and on the others by a shady lane, now overhung by the untrimmed trees and shrubberies within. Leaving his bicycle in the care of a publican, with whom he intended later to share a flagon of ale, Lott walked down the main road and then round the lane.

The question of approach and departure—if Sir Carle Venning really had come to Ferris to murder his "friend" that Saturday night—was engaging Lott's attention. Bent upon such an errand, the baronet would hardly have turned in at the drive and parked his car outside the front door. On the other hand, he would not risk leaving it in the main road, where it would almost certainly be noticed; he would be more likely to leave it in the lane, but as near as possible to the house, so as to cut short the time that it had to stay there. As he walked, therefore, Lott kept a look-out for a gate or some other means of entrance into the grounds from the lane. The "unclimbable" iron fence, however, though badly in need of a coat of paint, was otherwise in good condition and it was not till he was almost at the farthest point from the house, at the lowest, southern, end of the gardens, that the detective found what he was looking for.

Here was a small wicket-gate and Lott, hunting about for signs which might confirm his conjecture, soon found the very thing that he was looking for; in the soft earth of a little gutter which a recent storm had probably moistened and which the overhanging trees protected from the sun, was the clear mark of a motor tire—a large tire with the tread clearly defined. Without being an expert, Lott was sufficiently thorough in his work to know the principal makes of tire by sight; this, he knew, was a Braston—an expensive but hard-wearing tire much used by the drivers of high-powered cars. And Sir Carle's car, he had taken the trouble to find out, was a 30-80 Highflyer. This was certainly promising—all that he had hoped for—but it was far from being conclusive. It had yet to be proved that the Braston tire belonged to Venning's car.

Lott thought that it might be worth trespassing in

the grounds in the hope of finding something more. The shrubberies were so much overgrown that it should be possible to penetrate well into the garden without being seen, unless he bumped into somebody, and then he could either disclose his identity or pretend to be a reporter. As he moved cautiously along the weed-grown path, Lott took stock of his surroundings. On his left was a tennis-court and beyond it the ground rose to a terrace, which ended in a square brick building—evidently a garden-house of some kind. From there the terrace swung round right-handed and the ground rose again in more terraces till it reached the house, of which peeps were visible through the trees. A very fine situation, thought the detective.

The path which he was following sloped gradually upwards through the shrubberies, not rising in steps as it did on the other side, a difference, no doubt, to allow of the passage of wheelbarrows, etc. On this side, the approach to the house was almost entirely concealed, and as he met nobody, Lott was soon on a level with the house and found himself close to the lean-to shed which, as Dawle had told him, housed a convenient ladder. It would have been an easy matter to approach the study window by that method. But could he have got in unheard or unseen by his victim? That, at the moment, seemed impossible, and Lott realized that it was an obstacle in his course that would take some surmounting.

Looking at his watch, he realized that there was no time to do more now if he was to catch his train to Derby. Returning to the lane, he followed it till it rejoined the main road at the end of the village and was soon enjoying his well-earned mug of beer.

The ride back to Hylam and the train journey to Derby gave Lott ample time to think out his line of action with Captain Bowys. A good deal would depend upon the type of man he had to deal with, but the detective's experience had showed him that it was generally best to come straight to the point and avoid undue subtleties, though there were various shades of manner with which this could be done.

Lott had gathered from Sir Carle that his friend was "interested in horses," by which he probably meant that the Captain did a little mild horse-coping to eke out his pension. He lived, it seemed, on the outskirts of Derby, and Lott noticed a diminutive groom and a ratty-looking terrier in the backyard of the little house to which his taxi brought him. The house itself was a monument of discomfort; the little hall was cluttered with coats, hats and sticks; a combined smell of food and smoke and dog permeated everything; while the study or sitting-room into which he was shown was dirty and frowsty to a degree.

Captain Bowys himself, Lott thought, had been sleeping off his lunch in the brokendown armchair when the detective was announced. He struggled to his feet, however, shook hands rather effusively and waved his visitor to a sofa. He was a thin, haggard man, with clean-shaven lips and chin and very light blue eyes; probably about fifty but trying to be ten years younger. He was dressed in the conventionally exaggerated riding-breeches of his type, with a waisted, long-skirted check coat and canvas gaiters. Phil May would have reproduced him to the life in about three lines.

"Glad to see you, Inspector," he said, dropping back

into his chair, "though it's a bit of a surprise. Carlo sent you along, did he?"

"He told me where to find you, sir. I'm working on this Ferris Court case—the death of Captain Sterron, you know, sir."

Bowys's eyes widened to a stare. He sat up in his chair.

"Sterron? What, the chap who hanged himself? What's that got to do with me?"

"Only indirectly, sir. The unfortunate gentleman's death is a bit of a mystery still and we're obliged to follow up the movements of everybody connected with him. You knew him, I suppose, sir?"

"Never set eyes on the blighter, to the best of my knowledge. Don't think many people did—never hunted or went racin' or anything like that."

Lott had difficulty in not smiling at the inevitable clipped "g"; what an incredibly narrow type it was.

"No, sir? Still perhaps you wouldn't mind telling me what you were doing on Saturday night?"

There was a trace of anxiety in the look of astonishment with which Captain Bowys greeted this question. He shifted uncomfortably in his chair.

"Saturday night? I was . . . well, I was staying with Sir Carle Venning at High Oaks."

"You were at High Oaks all the time, or did you go anywhere else?"

The look of anxiety, or at least of discomfort, predominated now.

"Look here, Inspector," said Bowys, "why are you asking me all this? I tell you I didn't know this fellow Sterron."

Lott knew that he could not press the "anxiety"

pedal any further; a switch to "relief" might be useful.

"I only want to check what Sir Carle told me, sir," he said. "It's always useful to get a story corroborated."

But the "relief" did not register. Captain Bowys's cigarette-stained fingers fidgeted with his upper lip.

"Well, as a matter of fact, we went into Birmingham and did a show that night," he said.

"Dine anywhere, sir?"

"Yes, at the 'Herring Bone.'"

"And after the show, did you go straight back to High Oaks?"

There was a short but perceptible pause.

"That's right. Yes, we did," said Captain Bowys, lighting a cigarette.

"Which road did you come back by?"

Lott leant forward and spoke with slow deliberation.

"Which road? Eh? Why, there's only one road, isn't there? I really didn't notice. We were talking."

"About what, sir?"

"Well, about the show . . . and so on."

"I see, sir. And what time did you get back to High Oaks?"

Bowys's pale-blue eyes blinked as if the smoke of his cigarette had got into them; a dry cough added to the impression.

"About half-past twelve or one, I should think, but I really didn't notice."

The front door of the house slammed and a shrill voice cried, "Frank-ie!"

Bowys sprang to his feet.

"You must excuse me, Inspector," he exclaimed. "Some other time."

He ushered his guest out into the hall. A woman appeared from what was apparently the dining-room.

"Hallo; there you are. Oh!"

She stared at Lott, who, in turn, without staring, noted that she was garishly dressed, over made-up, older than she wished to appear, and—from the lines at the corners of her mouth—ill-tempered. He was glad that it was not his job to stay behind the closed door and listen to that shrill, penetrating voice.

"Who was that, Frank? Why didn't you . . ." The sound died away as Lott walked down the path.

Who was the yellow-haired lady? Lott had jumped to the conclusion that he was dealing with a bachelor—the untidiness of the house may have been responsible for that impression. Whoever she was, she seemed to have Frank Bowys well under her thumb. As Lott walked to the station he thanked his stars, not for the first time, that he had never got himself entangled with a woman.

The 4.50 from Derby got him to Birmingham at seven—a desperately tedious journey for a distance of barely forty miles, but it gave him time to get some food before starting on his quest. The fashionable "Herring Bone" grill-room was just beginning to fill up with theatre parties when Lott settled himself in a quiet corner. He ordered a mixed grill and a half-bottle of Clos de Tart and, with that passport to good-will, beckoned to the head waiter. Showing the man his official card, he explained that he was trying to get in touch with a gentleman whose evidence was required in a case of some importance but whose name was not known; it was thought that he had dined here on the previous Saturday night. He described the High Sheriff

—a description which the head waiter at once recognized as that of Sir Carle Venning, a fairly frequent client. An under-waiter was summoned who clearly remembered that Sir Carle and a friend had dined there on Saturday night, arriving at about half-past seven and leaving soon after eight. Lott thanked the two men, finished his dinner and climbed up to street level.

At the entrance door he approached a gaudy commissionaire who, with a little persuasion, was able to recollect Sir Carle Venning, whom he knew well, both arriving and leaving at approximately the times stated by the waiter. The two gentlemen had walked down towards Champion Street—yes, that would be the direction of the Pantodrome, where *Tickle My Ankle* had been in the bill the previous week.

A bare five minutes' walk took Lott to the big theatre, where even now crowds were flocking in to see the popular revival, *Lucky Little Lady*. The commissionaires and attendants were fully occupied with cars and tickets, so Lott judged it wisest to wait until the pressure should relax, amusing himself the meantime with watching the flow of Birmingham's Four Hundred. At last a commissionaire, the largest and most heavily bemedaled, appeared to have shaken himself free of the swarming pleasure-seekers; Lott approached him. It was evidently the detective's lucky evening; the commissionaire at once recognized his description of Venning, though he did not know his name; he was a gentleman who frequently came to see the musical shows, though more often in winter than summer, and who always had an affable word for an ex-service man. He remembered the gentleman coming for the evening house on Saturday; they had discussed the size of the houses which Jack Hallibut's shows always attracted; that would have been at about 8.15—after the first rush had gone in. Oh, yes, the gentleman had gone in all right. He also remembered him coming out; he had praised the show and said that it well deserved the big houses it drew. That would have been about 11.30; it was a long show and on Saturday night there had been flowers and speeches.

For the next hour, helped by a friendly word from the head commissionaire, Lott worked round the inside attendants, as and when he could get hold of them during the acts, trying to get a further check on Venning and Bowys. But nobody else seemed to have noticed the theatre-going baronet that night, though one or two knew him, or thought they knew him by sight. This did not discourage the detective—in fact he welcomed it. His theory was that Venning had gone in at 8.15, slipped out by a push-bar exit, motored to Ferris and got back again in time to mingle with the outpouring audience, at half-past eleven. It would have been a damn fine-run thing to get back in the time, especially as the murder could not have been committed till after ten, but it was possible; the thirty miles could have been covered at night in a high-powered car in a little more than an hour.

It would be worth, thought Lott, asking the Birmingham police if they had noticed a powerful car driven at high speed along the Hylam road at that time of night. In the meantime he would try the car park. But here his luck failed; the park attendant was a stupid and obviously unobservant man; he had a mort of cars to attend to on a Saturday night; how could he be expected to remember what they were like or when they came and went? Yes, he had a book of tickets with counterfoils, but he didn't have to enter any details on them; they only acted as receipts, both for car and fee. Disappointed, Lott made his way back to the New Street Station and caught the last train back to Hylam.

But his day was not destined to end on a note of disappointment. As he got out of the train at Hylam he was astonished to see the massive figure of Sir Carle Venning leave a first-class carriage just in front of him. Keeping as much as possible out of sight, Lott followed and emerged into the station yard as the baronet entered his car. As the door slammed, Lott slipped up to the back of the car and flashed his pocket-torch on to one of the tires. It was a Braston.

XIV. AN UNPROFITABLE INHERITANCE

O N the following morning Lott went round early to the Police Station and found Superintendent Dawle already at work on the routine affairs of his division. Having cleared these out of the way, Dawle turned a willing ear to his visitor. The C.I.D. man had slept well and breakfasted well, and was full of confidence, not untinged with condescension.

"Well, Mr. Dawle," he said. "I don't think I shall be bothering you with my presence much longer."

The Superintendent looked suitably surprised.

"What, giving it up?" he asked.

"When I've handed him over to you, yes," replied Lott.

"Ah, I see; you've made a bit of progress, eh? Well, I daresay it won't be long before the murderer's in our cells." Dawle paused to light a pipe. "Though he may not be the chap you're after," he added, complacently puffing.

Lott raised his eyebrows.

"You've been on the go, too, have you, Mr. Dawle? Any objection to letting me know about it? No point in having secrets between us, is there?"

"Not so far as I'm concerned. I've got no reputation to worry about," replied Dawle with a chuckle.

The Scotland Yard man looked slightly disconcerted at this innuendo, but he wanted to hear the Superintendent's story, so he produced an appreciative smile and listened attentively while Dawle told of the theory he had formed about Gerald Sterron's return to the study and the extent of the evidence in support of it. It was not until he came to Sir James Hamsted's new evidence, however, that Lott showed more than a polite interest; then he seized on the new point.

"That sounds more like my man," he said. "What time did Sir James hear the footsteps?"

"He didn't know, worse luck. Apparently he hardly noticed them consciously—didn't look at the clock or anything like that. But he thinks that he and Sterron must have been playing about an hour when he heard them."

"Eleven o'clock? That's not possible for Venning; he couldn't have got back to Birmingham in half an hour." Lott's disappointment was obvious, but he quickly recovered. "Still, he only *thinks* it was about an hour. If he was absorbed in the game he might have thought the time longer than it really was. If it was half-past ten he might have had time to get back by half-past eleven, though it would be the hell of a rush. Still, main road and no traffic to bother about—it might be done. We must find out if any one saw a car going that pace, Super."

"Aren't you a bit jumping to the conclusions you want, Mr. Lott, if I may venture to say so?" put in the Superintendent, tilting back his chair. "Surely the murderer wouldn't go tramping round the house so that every one could hear him?"

"Every one didn't hear him, so far as I can gather," returned the detective. "Hamsted only heard him subconsciously—not enough to distract his attention, and

Sterron—Gerald Sterron, that is—didn't hear him at all. Probably he had to cross that path and couldn't help making a slight noise; he'd be in evening shoes, not rubbers."

"Would he be coming down that side of the house? The library looks out on the west side. I don't know your theory yet."

Lott's face fell.

"And I don't know the house. I'm at a disadvantage. I must get out there, Mr. Dawle, and have a look over it. No, that doesn't fit in with my theory; I think he came up from the bottom of the garden; that would land him at the south-east corner of the house, and that's where the ladder is. He'd have no need to go down the west side—not if I'm right about where he left his car. What's your idea, Super.?"

Dawle made a slight grimace.

"One I'm not very proud of," he said. "I think that footstep may have been our man at Styne taking a look round in the ordinary course of his duty. I've never given the fellow a thought. I ought to have had him over and questioned him."

"Styne? Where's that?"

"Biggish village about three miles from Ferris. We've got a constable there—Bunning. He'd have a point out Lambon way; that'd take him through Ferris. I thought I'd run over there this morning and question him; better than telephoning."

Detective-Inspector Lott looked down his finely-chiseled nose, but was wise enough to make no comment on this typical example, as he felt it to be, of provincial slackness. Instead, he urged the necessity for his own early introduction to Ferris Court. Superintendent Dawle, feeling that he was for the moment at a disadvantage, did not press for an account of the other's doing but ordered a constable to bring his car round.

"By the way, sir; what about that second P.M.? Has it been done?" asked Lott as they got into the car.

"Not yet. The Home Office are sending Sir Hulbert Lemuel down; he couldn't get away yesterday. Dr. Tanwort 'll do any surgical work that's necessary, but he'll do it under Lemuel's eye. Lemuel's going to hunt the whole body over, too, in case Tanwort's missed anything else. Infernal nuisance, the delay; can't get at the will till he's been buried."

"Oh, surely the solicitor would let you see it?"

"Well, he didn't. I tried him," replied Dawle curtly.

Arrived at Ferris Court, Superintendent Dawle asked for Mr. Gerald Sterron and was again shown, with Lott, into the library. Gerald Sterron soon appeared, looking as cool and unperturbed as on the previous morning. Dawle realized that, if his own theory was correct, he was dealing with a man whom it would be difficult to trip up.

"I wanted to introduce Detective-Inspector Lott to you, sir, from New Scotland Yard," he said, watching Gerald's face as he spoke. The merchant raised his eyebrows but gave no sign of perturbation.

"Does that mean that you've definitely abandoned the suicide theory?" he asked.

"No, sir; nothing definite so far. But the Chief Constable thought it better to clear things up as quickly as possible—better for all parties."

"I quite agree," said Sterron. "I don't know much

about police procedure in this country. I rather thought the local police only called in Scotland Yard when they were stumped. You can't have been stumped in four or five days, can you?"

"Oh, no, sir; that's what gets into the papers. It does happen sometimes, of course, but it's much wiser, if you're going to have the Yard, to have 'em at once, before everything's cold."

Lott had difficulty in repressing a smile. This was a point of view more often heard in London than the provinces; still, it was true that this Constabulary had been commendably quick in calling in the Yard, whatever their reasons may have been.

"Well, now you're here, Inspector Lott, what can I do for you?" asked Gerald Sterron, turning to the younger man. "I've told Superintendent Dawle absolutely everything I know about my brother's death."

"I'm sure you have, sir," said Lott. "At the moment, I only want permission to have a look round the house and perhaps talk to some of the servants."

"It's not my house, Inspector, though I'm sure my sister-in-law will have no objection to your doing anything you may think necessary."

"On that point, sir; can you tell me who the house does belong to now?"

Gerald shrugged his shoulders.

"I suppose it's Mrs. Sterron's until the will is proved. After that, I don't know; it remains to be seen. Mr. Halfcastle might tell you; he's coming down this morning."

Lott pricked up his ears.

"That's very fortunate, sir; I was hoping for a word with him some time. When do you expect him, sir?"

"About lunch-time; he's coming by the nine o'clock from St. Pancras—12.30 at Hylam, I think."

"Then if I may see him for a minute when he comes, sir. Till then, I'll have a look round."

For the next two hours Lott, under the guidance of Superintendent Dawle, inspected the scene of the tragedy. The study had been sealed and undisturbed; save for the absence of the body and the presence of a perceptible layer of dust, it was as it had been when Gerald Sterron and Willing broke into it four days ago.

Lott paid particular attention to the windows, trying to find some sign of foot- or finger-mark to encourage his theory of an entry from the outside, but there was none. Still, it was practically certain that the murderer had left the room by the window, however he had entered it, and if he made no marks going he might have made none coming.

Superintendent Dawle was extremely skeptical of an entry by ladder; the victim must have heard it and been on his guard.

"If the murderer came from the outside, it's much more likely that somebody let him in," he said. "If it was Sir Carle Venning, what's wrong with Mrs. Sterron letting him in herself?"

"What, by the front door? Bit risky, wouldn't it be?"

"No, through her sitting-room; it's got French windows opening to the ground. On the north side, it is."

"I didn't know that," said Lott quickly.

"Didn't I tell you? One of the maids found a man's muddy footprint there one day, some time ago. It looks as if she made a habit of letting people in that way."

"Damn the old fool," thought Lott. "Why couldn't

he have told me that before?" But aloud he only said, "I'd like to have a look at that room, sir."

"Come along, then," said Dawle, leading the way out into the hall and down the little passage beyond the front door. Dawle's tap at the sitting-room door was answered by a woman's voice within. As they entered, Griselda Sterron looked round from the escritoire at which she was writing; beside her stood Grace Nawten. Dawle saw that, in spite of the black dress and the dark lines of anxiety under her eyes, Mrs. Sterron was looking more beautiful and much younger than he had ever seen her before. The loss of a husband like Herbert Sterron might well be an overwhelming relief to a woman, the shrewd policeman realized, however anxious and harrowing the circumstances of his death.

Having been introduced, Lott did no more than offer his condolences and again ask permission to carry on his investigations. If he was to question Mrs. Sterron, it would have, he realized, to be a searching and severe cross-examination which he could hardly carry out at his first meeting. He hardly noticed the quiet secretary, who looked singularly colorless next to her employer's vivid beauty.

"Very handy bolt-hole, that," he said when they were back in the study.

"Couldn't bolt *out* that way; not with this door locked on the inside," commented Dawle.

"You're sure it was?"

"Sir James Hamsted says he specially looked to see. He's a pretty safe witness. Coroner and all that."

"Well, that's the way the fellow came in, anyhow," said Lott confidently. "And that makes her an accessory before the fact. You must keep an eye on her, Super.; we can't have them bolting together."

"I wasn't born yesterday, young man," said Dawle dryly. "I've had a man watching Venning ever since the inquest. She won't go without him."

Lott stared.

"You never told me that, sir," he said.

"You didn't ask. We don't blow a lot about what we do down in the country."

This was unkind, but Dawle was feeling sore about Lott's unspoken criticism of the early morning.

"Then you know where he was yesterday?"

"I do. And I know you were interested in his back tire last night, though you haven't thought fit to tell me why."

Lott, to do him justice, could see a joke against himself. He laughed heartily—though not aloud.

"Well, I'm blowed. I give you best, Mr. Dawle," he said. "You've scored off me properly."

The Superintendent was instantly mollified. He grinned in return.

"That's all right, my lad. Perhaps you'll tell me all about it some time. Meantime . . ."

An electric bell somewhere in the back regions trilled melodiously.

"That'll be the solicitor," said Lott. "Let's get him before the family do."

He slipped out into the hall and, as Mr. Halfcastle gave his hat to Willing, the detective approached and handed him his official card.

"If you could spare me five minutes, sir?" he said.

The solicitor glanced at the card and his face instantly became grave.

"Certainly," he said. "Willing, tell Mrs. Sterron I will pay my respects to her in a few minutes. Come into the library, Inspector."

The room was empty and Lott quickly explained his presence. Halfcastle nodded.

"I thought there was something up when they adjourned the inquest," he said. "And when that Superintendent tackled me about the will."

"It would really be a very great help to us, sir, if you *could* let us know something about that. I realize, of course, that you are quite within your rights in withholding information at the moment, but I understand from Mr. Sterron that he is anxious to help us."

Mr. Halfcastle thought for a minute, then took his decision.

"Very well," he said. "I'll let you see the will; I've got it here." He opened his black bag. "I admit I was a bit short-tempered with the Superintendent, but he wasn't too tactful with me."

Lott smiled. He could imagine Dawle's direct line of approach.

The will, when he had digested it, proved to carry out the instructions contained in the notes which Grace Nawten had shown to Dawle, and by him to Lott.

"Then the bulk of the estate goes to Mr. Gerald Sterron, sir?" asked Lott quietly.

Mr. Halfcastle had watched the detective carefully as he read. He had also done some quick thinking.

"That is the case," he said. "Now I think, Inspector, that it may save you from misapprehension and every one else from a good deal of unpleasantness, if I explain to you just what this inheritance implies. Shall we sit down?"

"I wonder, sir," said Lott, "whether you'd mind me fetching Superintendent Dawle? He's in the study, and naturally it will be of great interest and help to him to hear what you have to say."

"Of course, of course. Fetch him in."

A minute later, Lott reappeared with Superintendent Dawle. Mr. Halfcastle held out his hand.

"I think I have to apologize to you, Superintendent," he said. "I was rather short with you on Tuesday."

"That's very handsome of you, sir. Of course, the fault was mine. Or we might blame it on the weather," Dawle said with a smile.

The three men seated themselves near one of the windows and well away from either door. When the Superintendent had run his eye over the will (he was not going to give Grace Nawten away) Mr. Halfcastle continued.

"I was telling Inspector Lott that I may be able to save him from a misapprehension. You will probably have grasped the state of affairs from my evidence on Tuesday, Superintendent, but I can perhaps amplify that now that I know what is in the wind. As I said then, the Ferris estate is very strictly tied up at the present time, and will be for many years to come. Captain Sterron in his young days . . . I can speak plainly, in confidence . . . gambled heavily and most foolishly in stocks. His intentions, I really believe, were laudable enough—to improve the finances of the estate, rather than to make money for his own amusements—but whatever the motive the result was disastrous. Everything in the way of stocks that he could lay hands on he sold, but most fortunately he did not attempt to realize the Liverpool property from which the bulk of the income was derived. If it had not been for the War, the family *must* have lost Ferris, but the War not only pulled him up but enabled substantial economies to be effected."

Mr. Halfcastle extracted a paper of notes from his bag.

"In 1924 he began to rebuild what he had so nearly destroyed. A trust was established—I hold the deed in my hand—for the accumulation and reinvestment of the whole of the income from the Liverpool property over a period of twenty-one years. It was hoped that by 1945 a sufficient sum would have been accumulated to provide an income adequate to an estate of this character. But in the meantime the income accruing to the owner of the estate is extremely limited and now that Captain Sterron is dead death duties will have to be paid—and there is no sinking-fund or insurance policy from which that can be done. The duties will have to be paid over a period of eight years, as provided by the Act. During that time there will not be a penny of income for Mr. Sterron, and very little with which to maintain Ferris. The place will have to be. let—if in these days it can be let—it is none too well supplied with modern requirements. Even after the death duties are paid off, it will be a long time before the estate can recover from this added blow—and then only by great care and sacrifice on the part of the owner."

"If you'll excuse me a moment, sir," interrupted Lott. "Has Mr. Gerald Sterron an income of his own apart from what he will eventually have from the estate?"

"He has, yes, but only enough for his present requirements. He has a family—a wife, two sons, and four daughters, all in the school or nursery stage. His own income, from what he has made in his business, is enough to keep him and his family in a comfortable house at Hindhead; it allows no margin for anything else. The one thing he can hope for out of this inheritance is to let Ferris for twenty-one years, by which time the estate, if all goes well, should be on its legs again."

Mr. Halfcastle paused and looked thoughtfully at his companions. Then he made his second decision.

"I tell you this, gentlemen," he said, "because I think you may be connecting this inheritance with Captain Sterron's death. You will probably realize now how impossible such a suggestion is. Would any man in his senses—leaving aside all questions of morality, honor, family ties and so on—would any man in his senses commit a murder and endanger his own life for a problematical advantage twenty-one years ahead? Bearing in mind, too, that the dead man was fifty-five years old and in none too robust health—that the inheritance might well come into effect in the ordinary course of nature long before the twenty-one years are up. I am sure you will agree with me that the idea is unthinkable."

The solicitor returned the will and his notes to the black bag and rose to his feet.

"I must go and see Mrs. Sterron now," he said. "I shall not be leaving till about four. If you want to see me, I shall be at your service."

As the door closed on him the two police officers turned to look at each other. Lott gave a mischievous smile.

"I think that knocks the bottom out of *your* theory, Mr. Dawle," he said.

XV. TIME OF DEATH

IN the meantime, a minor crisis had arisen in Hylam. Sir Hulbert Lemuel, the Home Office analyst, having announced his intention of coming down in the afternoon to do the second post-mortem, had, after the manner of indispensables, turned up in the morning—by the same train as had brought Mr. Halfcastle to Hylam. Finding neither Chief Constable, nor Superintendent, nor Scotland Yard Inspector to meet him, he saw fit to be crotchety, but when the Coroner—who fortunately was found and brought along at the double—offered to send for them, he replied that they had their work to do, that he did not in the least require their presence, and that he could say all he had to say to Sergeant Gable, who was doing his best to represent his absent chiefs.

While all this fussing was going on, Dr. Tanwort was anxiously waiting at the mortuary for the snubbing that he felt sure he was going to get. And which he certainly would have got had not Mr. Lovejoy exercised his privilege as a coroner and come along to watch the event. Nothing would induce Sir Hulbert to be rude to a colleague in front of a layman, so Tanwort, to his intense surprise and delight, found himself being treated with courteous consideration and so gradually recovered his usual spirits.

Having the body stripped of all covering, Sir Hulbert began a minute examination of every inch of the surface, from the skull to the toe-nails. He paid particular attention to the extremities into which the blood had flowed while the body was hanging, because in those parts the post-mortem staining was deepest and it was by no means easy with the naked eye to distinguish between staining and bruise. In one or two places Sir Hulbert asked Dr. Tanwort to remove a section of flesh, which he then examined under a microscope; in each case it was clear that the blood was not extravasated but was only bloody fluid issuing from the cut ends of the tissues—blood which was readily washed away, even in its present congealed state, by a gentle stream of water. There was no bruise, nor any cut, other than the ligature mark and the bruising on the inner side of the lips to which Sir James Hamsted had drawn attention and which had probably been caused by the pressure employed in smotheration.

Although there was no bruise or cut on the body, however, there was one mark on the back, over the right hip, which did interest the analyst. It was a rectangular depression, about three inches square, deepest below where the tissues were thicker and becoming less marked above where the flesh thinned over the bone.

"There's been some pressure there," said Sir Hulbert; "sufficient to press the flesh down but not enough to bruise it. Done after death, of course."

"How can you tell that, if I may ask, Sir Hulbert?" said Mr. Lovejoy, inspecting the place with interest.

"If it had been done before death the returning blood flow would have caused the flesh to resume its normal position as soon as the pressure was removed. It may have been caused at any time after death—perhaps even on this slab, if something was left under him. You might just enquire about that, Dr. Tanwort. By the way, did you notice this when you made your examination?"

Dr. Tanwort flushed slightly.

"No. No. I . . . er . . . I don't think it was here then," he answered.

"Well, he's been lying on something since that, then. I don't suppose it matters, but the police had better know about it. Now, Tanwort, this constriction mark: we'll have a section here, please."

Sir Hulbert pointed to a spot on the neck and Dr. Tanwort got to work again. It was not quite so neat a job as he could have wished because he was slightly flustered about that depression. Had he seen it—and not noticed it? Had he even looked there? Surely he must have; but it was true that he had been so convinced that the case was one of suicidal hanging that his examination of the body for signs of violence had not been as thorough as he could now have wished. And in any case, this was not a sign of violence; it was not a cut or a bruise, only a depression—a sign of pressure—gentle pressure—that was not violence.

"There you are, sir," he said, laying the section on its glass slide under the microscope.

Sir Hulbert spent a considerable time over his examination of this section, but the result was almost the same as before. Although the flesh had undoubtedly been bruised by the ligature it had been bruised after death—there was no sign of vital reaction—no extravasated blood, no ecchymoses; the discoloration round the edge of the depression was evidently due to the post-mortem hypostasis evident in other parts of the body.

A section taken from the lower lip, on the other hand, showed unmistakable signs of bruising on the inside. An examination of the lungs confirmed the presence of ecchymoses and larger sub-pleural hemorrhages already discovered by Dr. Tanwort; microscopic examination also revealed ruptures of the lung tissue and hemorrhages into the tissue, all these being symptoms of the asphyxia common to both smotheration and strangulation. The latter had been assumed by Dr. Tanwort because of the circumstances in which the body was found, whereas the former proved now to have been the cause of death.

Having given his decision and discussed with the Coroner the nature of the evidence which he should give at the resumed inquest, whenever that should prove to be, Sir Hulbert Lemuel prepared to depart. As soon as he emerged into the open air, however, he was approached by Sergeant Gable.

"I beg your pardon, sir," he said. "I got on to Superintendent Dawle on the 'phone ten minutes ago; he was engaged with Mr. Halfcastle, the solicitor, up till then, and I didn't like to have him disturbed. I told him you didn't want him to come back to meet you, sir, and he said I was particularly to ask you if you could give him an opinion on the time of death. Dr. Tanwort gave an opinion, sir, but Mr. Dawle would be glad to have it confirmed."

Lemuel turned to his companion.

"Have you got the data, Tanwort? It's very difficult for me to give an opinion now unless you can tell me on what data and assumptions you based your own."

Dr. Tanwort fished a note-book out of his pocket.

"I've got a note of the temperature here, I think," he said, flicking over the leaves. "Yes, temperature at 8 A.M. was 65°; there was just a trace of warmth still to be felt externally. Rigor was practically complete. Taking all this into account, I gave it as my opinion that death had taken place from eight to twelve hours previously, that's to say, between 8 and 12 P.M. the previous night. I think I subsequently reduced that to eight to ten hours, or from 10 to 12 P.M., in view of the fact that rigor is accelerated by heat, and Saturday night was hot. There is definite evidence, I believe, that he was seen alive at 10 P.M., so I'm probably not far out."

Dr. Tanwort was pleased with this speech. It showed care, knowledge and thought—and it was backed up by material evidence.

Sir Hulbert considered for a minute.

"Your point about the hot night cuts both ways," he said. "Although heat certainly accelerates rigor, it also tends to retain body warmth, which would point to an earlier rather than a later hour. There is also the fact that heat is well retained in cases of asphyxia, which also points to an earlier hour. I should say that twelve o'clock was too late; eleven o'clock, perhaps, or any time between that and ten, if ten really is the earliest possible in the known circumstances."

He turned to Sergeant Gable.

"Got that?" he asked.

Sergeant Gable was not quite sure of the technicalities but he gathered that, in Sir Hulbert's opinion, death had occurred at some time between 10 and 11 P.M.

"That's right, Sergeant. Tell your Superintendent that I shall send my written report to the Chief Constable tomorrow morning by messenger. He'd better have a look himself at one mark on the body that I shall refer to. After that, if Mr. Lovejoy here agrees, I see no reason to delay burial any longer. In fact, the sooner the better."

The great man took a brisk farewell of the lesser fry and hurried off to catch his express train back to London. Sergeant Gable, in his turn, hurried off to assure his chief over the telephone that he had got the information asked for. The Superintendent had, however, already left Ferris Court. Dawle had been considerably annoyed at hearing that the second post-mortem was taking place in his absence, and had been inclined to blame Sergeant Gable for not insisting on getting through to him earlier; still, he was just enough to realize that it is not easy to know when an interruption will be forgiven and Sergeant Gable had been expressly told by the Home Office analyst not to recall his superior officer.

Having finished his interview with Mr. Halfcastle and after spending some time in talking it over with Inspector Lott, Dawle had sent for the housemaid, Ethel, and questioned her about the library clock. He was an obstinate man and though what Mr. Halfcastle had told him now showed that the motive round which he had started to build his case could no longer be considered as a motive at all, he was still anxious to find support for his theory. He got no help from Ethel; the clock in the library was a good time-keeper; it was always set on Sunday morning by Mr. Willing and she had herself seen him set it this last Sunday morning, corpse or no corpse, and it hadn't been half a minute out. Mr. Willing, consulted, confirmed this. If, then, the clock had been put back on Saturday night, as his theory demanded, it had been put forward again before Sunday morning.

Considerably disgruntled by the apparent collapse of his case, Superintendent Dawle decided to take time to think it over before doing any more at Ferris. He would look up the constable at Styne on his way back to Hylam, where he would—he hoped—learn the result of the second post-mortem. Inspector Lott decided to accompany him.

They were soon at Styne and Police-Constable Bunning, who had been warned by telephone of their arrival, received them at his little cottage with respect mingled with nervousness; superintendents didn't often visit constables, but when they did it generally meant trouble. Dawle, however, was not one of those officers who liked to blame their own mistakes on their subordinates.

"It's about this affair at Ferris Court, Bunning," he said; "that's on your beat, isn't it?"

"That's right, sir."

"I ought to have seen you about it before. I don't suppose you noticed anything odd, or you'd have let us know. Were you out that way on Saturday night?"

"I was, sir. I had a point with Hummle half-way between Ferris and Lambon at 11.30 that night. That took me through Ferris at 10.45 or thereabouts and I had a look round the Court as usual."

"Everything in order?"

"Yes, sir, so far as I could see."

"Did you go round the south side?"

"Yes, sir; right round the house."

"D'you know which the study windows are?"

"Oh, yes, sir, I know the house well; my wife was a housemaid there."

Superintendent Dawle was too much interested in

his enquiry to notice the significance of this confession of familiarity with the inside of Ferris Court.

"Were the study windows open or shut when you went past?"

"One was open, sir, and one was shut, the near one. There was a light in the room, as there usually is."

The two senior officers were listening with intense interest. They exchanged glances of significance.

"Listen, Bunning," said Superintendent Dawle. "This point's of great importance; you mustn't mislead us, whatever you do. If you aren't sure, say so. Now, then, as you look at the house, which of the windows was open, the one on your right or your left?"

"The one on the right, sir; it always is till the Captain goes to bed."

Superintendent Dawle looked at Lott.

"That's the one he was found hanging in," he said. "He wasn't hanging then, at 10.45; he was still alive, then!"

XVI. TRY AGAIN

FOR an appreciable time the two police officers continued to stare at each other in something like consternation. Superintendent Dawle was the first to break the silence.

"What time did you say that commissionaire chap saw your man leaving the theatre in Birmingham?" he asked.

"Half-past eleven," replied Lott glumly.

There was another pause.

"Can't be done," commented Dawle.

"It can't be done, sir, as you say," agreed the detective.

"What about it then? Bit of a snag, eh?"

Lott stroked his smooth cheek.

"What about it, sir? Why, we've got to find the way round it."

Telling Police-Constable Bunning to say nothing to any one on the subject, the two seniors returned to the police car, in which they drove slowly back towards Hylam. Lott remained for a time sunk in thought.

"Will you tell me again, sir, what grounds you have for thinking there's anything up between Sir Carle and Mrs. Sterron?" he asked at last.

Dawle repeated what he had heard on the subject. Sir James Hamsted's statement that the two seemed to take "more than a little pleasure" in each other's company; the various statements of different members of the household—of junior members of the household,

Dawle had to admit; finally, Ethel's statement about muddy footmark in Mrs. Sterron's sitting-room which seemed to suggest the admission of a surreptitious visitor.

"A bit thin really, isn't it, Super.?" said Lott. "Venning certainly seemed uncomfortable when I questioned him about it, but I'm bound to admit he denied that there was anything in the suggestion."

He remained silent for a time longer, then suddenly shook himself briskly.

"Look here, sir," he said, "if I'm to go on with this Venning line, I must satisfy myself that there is something in it. I must tackle the woman herself. Will you take me back there?"

After leaving Styne the police car had had to come back through Ferris and was now only a little way beyond it. Without a word Superintendent Dawle stopped the car, turned it, and drove back towards the village. Stopping outside the gates of Ferris Court he turned to his companion.

"You're quite right to stick to it," he said. "One snag doesn't make a dam; you make sure the water's running the right way, then jump in and find the way round your snag. I've got two, if not three, snags in my way. I'm going back to Hylam to do a bit of thinking."

Lott walked up the drive and, as he approached the house, saw what Superintendent Dawle had seen two days previously—a pretty girl returning from a rose-picking expedition. He realized that she was the girl whom he had seen a few hours ago in Mrs. Sterron's sitting-room; he found himself wondering that he had not then taken more notice of so attractive a young lady.

"I thought you'd gone," said Grace Nawten with a smile.

"So I had, miss," replied Lott. "Something seems to have drawn me back."

Miss Nawten began to laugh but suddenly stopped; a shiver seemed to pass through her.

"It's difficult to realize that you are . . . hunting," she said in a low voice.

Lott felt slightly uncomfortable.

"I'm only doing my duty, miss," he said lamely. "I'm afraid I ought to ask you some questions."

"Yes, I suppose you must. Come back into the garden. I hate being questioned indoors; I always think somebody is listening."

They walked down on to the south terrace and turned towards the rose garden at the west end of it—the one bit of garden still well kept.

"I look after these myself," the girl said. "It's so awful to see them neglected—the lovely things."

"The rest of it is neglected?" queried Lott.

"Oh, yes, look. Captain Sterron was fighting—an uphill battle, Inspector. But he was going to win."

Lott saw a flash in the girl's eyes. She evidently felt a sincere interest in her late employer's struggle to regain lost ground.

"You never thought it was suicide, the Superintendent tells me," said Lott.

"No, I knew it wasn't."

"May I ask how, miss?"

Grace Nawten shrugged her shoulders.

"How does one know such things? It was entirely contrary to his whole object in life. He was trying to put the estate on its legs again; his death will undo all he has done; now there will be death duties and . . . extravagance."

The two walked down a length of the rose garden before Lott spoke again.

"Will you tell me, please, whether you think Captain Sterron was jealous of his wife's friendship with Sir Carle Venning?" he asked.

"Whether he was jealous, or whether he had grounds for jealousy?" asked the girl calmly.

"Both really, but especially whether he had grounds for jealousy."

"He was certainly jealous—or, at any rate, angry. As for the rest, have you asked Mrs. Sterron?"

"Not yet, miss, but I'm going to," replied Lott grimly.

"I should. After all, my opinion's not likely to be of much value, is it? There are only two people who can really *know*."

Inspector Lott looked thoughtfully at his companion.

"In cases of murder, Miss Nawten," he said, "it is the rarest thing in the world to have absolute knowledge of guilt—first-hand evidence; we have to rely upon the building up of a mass of circumstantial evidence. And yet, the majority of murderers are hanged and there is no known case of a man having been unjustly hanged. All the same, I will follow your advice and go direct to one of the principals for my information. I can't promise, though, that I shan't come to you again for your 'opinion.' "

"All right, Inspector; we'll leave it at that," said Miss Nawten calmly. "I think you'll find Mrs. Sterron in her sitting-room now."

Finding Mrs. Sterron involved all the formalities of

"enquiring" and "announcing" on the part of her butler. Lott swallowed his impatience and was beginning a polite re-introduction of himself when Mrs. Sterron cut him short.

"What were you talking to my secretary about?" she asked abruptly.

Lott always admired direct attack, and he certainly admired the animation with which this attack was launched. Anger suited Griselda much better than the pale languor or girlish high spirits which she more commonly affected. Lott met the attack with a *riposte*.

"About you, madam. I was asking Miss Nawten whether Captain Sterron had reason to be jealous about you."

Griselda was not expecting anything quite so direct as this, but she did not flinch from it.

"And what did Miss Nawten see fit to tell you?" she asked haughtily.

"She told me to come and ask you, madam," replied Lott in his blandest voice. "That's why I'm here."

For a moment Mrs. Sterron hesitated, then pointed to a chair.

"You'd better explain what you're talking about," she said curtly.

"Yes, madam, certainly. I am here, as you know, investigating the death of your late husband. It was at first thought to be a case of suicide, but there is now a suggestion that it may have been murder. In either case we have got to find the cause of it—the motive for it, I should say. There has been some talk of Captain Sterron having felt jealous of your intimacy with another man; if that is really the case, it might provide grounds for either suicide or murder. I am inviting you, madam, to tell me whether he had such cause, but I am bound to warn you that you need not make any statement at the present time if you think it wiser not to."

Griselda paid no attention to this ominous warning. Her face was expressionless; she was certainly not acting now, whatever she may have been doing before.

"What man are you talking about?" she asked.

The detective raised his eyebrows in well-feigned surprise.

"Is there more than one man in question, madam?" he asked.

Griselda made a gesture of anger, but controlled herself.

"You are impertinent," she said. "I don't know whether you are acting under instructions or whether you are within your rights in speaking to me in this way. I don't really care. But I want to know what man you are talking about."

It was well done. Lott felt uncertain whether her indignation was genuine or a cloak to another emotion. In any case, he had not yet learnt what he had come to find out. This woman was as able a fencer as himself; he must use a heavier weapon.

"I am talking about Sir Carle Venning, madam," he said, watching carefully the handsome face in front of him. There was a slight narrowing of the eyes; that was all.

"I thought you probably were," said Mrs. Sterron calmly. "Does he know you are making these suggestions?"

"That is no answer to my question, madam, if you will forgive my bluntness," said Lott, beginning really to feel that he was not getting the better of this contest. "I asked whether there was any ground for Captain Sterron feeling jealous of your association with this gentleman."

"Certainly not. I've only your word for it, Inspector, that he did feel jealous."

Griselda took a cigarette from a silver box beside her and blew a delicate feather of smoke down her fine nose.

"You deny that there was any ground for jealousy; do you deny the association?"

"I don't know what that means. It sounds like company-promoting."

Mrs. Sterron smiled pleasantly as she watched the smoke rising in a gray spiral from her finger-tips.

"I will try to be more exact, madam. Do you deny that your relations with Sir Carle Venning were of an intimate character; that you were something more than friends?"

"Oh, yes, certainly. We were friends, perhaps intimate friends, but nothing more."

This was leading nowhere. Lott fingered his sharpest saber. He leant forward.

"Do you admit your other friends to this room at night?" he asked sharply.

That had gone home. Griselda's hand with its pink-tipped cigarette stopped half-way to her mouth, then slowly descended to her lap. There was no point in waiting for an answer; now was the time to strike.

"Three weeks ago you admitted a man to this room after the house had been shut up, madam. It had been raining, and the mark of his footstep was found inside the window the following morning. Was that man Sir

Carle Venning? I warn you again that you need not answer if you do not wish to."

But Griselda Sterron had answered. Her face had turned white—a deathly white against which the scarlet lips stood out in a vivid gash. Her eyes wavered—and returned to the Inspector's face. She rose quietly to her feet.

"I am quite sure that you are exceeding your duties, Inspector," she said in a voice that was almost calm. "I shall not answer any more of these absurd and impertinent questions."

She walked to the fireplace and touched a bell beside it, then sat down at her writing-table again and picked up a pen. It was a fine recovery—but Lott had got his answer. Without waiting for the bell to be answered he left the room.

Although each of the two principals had denied that a guilty liaison existed, and although the evidence in support of it rested largely upon gossip, Lott no longer felt any doubt in his own mind that Griselda Sterron and Carle Venning were lovers. Whether their love was guilty to the extent of murder was still open to conjecture; at the moment there was strong evidence to the contrary in the apparent alibi which Venning had established in Birmingham. But the detective had before now known alibis as cast-iron as this which, on close investigation, had broken down. It was his duty to test this one to its utmost before he was satisfied that Carle Venning was not guilty of the murder of his lover's husband.

How was that alibi to be tested? On what was it based? On what did it depend? It depended upon the time factor. The period within which the murder could have been committed had now been reduced to little more than an hour, if the evidence of the doctor was to be believed. Captain Sterron was known to have been alive at 10.45 P.M.; Dr. Tanwort had said that he must have been dead by midnight. And right in the middle of that period—at 11.30 P.M.—Venning had been seen in Birmingham, thirty miles away. But had he really been seen there? That depended so far upon the evidence of one man—a man about whom Lott knew nothing. It was a point that must be much more closely tested.

Obviously he must return to Birmingham and go much more closely into that alibi. But first of all, there were two points that he would like cleared up nearer at hand. He wanted further evidence as to the time at which Sir Carle Venning had returned home on Saturday night, and he wanted to know what that gentleman had been doing in Birmingham the previous day. For the latter point, he had only to ask the man who had, by Superintendent Dawle's orders, been shadowing the High Sheriff; in the rush of the morning's work he had forgotten to ask Dawle to elaborate the little score that had given him such pleasure. For the first point, he would go to High Oaks and try to get some information out of the household.

Superintendent Dawle had promised to send a police car back to Ferris for Lott and this the detective found already waiting outside the gates. In it he drove to High Oaks, a distance of ten miles; ten miles, he learnt from the constable driving, on the other side of Ferris from Birmingham. So that whereas Birmingham was thirty miles from Ferris, it was forty miles from High Oaks. Venning had said that he had got back at "about half-past twelve" on Saturday night; which seemed hardly possible, but on the other hand he had been calculating upon the basis of leaving the theatre at "about eleven"—the usual time—he might quite reasonably have forgotten that the speeches had prolonged the performance that night to a later hour—half-past eleven, according to the commissionaire. The point did not seem of great importance, because according to the doctor, Captain Sterron was dead by twelve o'clock. Still, Lott believed in checking *all* statements connected with an alibi.

The detective saw no point in having another encounter with Sir Carle at this stage of the enquiry, so he left the car outside in the road and walked round to the back door. The bell was answered by an untidy-looking scullery-maid whom Lott asked to tell Mr. Stainer (name previously ascertained from the Hylam police) that a "gentleman" would be glad of a few minutes' conversation with him. The hard-faced man-servant shortly appeared and, as soon as he realized the identity of the "gentleman," showed every sign of regretting that he had so readily responded to his call.

"Sir Carle's not in," he said shortly, remaining in the shadows of the back hall.

"That's all right," responded Lott blandly. "I came to see *you* this afternoon. May I step inside?"

It was too late to find an excuse and futile to attempt force against the police. Mr. Stainer led the way into the pantry and, shutting the door, waited sullenly for the detective to disclose the object of his visit.

"Nice little place you've got here . . . er . . . Stainer, isn't it?"

"That's my name," replied the man.

"I thought it might be, but I wasn't sure. Now, I

want a little information from you about last Saturday night. You can tell me, can't you, what time your master and Captain Bowys got back from Birmingham?"

"No, I can't," replied Stainer. "I was asleep."

"Oh? What time did you go to sleep?"

"I don't know, but I was asleep when they got back."

"How do you know that?"

"I should have heard them if I hadn't been; my bedroom looks on the yard."

"Ah, that's interesting. So if I tell you that they got back at eleven, you must have been asleep by then?"

Stainer eyed his questioner doubtfully.

"Yes," he said after a pause.

"And if I tell you that you weren't asleep by eleven, then they can't have been back by then? Not even if they say they were?"

Stainer shifted uneasily.

"I tell you I was asleep by eleven," he said doggedly.

"Oh, you were? And how did they get in?"

"Sir Carle's got his latchkey."

"And nobody sits up for him?"

"No."

Lott rose to his feet.

"Well, then I'm afraid you can't help me much," he said, watching Stainer's face—which at once reacted with evident relief.

"Oh, just one thing more," said Lott casually, pulling out his note-book and extracting from it a shiny white card. "Just as a matter of form, I'd be glad if you'd let me have your finger-prints."

The man drew back as if he had been stung.

"What are you getting at?" he snarled. "You've got nothing against me?"

"Think not? What about a little matter of forged references?"

It was a guess, but one based upon experience, and it came off—Stainer collapsed into a chair, his face white and haggard.

"You can't prove it," he said. "I deny it."

"I shan't bother about it at the moment if you tell me the truth," said the detective. "Now, what time did Sir Carle get back on Saturday night?"

"I tell you I don't know. I was asleep."

"I don't believe you," said Lott sternly. "Now, look here, Stainer, or whatever you like to call yourself, this is a case of murder; you know very well that if you withhold information or mislead the police, you're making yourself liable as an accessory—before or after the fact. Come on, now; answer my question."

Stainer buried his face in his hands. At last he looked up.

"For God's sake don't tell him I told you, or he'll kill me," he said. "He didn't get back till half-past two."

XVII. "TIME TO THINK"

AFTER dropping Inspector Lott at Ferris, Superintendent Dawle had driven back to Hylam and arrived just in time to change into his newest and tightest tunic for a foundation-stone ceremony by some minor royalty that he had forgotten all about. As he stood about for hour after hour—or at least, half-hour after half-hour—in the sweltering heat, Dawle cursed the waste of time that these functions represented to busy men. He could not even pass the time in thinking out his problem, as constant trivial interruptions occurred to break his chain of thought. When it was over he gratefully removed his tunic and settled down to a cup of tea and a pipe; as the third puff and prod settled the tobacco down into good drawing condition, the Superintendent's mind gradually slipped into the state of unconscious reverie which makes real thought possible.

His own "line," he realized, had fallen to pieces; not only would Gerald Sterron not gain by his brother's death but, in the paying of heavy duties, he might even, for the next ten or twenty years, be a loser by it—and what man of fifty-four is going to commit murder for a problematical gain twenty, or even ten, years hence? His theory of a return to the study and a faked clock also had come to nothing, because though it still held as a theory there was now no point in it—if Herbert Sterron was alive at 10.45 there was no sense in supposing that his brother went through all that per-

formance at ten or ten-fifteen; he could not possibly
have deceived Sir James about the time to the extent
of three-quarters of an hour.

Where, then, was he to look next? Was Lott on the
right line, after all, in spite of the alibi snag? Or was
there a third line that had hitherto escaped him?

Reaching for his note-book, Dawle methodically
turned over the leaves to see if there was any point that
he had forgotten. On an early page a rough sketch of
a finger-print caught his eye—the scarred finger-print
which had been found on the outside of the study door.
So far, that had not been identified, though prints of
every one known or believed to have been in the house
on Saturday night had been checked. Probably it had
been on the door for days before the tragedy; Dawle
did not know how often doors were "rubbed down,"
nor how long prints would remain if untouched—that
was a point for Sergeant Gable.

There were the account books, of course; he had not
plowed his way through them in detail yet, nor yet
through the files of private correspondence and business letters which the dead man's writing-table had contained. With a weary sigh Dawle rose to his feet and
made for the cupboard in which these things were kept;
he was just starting on the "Personal" file when Inspector Lott appeared.

Dawle listened with interest to the detective's account of his interviews with the two ladies at Ferris, and
still more to the revelation by Sir Carle Venning's manservant of the real hour at which his master had returned home on Saturday night.

"Don't quite see how that helps," said Dawle. "Dr.
Tanwort gave twelve midnight as the latest possible

time of death, and this Home Office chap, Gable tells me, puts it at eleven."

"What's that?" exclaimed Lott.

"Ah, you haven't heard that, of course," said Dawle. "Gable rang us up at Ferris to tell us, but we'd just left. It seems that Sir Hulbert Lemuel puts the latest limit of the time of death at eleven, not twelve, as Dr. Tanwort did."

Lott's face had fallen as the Superintendent spoke.

"That makes things worse than ever," he said. "I thought I might have been able to shift Venning's alibi enough to get him to Ferris by twelve, but if he's got to be there between 10.45 and 11, and back in Birmingham by 11.30, it can't be done. At least, I don't know; if that 11.30 alibi's a fake, it's still possible, though I don't see where the return at half-past two comes in; there seems no sense in that."

For several minutes he remained sunk in thought, while Dawle methodically worked his way through the file in front of him. At last Lott looked up.

"I must get back to Birmingham and shake up that alibi," he said, "but look here, Super., what was Venning doing in Birmingham yesterday? You say your man followed him there?"

Dawle laughed.

"Funny thing you never saw him," he said. "You seem to have followed much the same track, only backwards. Sir Carle got to Birmingham at half-past five, went to a couple of shops—I've got their names if you want them—and at six o'clock into the 'Blue Pearl' bar. He came out of there a little before seven and went along to the Pantodrome, where he went in at the stage door. . . ."

"Stage door?" exclaimed Lott.

"That's it. He stayed inside till nearly eight, came round to the front and had a talk with a commission-aire. Then he went along to the 'Herring Bone,' and probably had dinner there; anyway, he stayed there till about half-past nine, when he walked to the station and caught the train back to Hylam—the same train as you, I gather, Mr. Lott."

The C.I.D. man had listened to Dawle's recital with something like dismay.

"He was talking to that commissionaire five minutes before I got there, then?" he exclaimed. "Filling him up with his alibi, I suppose. Well, I'm damned if that wasn't pretty cool—and I got properly sucked in. All right, Mr. Commissionaire, there'll be something coming to you for this! But look here, Super.; you say he went from the Pantodrome straight to the 'Herring Bone' just about eight o'clock; how was it I didn't meet him? I went straight from the 'Herring Bone' to the Pantodrome—down Champion Street, I think it's called."

Superintendent Dawle permitted himself a broad smile.

"You did meet him," he said. "Or rather, you passed him, on the opposite side of the street. My man noticed you going along with your nose in the air and your eyes . . . well, I won't say shut, Mr. Lott, but they can't have been very wide open. Callender didn't know who you were then, but when he saw you flashing your torch on the tire at Hylam Station he remembered see-ing you and guessed right."

The Scotland Yard detective looked thoroughly crestfallen; it wasn't often that he fell down before the provincial police like this, but Superintendent Dawle was a good fellow and wasn't crowing over him offensively; lucky that he hadn't himself been offensive to Superintendent Dawle as, he was bound to confess, he sometimes was to the county constabularies.

"I've got to do my Birmingham job all over again," he said, "and this time I'll do it with my eyes open. What time's the next train, Mr. Dawle?"

"Going back there tonight? Well, nobody can accuse you of not being a worker." Dawle knew when to apply a word of comfort. He pulled a railway time-table out of a drawer.

"There's a train at 6.20," he said, "gets you in at 7.13. Have something to eat before you go; I can see you aren't going to sit about much in Birmingham."

"You're right, I'm not. I'll slip into that little café in the High and get a poached egg."

Superintendent Dawle looked at his watch.

"It's twenty past five now," he said, "that gives you an hour. Like to slip down to the mortuary with me and have a look at that body before you have your poached egg? Gable tells me that Sir Hulbert found a mark on it and they want to get it buried."

Lott made a wry face.

"Not much of an appetizer for an egg!" he said. "Still, I may as well see it. I can't afford to let anything slip after this."

Superintendent Dawle heaved himself into his tunic and shoved his pipe into his pocket.

"Got some fags on you?" he asked. "You'll want to smoke in there."

The heat of the afternoon was beginning to wear off as the two police officers made their way towards the hospital. Superintendent Dawle received respectful salutes from several of the townspeople, whilst many a glance of interest was turned on his companion, whose identity was beginning to leak out. Sergeant Gable had gone on ahead on a bicycle and was waiting for them outside the mortuary with the hospital porter and the key. To his own great disappointment the latter official was dismissed as soon as he had handed over his charge.

In anticipation of this visit, the body had been left face downwards, so that the police officers were spared the unpleasant task of turning it over; spared, too, the sight of most of the wounds caused by the two post-mortem examinations. Even so, the kindly Superintendent felt a sensation of pity for the unfortunate man who even after a violent death could not be left in peace.

"Poor devil; it's a shame to treat him like this," he said, puffing placidly at his pipe.

Inspector Lott, whose cigarette tobacco was of a less pungent character, enjoyed sensations of a different nature. He preferred not to speak.

Sergeant Gable, unemotional and efficient as ever, pointed out the rectangular depression above the hip joint which had been shown to him by Dr. Tanwort.

"The doctors said it was done after death," he said. "But it's not a blow. They thought he might have lain on something in here, though Dr. Tanwort didn't know what it could be."

Superintendent Dawle bent down and examined the mark carefully, a frown of thought on his rugged face. Suddenly his expression changed into a grin.

"Why, I know what that is!" he exclaimed. "That's

his cigarette-case! I took it out of his hip pocket my-self before the body was brought away from the house. He was lying on it after we laid him on the sofa, of course."

Lott turned and walked out into the fresh air.

"If that's all, it wasn't worth it," he said as Dawle joined him. "You can have my poached egg, Super.; I'm going to walk it off."

The Superintendent laughed.

"Squeamish, you London chaps," he said. "Well, you get yourself a bite some time, or we'll be having you fainting on us next. Not accustomed to hardship in Whitehall, eh?"

Before returning to his task with the correspondence files, Dawle went round to Mr. Lovejoy's house to re-port that, as far as he was concerned, the body might now be buried. The Coroner agreed to give his certifi-cate for burial and to notify the family accordingly.

As he walked back towards the Police Station, Dawle's way took him past the old house which sheltered the Hylam Fathers. It occurred to him that he would go in and have a word with Father Speyd, perhaps even persuade him to explain a little more lucidly the cause of his Sunday morning outburst. The priest was in and greeted Dawle with a friendly smile in the small, sparsely furnished room which served him as an office and study. For a few minutes the two men exchanged commonplaces about the weather, the afternoon's cere-mony, and other subjects equally removed from their thoughts. Dawle thought that "the padre" was looking even more ill and emaciated than when he had last seen him; too much fasting and too little fun was his diag-nosis of the case.

"I've been wondering, padre, whether you feel able to tell us a bit more about the relations between Captain and Mrs. Sterron," said Dawle, broaching the subject at last.

Father Speyd's expressive eyes showed the distress which he naturally felt at this painful subject. He sat for a time, looking at the bare table in front of him. At last he seemed to come to a decision.

"I'm sorry, Dawle," he said. "I know I've brought this on myself by my ill-advised outburst on Sunday morning—I was greatly upset by the distress and misery in which I found Mrs. Sterron. I can't tell you anything. All that I know I was told under the seal of the confessional and that is a sacred and inviolable trust. There can surely be no point in dragging the lives of these unhappy people into the light of public knowledge? The man has paid on earth for his sins; it is for his Heavenly Father to forgive or to punish further. Why cannot we leave it in His hands?"

Dawle shifted uneasily in his chair; this was ground on which he was unaccustomed to tread.

"It's not quite what you think, sir, I'm afraid," he said. "You probably still think he killed himself; he didn't; he was murdered."

Father Speyd shrank back in his chair as if he had been struck. His white face grew even more ashen and drawn; he buried it in his thin, finely-chiseled hands. Dawle heard him muttering what sounded like a prayer. At last he raised his haggard face and stared at his visitor.

"You know that?" he asked, his voice dry and anguished. "Is that certain?"

"I'm afraid so, sir. I'm not at liberty to tell you how we know, but you can take it as a fact."

Father Speyd rose abruptly to his feet. A rare smile lighted up his eyes as he held out his hand.

"You must give me time to think, Dawle," he said. "This is terrible news and a terrible problem; I must . . . I must have time. If I feel . . . when I am told —and I shall be told—where my duty lies, I will speak to you again. You will forgive me if I ask you to leave me now? Come, I will show you to the door."

Leading the way down the narrow passage, Father Speyd was met by another priest, who murmured something to him. "I will see her, of course," he said.

In the little hall an old woman was standing, a basket over her arm. Her lined old eyes lit up when she saw Father Speyd. She dropped a half-curtsey.

"I've brought ye these, Father," she exclaimed eagerly, turning back the white cloth from her basket. "They're new laid an' the lettuce is fresh cut this evening. Ye've to eat 'em yerself, mind; starvin' yerself as ye are."

"Of course I will, Mother," he said. "And a lucky man I am to have such a good friend. How's Biddy this evening?"

"Poorly, Father, poorly. I must get back to her. But she wouldn't rest till I'd brought ye the eggs an' the lettuce. She said, would I bring her y'r blessin'?"

The old woman dropped on her knee and Dawle, with the Englishman's embarrassment in a scene of emotion, turned away his head. But as he turned, his eye caught the right hand of the priest raised in benediction; down the center of the forefinger ran a clear-cut scar.

XVIII. MR. GOTTS

SUPERINTENDENT DAWLE walked away from the Community House in a state of considerable perturbation. Although the glimpse which he had caught of Father Speyd's upraised hand had been only a fleeting one, he had not the slightest doubt that the scar on the priest's forefinger was identical with the print found on the outside of the study door at Ferris Court. There was, of course, nothing to prove that the impression on the door had been made on Saturday night—it seemed impossible that it could have been—but Dawle had a clear impression of Father Speyd telling him the next day that he had not been received at Ferris Court since his first visit shortly after his arrival in Hylam—a matter of two or three years ago. He might, of course, have made the print on Sunday morning, when he was summoned to Ferris to see Mrs. Sterron; until the arrival of the police, nobody had been keeping watch outside the study, though the door was sealed; but why on earth should he have touched the door—and touched it in that position, as if he were pressing on it? It was a disturbing problem and one that must be most thoroughly investigated; the present state of the case was so unsatisfactory that not a single clew must be overlooked.

As he strode through the streets, unconscious now of his surroundings, Dawle pondered how best to follow up his discovery. He could, of course, ask Father Speyd (having first satisfied himself that the print on the door really did coincide with Speyd's finger-print) when and why he had touched the door. But to do so would be to reveal a knowledge that might be better kept to himself. Dawle's mind flew back to that first outburst of the emotional priest: "I am responsible!" Could that have been a confession? A confession hastily withdrawn and amended into a rather highfalutin and nonsensical speech about "the wrath to come"? But what earthly ground could there be for such an idea? Why should Father Speyd kill Herbert Sterron of whom, obviously, he disapproved but whose affairs could be of no more than professional interest to him? The idea was absurd. Still, Dawle did not propose at this stage to let Father Speyd know what he had found.

What should he do, then? He could enquire at Ferris Court as to whether Father Speyd had, or could have, touched the study door on Sunday morning; but that would instantly give rise to the most undesirable speculations, as would even an enquiry as to whether the priest had been to Ferris on any occasion other than Sunday morning. The same objection applied to enquiries of a similar type among Father Speyd's acquaintances. No; in the first place the investigation must be secret.

Once again, then; what should he do? The obvious, routine thing to do would be to watch Father Speyd's future movements, in case he did anything that threw light on the problem. Obvious routine things were, in Superintendent Dawle's experience, often the best, and therefore, on his return to headquarters, he sent for Sergeant Gable, who had been struck off other duty in order to be free for work in this case. Sergeant Gable was, Dawle knew, not only efficient but absolutely trustworthy; to him, therefore, the problem was unfolded. Gable was naturally thrilled to hear that his precious finger-print had been identified and agreed that the clew must be followed up at whatever pains. He offered to do the watching himself, and to this his Superintendent agreed.

"But you'll want some one to help you," said Dawle. "You can't watch twenty-four hours out of the twenty-four and it's impossible to tell when he may do something that ought to be watched. If he's really on the crook, it'll be at night and so you'd better take the night. We'll put Moler on to the day work; he can be trusted not to make a fool of himself. Now, how shall we set about it?"

After a good deal of discussion it was arranged that Moler should—by arrangement with the postal authorities, who need not be told who was to be watched—be set to do some repair work to a telephone cabinet in the same street as, and about a hundred yards away from, the Community House. That could not be continued for many days, of course, but it would do for a start. Sergeant Gable was to take up his quarters after dark in an empty house from which a view could be obtained of the small door which opened from the garden of the Community House into a back street. This door was normally kept locked and was never, so far as the police knew, used by the priests, but if Father Speyd was really up to mischief it was more probable that he would use that exit than the public one in the main street.

"Mind you, I think you're on a wild-goose chase," said Dawle. "But at the moment there's nothing better we *can* chase."

Sergeant Gable went off to make arrangements for

the watch, and Dawle settled down to his interrupted search of the correspondence files.

In the meantime, Inspector Lott had made his way to Birmingham and begun his second examination of Sir Carle Venning's alibi. There was no point in going through the "Herring Bone" part of it again; Venning had left the grill-room soon after eight and Captain Sterron was still alive at ten—certainly alive at ten, inferentially alive at 10.45. It was the theatre alibi that mattered; was the baronet really there at 11.30? In addition, Lott wanted to know what he had been saying to the commissionaire on Wednesday evening ten minutes before Lott's own talk with that bemedaled functionary, and what he had been doing at the stage door an hour before that.

Inspector Lott was not himself a devotee of the theatre, certainly not of its musical and variety branch. He had but the haziest idea of what went on at a stage door, though he had been brought up to believe that it concealed all that was wickedest—and most seductive— in life. In his ignorance he believed that its activities were confined to "between the acts" and "after the show," consisting then of a parade of pimply and weak-chinned young men with large bouquets concealing surreptitious notes. Knowing that the commissionaire would be busy with the arriving audience until well after the rising of the curtain, the detective thought he would fill up time with whoever was in charge of the stage door; he presumed that there was such a person. There was. And he was Busy. Mr. Gotts was always busy, even when he was sitting in his little glass-fronted box studying the evening paper with the aid of a toothpick and a cup of something hot. Just now he definitely was busy.

Ladies of the chorus constitutionally incapable of arriving at anything but the last minute, yet found just ten seconds extra in which to argue that there "must be something for them"; young gentlemen of all ages with small parts, not "on" in the early scenes, had greater leisure in which to discuss the racing results, lodgings, girls, salaries, and interminable shop with Gotts; messenger boys with parcels required chits signed; the assistant stage-manager wanted to know where the blazing hell the deputy-assistant-stage-manager was, and the deputy-assistant-stage-manager, when he did turn up and heard of these enquiries, wanted to know why to sublimated heavens the assistant-stage-manager couldn't remember that he had himself sent the deputy-assistant-stage-manager up to London to see the Boss and how could he get back before the train did. Yes, Mr. Gotts was busy.

Fearing lest the commissionaire, being a very "head" commissionaire, might elect to go off duty till the end of the show if he were not quickly tackled, Lott gave up the stage door for a while and returned to the front of the house. It was a well-timed move; the head commissionaire was just pocketing his gloves preparatory to slipping round the corner for "something."

Lott turned on his most official manner. He never bullied; he got better results by being cold, relentless and deadly.

"I want a word with you, Commissionaire," he said curtly, noting as he did so a slight look of discomfort on the other's face.

"Better come and have one with me, then," said the commissionaire affably. "There's a quiet room."

In the quiet room Lott refused a drink and came to business.

"I'd like your name first, please," he said, producing his note-book.

"Appling's my name; anything wrong with it?"

"Nothing at the moment," responded Lott calmly.

"Sergeant-Major Appling, 2nd Quenshires," added the commissionaire defiantly.

"Ah, yes; I'm an ex-service man myself, N.C.O., too," said the unmoved detective. "Corporal in the R.A.S.C."

Sergeant-Major Appling snorted but was wise enough to remember their respective present positions.

"Now, Appling; I asked you yesterday about a gentleman who was here on Saturday night—at your show. You told me that you saw him both arrive at 8.15 P.M. and leave at 11.30."

"That's right," said Appling. "Remember him quite clearly."

"You didn't remember to tell me that you'd been talking to him ten minutes before I asked you about him," said Lott sternly.

Appling's ruddy color paled slightly. He took a pull at his tankard.

"Why should I tell you?" he said in a surly voice. "You didn't ask me that. It's not my job to volunteer information."

Lott ignored the point.

"What was he saying to you?" he asked.

"Passing the time of . . ."

"Now, then, I don't want any of that," interrupted the detective. "He was talking to you about the same thing that I talked to you about ten minutes afterwards. What did he say?"

"If you know all that, you know as much as I do." Ex-Sergeant-Major Appling rose to his full six and a quarter feet. "I'm going back to my job."

"No, you're not—not till you've answered me. I want the truth this time, Appling; what time *did* you see Sir Carle Venning on Saturday?"

"At the times I told you. I've had enough of this."

"You'll have more if you aren't careful, and in a different place. I warn you, Appling, if you want to be charged with being an accessory to murder you're going the right way about it."

"Murder?"

Appling's heavy jaw had dropped. He stared at his companion in consternation.

"Murder."

"You didn't say anything about murder yesterday. Some rot about tracing a witness."

"Well, I'm saying it now. Come along, the truth, please."

"But I've told you the truth. I can't say more than what I know."

"You stick to it that you saw him at 11.30?"

"Certainly I did; coming out from the show with the others."

Lott felt a twinge of disappointment. He had hoped to beat down that statement.

"And last night; what was he saying to you then?"

"Asked me if I remembered seeing him on Saturday night. Asked me what time it was. Said he wanted to know because he'd had a bet with a friend who said it couldn't be so late. That's all he said."

"And he told you not to tell me that he'd been talking to you?"

"Didn't say anything about you. There, I've told you everything; you've got to take it or leave it. I must get back to the theatre or I shall lose my job."

There was no use in pressing the man further. Either he was telling the truth or he would continue to lie; nothing short of arrest would force him now, and there were no grounds for arrest. Yet Lott felt profoundly dissatisfied with the commissionaire's story; what innocent man would come all the way to Birmingham to ask a question like that? And the bet, what a futile story! Still, it would be difficult to shake it if Appling stuck to his guns. It would be necessary to find out something about his character, his veracity; the city police might be able to tell him something about that.

Lott was moving off in search of a policeman when he remembered that he had not yet made his stage door enquiry. Was it worth the bother? What could members of a company which had only arrived in Birmingham this week tell him about the events of the previous Saturday? Surely . . . Lott pulled himself up sharp; he knew that he was arguing with himself because he didn't *want* to make the enquiry—he felt out of his element at that stage door, positively shy. He returned to the stage door and found it for the moment deserted. Deserted, that is, save for Mr. Gotts, who, it was commonly believed, ate, slept, prayed and would die at his post—had, indeed, probably been born there.

Lott approached the little glass cubicle.

"I beg your pardon," he said; "can you tell me whether Sir Carle Venning is here tonight?"

Mr. Gotts raised a pair of slightly bloodshot eyes from the evening paper that he was perusing.

"Is 'e be'ind, d'ye mean?"

The detective looked slightly at a loss.

"Did he come through this door, I mean?"

"Not tonight, 'e 'asn't. 'E may 'a gone through the pass door."

"He was here last night, wasn't he?"

Mr. Gotts eyed his interlocutor warily.

"What are you gettin' at, laddie?" he demanded.

This was an awkward question. Some instinct warned the detective not to play his official card here, and yet he could expect to get no information of any value without displaying a curiosity that must be backed by some explanation.

"I'm an enquiry agent," he said in a confidential undertone. "A client of mine is interested in a theatrical venture upon which Sir Carle Venning thinks of embarking, but my client is uncertain whether Sir Carle is engaging the right principals. He's anxious to know. . . ."

"Oh, come orf it; I'm busy," said Mr. Gotts, raising his newspaper close to his eyes.

"The information would be worth something to my client," tried Lott.

The newspaper dropped slightly; Mr. Gotts' eye engaged itself with the ten-shilling note which Lott was fingering.

"What does 'e want to know?" enquired this Cockney in a Midland world.

"He wants to know who Sir Carle came here to see yesterday."

Mr. Gotts silently stretched out his hand and, having received the ten-shilling note, shoved it into an upper waistcoat pocket from which a pen, a pencil and a comb emerged.

"Comes to see some o' the girls," he answered.

"Can you tell me their names?" asked the mystified detective.

Mr. Gotts scratched his graying hair beneath the ancient bowler in which, like his cubicle, he was commonly believed to eat, sleep, pray, etc.

" 'Ow can I remember all these girls' names, comin' an' goin'?" he asked. And yet this was the very feat which was one of Mr. Gotts' most miraculous accomplishments.

"Well, of course, I don't rightly know 'oo 'e came to see last night. Stric'ly speakin', nobody's allowed be'ind, except on business, but Sir Carle's a good client of the the-aytre an' the guv'nor tells me I can let 'im through when 'e wants. All I know about last night is that two o' the girls come to the door to see 'im orf; it was just before the show started an' I told 'em to 'op it back. They was dressed."

Lott would not have thought it, perhaps, if he had seen them, but he got the correct impression.

"D'you know their names?"

"Miss Peel and Miss Wilters they was." Gotts gave a short laugh. "Principals, did you say? The only show they'll be principals in is a breach o' promise case."

Lott wondered what his next move should be; he did not want to spend another day in Birmingham and yet he could not afford to miss any possible source of information—he must have a talk with these girls.

"Could I go through and have a talk with these young ladies?" he asked.

Mr. Gotts eyed him with pity.

"You could not," he said. "Lose me my place to let you through there."

"Then how am I to see them?"

"You can see 'em if you goes round in front and pays yer eighteenpence."

"Yes, but I want to talk to them."

"Why don't yer take 'em out to supper, then?" asked the doorkeeper contemptuously. "Girls 'as to eat."

The idea had never occurred to Lott; the very thought of it made him nervous. But it *was* an idea.

"How can I do it?" he asked. "I don't know them."

"Send 'em a note. 'Ere, I'll see about it if yer makes it worth me while."

A second note changed hands.

"All right. Orf you go an' I'll see that they're ready after the show. Not s'many free suppers goin' in Birmingham since the income tax went up. There's the bell. 'Op it; I'm busy."

XIX. UTILITY DANCERS

THERE was still plenty of time before the show ended and Lott's first—and probably last —theatrical supper-party began, but there was also a good deal still to be done. In the first place, the detective went round to the headquarters of the City Police, but the offices were shut and the constable on duty advised him to go round to the Gordon Street police station, where the Superintendent in charge of the Central Division, in which the Pantodrome was situated, might be found. The Superintendent, however, was out investigating a burglary at a big jeweler's and the charge-sergeant did not himself know anything about Commissionaire ex-Sergeant-Major Appling. He advised Lott to come round again in the morning, when the Superintendent was pretty sure to be in. As his supper-party in any case necessitated his sleeping in Birmingham this involved no undue delay, and Lott returned to the Pantodrome, stopping on the way at a quiet hotel to book a room for the night.

For the next hour he repeated the performance of the previous evening, questioning every attendant he could find in the Pantodrome in the hope of getting some further news of Sir Carle Venning. He was no more successful than before, except that he picked up one piece of information that might or might not have a bearing on the case; a program-seller in the stalls had noticed that two stalls in one of the front rows were unoccupied for most of the performance, which was unusual in so popular a show as *Tickle My Ankle* had proved to be. They had, however, been occupied before the end of the show, she thought by two gentlemen, though she had taken no particular notice of them and did not recognize Lott's description of either Sir Carle Venning or Captain Bowys. Before he could press the girl further the final curtain came down and she had to attend to her duties.

With feelings of mingled curiosity and nervousness Lott made his way round to the stage door, where a little crowd of loiterers had now gathered. There were few of the gilded youths of Lott's imagination, perhaps because of the income tax, as Gotts had suggested. One or two elderly gentlemen of not very attractive appearance were waiting in the narrow passage, talking to Gotts or eyeing each other askance. Soon a trickle of employees began to emerge and the swing door was constantly on the move. Musicians, stage hands, electricians, came first; then actors, the young ones talking and joking together, the elder lounging out with somber, harassed looks on their still greasy faces; actresses came last, in giggling, chattering groups if they were of the chorus, or stalking in solitary disdain if their parts extended beyond five lines and a dance.

Lott watched the girls emerge and wondered which would prove to be Miss Wilters and Miss Peel. A sense of growing disappointment crept over him as he saw how far removed most of them were from the seductive damsels of his imagination, even from those creatures of flesh and blood of whom he had recently caught glimpses across the footlights. Still there came no sign from Gotts; the elderly gentlemen had gone off with their not very attractive captures, the loiterers were thinning, the door had ceased to swing. Had Gotts forgotten? Had the girls refused to come?

The door swung again and two girls, chattering loudly, emerged into the passage and stopped in front of the glass cubicle. Mr. Gotts cocked his head at the detective.

" 'Ere you are, laddie," he said.

Lott advanced and raised his hat.

"On my right, Miss Wilters, on my left, Miss Peel; seconds out o' the ring," murmured Mr. Gotts.

"Stow it, Gotts," said Miss Wilters, "you're making the young man blush."

This was indeed true, and Lott felt the blush deepening at the remark. The whole thing was a new experience to him, but he was determined to rise to the occasion. The two girls were much younger and simpler-looking than he had expected; they were also, in voice and manner, a good deal more common; did sprigs of the nobility really marry girls like this? Nice girls as they might be, Lott hardly saw them as future duchesses. He did not realize that there is a shade of difference between the chorus of a West End show and the chorus of even a No. 1 Touring Company—the *Lucky Little Ladies*, as it happened, were not even that—the Pantodrome's season had not quite filled with No. 1's this year—income tax again; do Chancellors realize how far the ripples of their sixpenny pebbles spread?—and a No. 2 had been slipped into the bill this week as a stop-gap.

All this the ingenuous detective could not be expected to know, and he continued to regard himself as the cavalier of embryo peeresses. Of these, one—Miss Wilters —was a vivacious brunette, whilst the other was a tall blonde. Both were distinctly pretty and—though Lott was not yet conscious of the fact—had exceptionally good legs, factors which accounted for their presence in the front row of the chorus just as surely as their voices and manners would prevent them from leaving it.

"It will give me great pleasure if you two ladies will take supper with me," said Lott, wondering what his chapel parents would say if they could see their Bertie now.

"Pleased to meet you, Mr. Lott," said Miss Wilters, who was to do most of the talking. "This is Dulcie; I'm Rose."

The three shook hands, Dulcie Peel with a manner which was intended to be aristocratic and resulted in being silly.

"Where shall we go?" asked Lott. "You ladies must advise me; I'm a stranger in Birmingham."

Rose Wilters had already summed up her escort. This was no case for the "Herring Bone" or the "Imperial"; if she took him there, he would be shy and uncomfortable and worrying all the time at the cost of everything; much better have a jolly supper at some cheaper but still amusing place. To do Rose Wilters justice, she was thinking of her new friend's enjoyment as well as her own.

"What about the 'Avante Savoia'?" she said. "It's a new Italian place; quite amusing and the food's ever so good."

"That will suit me very well," said Lott. "Do you agree, Miss Peel?"

"Oh, I expect it will do, if you laike it," replied Dulcie, looking down her patrician nose.

Rose Wilters saw at once that Dulcie was going to

be tiresome; she expected all men to be the same, equally rich and equally silly. Rose knew better than that, but she didn't want the evening spoilt.

"You don't know another boy who'd like to come, too, do you?" she asked. "You mustn't be selfish, you know. A fellow oughtn't to keep two girls all to himself."

Lott felt uncomfortable. He did not quite know where this evening was going to stop. With his upbringing he could hardly be expected to.

"I'm afraid I don't know a soul. That's why I'm so glad to have met you ladies," he added gallantly.

"Oh, well; it'll be great fun, won't it, Dulcie? Cheer up, dear; you're as bright as a wet Sunday in Wigan. Here's the 'Avanty'; let's hope there's a table; I could eat a flock of partridges—they're in season today, you know."

They were fortunate in finding a corner table just vacated by an early party. The newly-opened restaurant was doing brisk business, even in these quiet times. There was an air of bustle and cheerfulness about the place that was certainly attractive and the proprietor, Signor Cantolini, was wreathed in hospitable smiles.

"I'm a bit hungry myself. I've had nothing to eat since breakfast," said Lott as they settled into their seats, a large typewritten menu in front of each. He wondered what these girls would think if he told them why he had eaten nothing all day.

The dinner was chosen by a committee of two, to which Signor Cantolini himself was appointed adviser. Lott listened with amusement to the discussion, which was carried on with a seriousness and concentration worthy of a Scotland Yard conference. *Hors d'œuvres variés* were to be followed by Minestrone soup, whitebait, chops and chips, and a Neapolitan ice—the latter insisted upon by Dulcie; it was fairly evident that the front row of the chorus had not fed heavily at its own expense that day. A bottle of Asti Spumante was recommended by Signor Cantolini.

Though not a connoisseur's wine, the Asti had an admirable effect upon the spirits of the party; Dulcie forgot that she was not at the "Imperial" and Lott that he was breaking mother's heart or, alternatively, in search of a clew with which to hang a man. The restaurant was beginning to empty before the detective suddenly came to his senses.

"Now, girls," he said—they had long ceased to be "ladies"—"I've got to talk business a minute. Did the fellow at the door tell you what I was after?"

"Old Gotts? We gathered it wasn't altogether our bright eyes you were after, dear. Something to do with a show, isn't it?"

"Oh, bother business," exclaimed Dulcie, who had improved as the varnish dropped from her. "Let's go and dance."

"Don't be silly, darling. Mr. Lott may have got a good shop for us both. What is it, dear? Comedy or revoo?"

"I'm afraid it's neither," said Lott, beginning to feel rather mean. "Fact of the matter is, I'm a detective."

Rose Wilters, who had been leaning confidentially against Lott's shoulder, sat up as if he had struck her.

"What! A 'busy'?" she exclaimed in horror. Dulcie stared stupidly at her friend.

"Yes, I'm afraid so. I'm trying to trace the movements of a man, and I believe he's a friend of yours.

At least, he came to see you at the theatre yesterday evening—Sir Carle Venning."

The girls exchanged glances.

"What d'you want him for?" asked Rose, taking a cigarette from the box which Lott had ordered.

"Perhaps I don't want him at all. D'you mind telling me what he came to see you about yesterday?"

Rose blew a cloud of smoke down her nostrils.

"Not very flattering, are you?" she asked. "Most boys come to see us because they like us."

"So I can imagine," said Lott gallantly. "D'you mind telling me how long you've known Sir Carle?"

Rose looked at her friend.

"How long have we, darling? Couple of years, on an' off."

"But how d'you manage that? Aren't you a touring company?"

"The show is, yes, but we're local. Dulcie and I belong to the 'Tripping Troupe,' reely, but that's been resting most of the summer. We get shops with the touring companies when they come to the Panto; it's so big their own girls aren't enough to fill the stage, so they're always glad of one or two extra girls who can dance an' look decent. 'Utility dancers,' the agents call us. We've done a lot of work that way this summer, haven't we, Dulce?"

Dulcie, from whom the Spumante was now beginning to evaporate, nodded sleepily. Lott was thinking hard.

"Then if you've known Venning some time . . ." he asked, then changed his line. "When did you see him last before yesterday?"

"Saturday night," replied Rose promptly.

Lott stared.

"You were in last week's show?" he asked.

"Rather. *Tickle Me Ankle*. It was a scream."

"And you saw Sir Carle Venning on Saturday night. When?"

"Want to know a lot, don't you?" Rose curled her pretty lip. "What's it got to do with you, duckie?"

Lott was uncertain how to deal with a witness of this type; she was new to him. He felt instinctively that it was no good being too official. He tried a confidential note instead.

"Well, it's my job," he said with a smile. "If I get results, it's good for me—and good for my friends."

"That's something, anyhow," said Rose, perceptibly brightening. "I don't mind if I tell you about Carlo; I've got nothing to be ashamed of, I'm sure. What is it you want to know, anyway?"

"When and where and for how long you saw Sir Carle Venning on Saturday night."

"You want to know a l— Oh, I said that before, didn't I?" Rose laughed boisterously. "Well, he was behind part of the show and he took us out to supper after, didn't he, Dulce?"

"Yes. The 'Imperial,' " murmured Dulcie.

"D'you mean he came to see you behind the scenes?" asked Lott, trying not to sound shocked.

"That's right, dear. Of course, it's not allowed, but Mr. Samuelson lets one or two gentlemen come behind sometimes."

"What time was that?"

"I'm sure I couldn't say. First interval he came, I think, and hung about till after the second. Of course, we were on most of the time."

"What time are the intervals?"

"You'll have to ask some one else that; I never look at the time."

"But roughly. How many intervals are there?"

"Depends on the show; there were two last week, one after Act I and one after Act II. The acts were about the same length, so you can do a little sum, Big Boy."

Roughly, from nine to ten, that meant. Did that matter? Perhaps not, if the murder was at 10.45.

"And what time did he take you out to supper?"

"Oh, after the show—quarter- to half-past eleven, I suppose."

"And he stayed with you till when?"

Rose screwed up her pretty face and made a long nose at the detective.

"Aren't you getting just a little inquisitive, dear?" she asked.

Lott felt himself blushing again.

"Well, tell me if you'd finished supper by twelve," he said.

"Heavens, no; nor yet by half-past. We danced, didn't we, Dulce?"

"Yes. The 'Imperial,'" murmured Dulcie, whose ideas were evidently not catholic.

Lott felt his spirits sinking. He had thought at first that the girls had been bribed to put up an alibi for Venning, but they could hardly fake a supper and dance party at a place like the "Imperial." Was his case falling to pieces after all? Was there a mistake, a catch somewhere?

"Was he alone, or was there another man with him?"

he asked, without any particular reason for doing so. He saw the girls exchange a quick glance.

"Oh, yes, Tommy was with him," answered Rose promptly.

"Tommy? Who's he?"

"Tommy Tratton; don't you know him? He's one of the lads."

"Nice boy. Took us to the 'Imperial,'" murmured Dulcie.

"What did he look like?"

"Oh, slim, blue eyes, one of those Ronald Colman mustaches. Rather a pet."

What, then, had become of Bowys? Lott shrugged his shoulders; Bowys didn't matter to him; Venning was his game and Venning, it seemed impossible to doubt, had been in Birmingham between 8 and 10, and again between 11.30 and 12.30, on the night of the tragedy. Could he conceivably have motored thirty miles to Ferris, committed a murder, thirty miles back, parked his car and rejoined the theatre crowd all in one and a half hours? It was impossible.

Dejectedly Lott called for his bill, ruefully paid it —he doubted whether the Receiver would stand for this supper, even if his own chief passed it. Dulcie yawned widely and stretched her graceful limbs; Rose blew a kiss to Signor Cantolini and led the way out into the fresher air of Little Haymarket.

"Well, I'm sure it's very good of you ladies to give me your company," said Lott, slipping back to his normal manner.

Rose raised her eyebrows.

"Aren't you going to see us home?" she asked. "We live together; it's not so far."

Oh, help. What did one say to that?

"I . . . I don't . . . I . . . I can't . . ." stammered Lott.

"Heavens! What's worrying you? You aren't my fancy boy, darling," exclaimed Rose. "But Dulcie and I don't want to walk home alone; we've got our characters to think of."

The girl slipped a soft arm through Lott's.

"Come on, Dulcie, take his other flip. 'Tisn't so often we go home under p'lice escort. The Brummagem bobbies'll be ever so jealous."

And so, in the small hours of the September night, Herbert Lott, Police-Inspector and Puritan, might have been seen promenading through the streets of Birmingham in the arms of two fair ladies of the lighter order. But he was not; not, that is, by any one that mattered. And so they came to a lodging-house in an obscure street. Rose opened the door with her latchkey; Dulcie, with the barest murmur of farewell, passed inside.

"Good night, Mr. Parker," said Rose, then quickly slipped a soft arm round the neck of the astonished detective. "You're not such a bad old Nosey, really."

Mr. Lott, hot with pleasure and dismay, was alone in the night. He had been kissed by a chorus girl.

XX. TIME TEST

THE following morning, Inspector Lott, still experiencing curiously mixed sensations of shame-facedness and elation, set about completing his enquiries in Birmingham. His first visit was to the Gordon Street police station, where he found Superintendent Vidal already deep in the routine work of his division. Having introduced himself and made tactful enquiries as to the jewel robbery, Lott explained his quest and his needs. Superintendent Vidal, who happened to be senior Superintendent and Deputy Chief Constable of the City, listened to the story with a lofty detachment that Lott found slightly irritating; the impression given was that a murder in the lesser world without was of trifling importance compared with a robbery within the bounds of the City of Birmingham. A sergeant was sent for to give any information that might be required, but in the meantime . . . Superintendent Vidal resumed the perusal of his monumental correspondence.

Detective-Sergeant Mascott fortunately proved to be of a very different type. He was a young man, keen, intelligent and delighted at the opportunity of meeting and talking shop with a C.I.D. man. He knew something about Sergeant-Major Appling, the Pantodrome commissionaire, believed him to be honest though bombastic, and could produce a police-constable who would know a great deal more. Together the two detectives trammed and walked down to the little house in the outskirts of the City where P.C. Hollocott was now spending his hours off duty.

Police-Constable Hollocott was one of those honest, reliable, hard-working men, common both to the police and to the fighting services, who yet never achieve promotion; sometimes it is stupidity, sometimes an early black mark, sometimes sheer constitutional dislike of responsibility; whatever the cause, they are to be found in every company and every force, and in times of trouble they are towers of strength to their superiors. Hollocott had served for nearly thirty years in the City Police, his pension was now guaranteed, but his service annually extended to the mutual satisfaction of himself and the Watch Committee. At the moment of the detective's call P.C. Hollocott, who had been on duty till midnight, was finishing a belated breakfast, clad in a pair of uniform trousers, carpet slippers, and an "army" shirt; his chin was as yet innocent of razor and his hair uncombed. At sight of Sergeant Mascott he rose smartly to his feet.

Introductions effected and two extra cups of tea provided by the hospitable and insistent Mrs. Hollocott, the enquiry was launched. The Pantodrome was on P.C. Hollocott's beat and he often had occasion to pass a remark or two to its head commissionaire; moreover, he had often watched him regulating the stream of arrivals and departures, a task which the ex-sergeant-major carried out, in Hollocott's opinion, not only efficiently but fairly. The commissionaire accepted tips, of course—why should he not?—but he was always courteous and helpful to those from whom no tips, or only minor ones, could be expected, "and that"—as Hollocott shrewdly observed—"was where a man was apt to give himself away." It was impossible for him to say, of course, that Appling was beyond the reach of temptation—that he might not actually fall for a heavy bribe—but Hollocott was definitely inclined to think that he would not, partly because he appeared honest, and partly because, for all his bombast, he was no fool.

"What sort of a party might it be, sir, that you're thinking bribed him?" asked Hollocott.

Lott described his quarry with some care and was instantly rewarded by the shattering of his last hopes. Hollocott himself knew Sir Carle Venning by sight, even by name, and had seen him outside the theatre on Saturday night at about the time mentioned by Appling. There had been an unusually large audience of "car folk" that night and Hollocott had turned up to help with the regulating of the traffic. He had seen Sir Carle among the emerging theatre-goers—Sir Carle was a man you couldn't overlook; he had not noticed his companion, nor which way he had gone, but apparently not directly into a car or taxi. No, P.C. Hollocott had no doubt at all about it, either as to its being Sir Carle or as to its being Saturday night—the lateness of the hour, 11.30, within five minutes one way or the other—was proof enough of that.

Here, then, was one part of Venning's alibi firmly established; wherever else he may have been that evening, he was in Birmingham at 11.30 P.M. According to the two girls he had been there both before and after that hour—continuously from about 9 P.M. till after midnight. That, of course, conflicted with the account given by Venning himself and by his friend Captain Bowys, both of whom had said that they had driven straight home after the show and were back at High

Oaks by 12.30. The latter statement, however, had been confuted by the manservant, Stainer, who had given the time of their return as not 12.30 but 2.30. It was a curious muddle. If the alibi had in some way been cooked, why the divergent stories told by Venning on one side and the girls on the other; would they not have agreed on the same story? But the fact remained that the stories did differ, and to a very important extent; there must be some explanation of that. Well, the only thing to do was to keep on testing the story at every point until it emerged which—if either—was the true version.

Lott divided his remaining task in Birmingham into two portions: the period from, roughly, 8.15 to 11.30, and the period from 11.30 to 1.30. 8.15 itself was fairly well fixed by the evidence of the waiter and the commissionaire at the "Herring Bone" and by Appling at the Pantodrome. Between that time and 11.30, Lott had only Rose Wilters' statement that "Carlo" and his friend had been "behind" part of the time—probably 9 to 10 P.M.—and the statement of the program-seller about the two empty stalls, which might or might not have a bearing on the case. After 11.30, again, there was so far only the word of the two girls that Venning had been with them at the "Imperial"—a story conflicting with his own statement that he had driven straight home. In order to check the girls' story as to the pre-11.30 period an examination of the stage staff would have to be made—the staff in the front of the house had already been examined twice and produced practically nothing. For the post-11.30 period, the staff at the Imperial Hotel must be questioned.

Lott groaned in spirit at the prospect of having to spend another evening, possibly another night, in Birmingham, but here Sergeant Mascott came to his rescue. The stage staff, the Birmingham man pointed out, were permanently employed at the Pantodrome—not fleeting visitors; many of them would be at work there even at this time of day, whilst others could be found at their homes. The same applied to the staff of the "Imperial." If Inspector Lott would accept his help, Sergeant Mascott would undertake to produce ample evidence one way or the other before evening. Lott accepted with enthusiasm. The enquiry would be greatly facilitated if a photograph of Sir Carle Venning could be procured. To this end a tour of the Birmingham photographers was made—and made in vain; Sir Carle did not apparently patronize the Birmingham studios, if any. A brainwave on the part of Sergeant Mascott, however, took them to the offices of the *Birmingham Pictorial*, where the illustrations editor produced a snapshot of Sir Carle returning to his ancestral home after his father's death; it was a younger Sir Carle but quite passably like him.

Armed with this the two detectives launched their campaign. Owing to initial failures it lasted longer than Sergeant Mascott had foretold, and when every available witness had been tested it remained a partial failure. Two or three stage hands at the Pantodrome knew Sir Carle Venning by sight, none by name; none of these could be certain when they had last seen him at the theatre, though one was pretty sure the subject of the snapshot had been behind on Wednesday night, and another thought he had seen him on Saturday. A fair number of gentlemen came behind from time to time, though there was a rule against it; nobody paid any attention to them—stage hands were busy men. So much for the Pantodrome. At the "Imperial," on the other hand, Sir Carle was recognized by a hall porter, a lavatory attendant, and two waiters. The baronet had been in to supper on Saturday night with two young ladies and another gentleman—the other gentleman was not known at the "Imperial"; he was described by the hall porter as tall and elderly, with a military mustache, by one waiter as clean-shaven, by the other as mustached but barely middle-aged, and by the lavatory attendant as wearing the fashionable black mustache described by Rose Wilters as a "Ronald Colman." The party had remained at the "Imperial" till nearly one, dancing, supping and watching the cabaret show.

So much, then, for 11.30 P.M. to 1 A.M.; Venning was undoubtedly in Birmingham between those hours; about the earlier period—8.15 to 11.30—there was much more doubt. But only the end of this period was of any interest; Captain Sterron was known to have been alive at 10 P.M. and was almost certain to have been alive—or at least the murderous business, the suicide faking, not completed—at 10.45. Was it possible that Venning could have got back from Ferris to the Pantodrome, including the hanging of the body, the return to his own car in the lane, the journey—a matter of 30 miles—the parking of his car in Birmingham, and the return to the theatre between those limits of time 10.45 and 11.30? Even allowing a slight error of time judgment at either end, by P.C. Bunning at Ferris, by P.C. Hollocott and Commissionaire Appling at the Pantodrome, the time available could not have been more than an hour. It seemed impossible, but the only way to make sure was to do the journey under as nearly as possible similar conditions.

The enquiry had taken so long that it was already

evening. Lott decided that, if he could obtain a suitable car, he would make a thorough job of the thing and do the journey at the time Venning must, if he were guilty, have done it. As for a car, Sergeant Mascott, who knew his Superintendent, thought that it was no use trying to borrow the City Police "chaser"; on the other hand, he knew of a young man who owned a fast car and who, being a bit of a "crime fan," would be only too delighted to have it used for a private test of this kind.

So, while Mascott went off to find his friend and charter the car, Lott returned to the Pantodrome for a final rake over, but learned nothing new—except that he himself was beginning to be regarded as a bit of a nuisance. At eight o'clock the two detectives and Mr. Leonard Buss, car owner, forgathered for a meal at a quiet restaurant, where—by way of reward—the outline of the case, with names omitted, was given to the thrilled Mr. Buss, and at a little before nine the test started. Mr. Buss's Rattalini was at least as powerful a car as Sir Carle's Highflyer, and it was felt that if this run could not be done in three-quarters of an hour, Sir Carle's alibi would be complete. Thirty miles in three-quarters of an hour does not sound a difficult task for a powerful car, but in practice it will be found that a sustained average of forty miles an hour requires clear roads and few obstructions. At the very start it became evident that neither of these conditions would obtain; although there was not much traffic, the streets were crowded with people, who seemed quite oblivious to the danger of strolling upon them with their heads in the air. The automatic light signals caused inevitable delays, and tram lines are always a hindrance to fast driving. By the time Birmingham and its suburbs were cleared more than ten minutes had elapsed.

For a time Buss was able to let the car out and the Rattalini roared along the broad highway at eighty miles an hour, its glaring searchlight illuminating the white ribbon far ahead. At one point, a policeman, leaping hurriedly from his bicycle, made frantic signals of remonstrance; Lott wondered whether Sir Carle, at this speed, could have escaped similar attention. Periodically, a car, traveling in the opposite direction, necessitated a dimming of the searchlight and a temporary diminution of speed. Then a village, with an awkward double bend brought the Rattalini down to a crawl and a stretch under repair prevented, for half a mile, the resumption of racing speed. At the end of half an hour they were only passing the sixteenth milestone from Birmingham, and though very little traffic was met after that point it was not till fifty minutes from the start that the car began to slow up on the approach to Ferris. Fifty minutes from a flying start, no parking, no walking a hundred yards to a car left in a lane, no allowance for slips or errors, and the road as clear as it was humanly possible for it ever to be. It was, Lott was sure now, inconceivable that Venning could have murdered Sterron at or after 10.45 and been back at Birmingham by 11.30. Sergeant Mascott and Mr. Buss, after dropping Lott at Hylam, were going to time the return from Ferris to Birmingham and let him know the result next day, but the C.I.D. man no longer had any doubt. The alibi was complete.

Disconsolately Lott watched the shadows on the road which the brilliant light forced from behind every bump and wrinkle, clearer now as the car slowed down

to stop opposite the Ferris Court gates. The black figure
of a bicyclist, his headlamp hardly visible in the glare,
turned in at the gates and disappeared down the drive.

"Better turn off that searchlight. We don't want to
draw attention to ourselves," said Lott, who wanted to
do a starlight prowl round the house.

The change from searchlight to parking lights almost blinded the occupants of the big car for a moment,
and Buss had to swerve sharply at the last moment to
avoid two other bicyclists who emerged unheralded
from the gloom.

"Where the hell are your lights?" called Buss indignantly, but the two figures flitted past in silence. Not,
however, before—even in the dim lights of the car—
they had revealed themselves to Lott as Superintendent
Dawle and Sergeant Gable.

"Mr. Dawle!" called Lott gently.

The heavier figure wavered and stopped, while Lott
jumped from the car.

"What's up?" he asked eagerly, as the Superintendent
reached him.

"On to something," whispered Dawle. "You remember that scarred finger-print on the study door I told
you about? Well, I found out last night whose it was;
it belongs to Father Speyd, the priest who acts as a confessor to Mrs. Sterron. He's supposed not to have been
in this house for years till Sunday morning, but I've
had him watched; this evening he slipped out of the
back door of their garden with a bicycle and Gable here
'phoned through to me; I followed at once and caught
'em up just out of Ferris. Speyd's turned into the drive;
I'm going to find out what he's up to; you'd better
come and lend a hand."

XXI. CONFESSION

IN the sitting-room at Ferris Court a man and woman stood close together, hand clasping hand, but their heads turned toward the door of the room. As each one's eyes watched the slowly-turning handle, a look of anxiety deepened into consternation—on the face of Luke Speyd, almost of fear.

A sharp tap came on the door.

After a quick glance at her companion, Griselda Sterron answered.

"Who is that? I don't want to be disturbed."

"This is Superintendent Dawle, madam. I want to speak to you, please."

At the sound of the voice, a sharp intake of breath, almost a hiss, had come from Father Speyd. He stepped quickly away from his companion. His eyes darted from side to side; the eyes of a creature in a trap.

"It's quite impossible for me to see you tonight. Come in the morning, please," said Griselda, her voice as calm as if she were giving a direction to her maid.

"I'm sorry, madam, but I'm afraid I must press it," came the inexorable voice of the law.

Speyd stepped softly up to his companion and whispered in her ear.

"You can't stop him. He'll get more suspicious, I must go—through the window again."

For a moment Griselda thought, a slight frown puckering her brow. Then she nodded and stepped softly to the window. With infinite care she opened the shutters, then the French window itself. Father Speyd was stepping forward to pass through when the figure of a man appeared in the opening.

Speyd shrank back with a gasp; even Griselda's face reflected her consternation.

"I'm sorry, sir; not just yet," said Inspector Lott.

Coming into the room he stepped quickly across to the door and unlocked it, admitting the uniformed figure of Superintendent Dawle. Sergeant Gable remained discreetly in the passage. Both police officers looked at Father Speyd, whose expressive face revealed the flashing torments of his spirit—horror, remorse, humiliation, shame.

Griselda Sterron, as usual, recovered her poise almost immediately. Her eyes sparkled with excitement —almost with exaltation.

"We are not ashamed!" she exclaimed. "What has been done was done to save me, but I am equally responsible. We will face anything that is before us— together."

Speyd turned away to hide the agony on his face.

"Oh, no, no," Lott heard him mutter between closed teeth.

Superintendent Dawle came to a quick decision. He really had no idea what Mrs. Sterron was talking about and he would run a big risk if he took a strong line which proved to be mistaken, but at the same time here was an opportunity, which might never return, of getting this man and woman to speak while their emotions were still swaying their senses.

"It will be best to take your statements separately," he said. "If you will kindly make yours to Inspector Lott, madam, I will take Father Speyd into the library.

You are not either of you at the moment being charged with anything, but I should warn you that you are not obliged to say anything unless you wish to."

Speyd turned one look of agonized appeal upon his companion, but she was blind now to anything but the dramatic effect of the scene. With head erect, incredibly handsome and proud, she looked straight in front of her; with bent shoulders the priest dragged himself from the room in the wake of Superintendent Dawle.

The library was empty, Gerald Sterron being, as Dawle had already learnt from Willing, away in London. Sergeant Gable, at a sign from Dawle, followed them into the room and, extracting some sheets of foolscap from his pocket, seated himself at the writing-table. Luke Speyd watched the preparations with eyes of misery.

"Now, sir," said Superintendent Dawle, retaining his official manner. "I must repeat my warning that you need not speak if you don't want to, but in view of Mrs. Sterron's remarks I am bound to detain you until I have a satisfactory explanation of them. Anything you say will be taken down by Sergeant Gable and read over to you and you will be asked to sign the statement."

"I . . . I . . ." began Speyd, then staggered and would probably have fallen had not Dawle quickly supported him and eased him gently into a chair. The look of compassion on the policeman's face would have given Luke Speyd strength if he had seen it.

"I'll get you a drop of something, sir. You keep still where you are," said Dawle firmly, moving towards the door.

Speyd lifted his head.

"No, no. I cannot take anything—any spirit. Some

water, perhaps. It is only that I am . . . that I have eaten nothing today. It is Friday."

Dawle grunted angrily.

"You're going to have a drop of warm milk and a biscuit, if we have to forcibly feed you," he said with kindly gruffness. "Damned starvation nonsense," he added to himself, as he made for the pantry.

In a few minutes he was back and stood over his patient till the milk and biscuits had disappeared. A touch of healthier color came into the priest's haggard cheeks.

"Thank you, Dawle," he said simply. "It is absurd for me, having swallowed a camel, to strain at a gnat."

He pulled himself together, but in response to a sign from the Superintendent retained his seat.

"It is no good trying to conceal anything now," he said. "It would only lead to further deception and misunderstanding, and perhaps to trouble for innocent people. I have sinned greatly, Dawle; not as you may suppose, but spiritually. For months I have nursed in my heart feelings for a woman—and a married woman —which are utterly forbidden to the members of my community. It began in all innocence, when she brought her troubles to me at the confessional. Then, as it became more and more difficult for her, under her husband's jealous eye, to lead her own life and to come regularly to our church, I took the grave—the terribly mistaken step of coming here clandestinely to talk to her, to advise her, as I hoped, to help her. Gradually there has grown up in me a feeling, first of human sympathy, then of anxious solicitude, of friendship, of affection, until suddenly I found that I had kindled and tended in my heart a flame that I could not subdue, unquenchable, insatiable."

Father Speyd leaned forward and pressed his face against his emaciated hands. For minutes there was silence in the room, while Dawle waited in sympathetic silence, and Sergeant Gable calmly read over and touched up his notes. Presently Speyd again raised his head.

"You mustn't think, Dawle, that she is in any way to blame for this. To her I am only a friend; she can have no knowledge of the depth of my feeling for her. But she believes—Heaven help me—that I killed her husband! Nothing I can say will dissuade her—and I cannot blame her, because I lied to her. Yes, I, a priest, an adviser of others, a Father Confessor—I have lied, not from necessity, not for a worthy motive, but from moral cowardice, to save myself from being degraded in her eyes."

"Just a second, sir, please," murmured Sergeant Gable. "You're going rather fast."

The realization that this confession of his utter shame was being recorded on paper sent a shudder of horror through the priest's thin body, but he pulled himself together and continued.

"I told you that I had formed the habit of coming out here, to advise her, I pretended, to see her, to be near her, as I knew in my heart. As I was not received by her husband I had to come secretly, in the dark. I came, as perhaps you saw me tonight, on my bicycle and was admitted to her room through the window. No one ever saw me; we thought it was safe. I came on Saturday. She had told me that there were people staying here, but that she could easily make an excuse to get away after dinner. She told me then that it could not go on—that her life with her husband had become intolerable. She spoke of leaving him, of . . . oh, she spoke wildly—wickedly, if you will, but who shall judge a woman suffering as she has suffered?"

"Just a minute, sir," interrupted Dawle. "Just what was she suffering? I can't get any one to tell me that."

Father Speyd swung his head from side to side on its thin neck. He clearly found it difficult to put ugly things into words.

"Can't you understand?" he asked. "To live with a man . . . to be wife to a man . . . with his trouble . . . a man who should have lived a life of strict celibacy. Can you not understand what it must mean to a woman of refinement, of delicate sensibilities? And then, the danger . . . the awful danger. . . ."

Superintendent Dawle saw that he could expect nothing more definite from this man.

"But what had all this got to do with you, sir?" he asked.

"You may well ask that, Dawle. I have asked it of myself. I have tried to deceive myself into believing that it was my duty as a priest to free one of my flock from this tyranny, this cruelty. But in my heart I know that my reason for helping . . . for trying to help her . . . has been of a very different character. My own heart, my very flesh, have rebelled against the suffering that she has endured, the sacrilege, the indignity, the vile cruelty to her soul and to . . ." Father Speyd's voice dropped to a whisper which Dawle could hardly catch, ". . . her body."

The anguished voice stopped, but in the deep-set eyes the agony remained. Staring in front of him, Luke

Speyd twisted his long fingers together in an unconscious writhing movement. Dawle watched them, fascinated.

"And so you did what, sir?" he asked abruptly.

Speyd looked up.

"I told her," he answered in a calm voice, "that I would speak to her husband again—reason with him, plead with him, warn him—not only of the punishment in another life that his cruelty would earn—as I told you on Sunday—but of the risk he ran of losing her altogether. I knew, from my experience in the morning that the man had no fear, no thought for what might happen in a future life, but I believed that he might fear for the present, that the thought of losing her might bring him to reason. I told her that I would go then, at once, to her husband; at first she urged me not to go, then she agreed."

Speyd looked round him and seeing the jug of milk which Dawle had brought on the table beside him, refilled the glass and drank greedily.

"I opened the door of her sitting-room and was about to walk out into the passage and across the hall to the study, when the door of the study opened and the brother, Gerald Sterron, came out. He stopped for a moment to say something to whoever was in the study, and I went quickly back into the sitting-room. He had evidently not seen me, in fact he was not looking my way at all. I waited for a time and then opened the door again and . . ."

"One minute, sir, please. Any idea how long you waited?"

"Oh, a minute or two—just to give him time to leave the hall."

"You didn't see which way he went?"

"Yes, as I was shutting the door I saw him turn down the passage that leads . . . I don't quite know where it leads . . . perhaps it is to that door?"

Speyd pointed to the library door that opened into the little ante-room. Dawle nodded.

"What time would that have been, sir?" he asked.

Speyd shook his head.

"I have no idea," he said. "I left Hylam as soon as it was dark—about nine, I suppose. It would take me half an hour to bicycle out here and we were talking together for a little time. It cannot have been far from ten o'clock."

Dawle nodded.

"Go on, sir, then. I don't want to interrupt you."

"I opened the door again, and listened, but could hear nothing. I walked quietly down the passage through the hall to the study door. As I walked, Dawle, I felt the resolution gradually oozing out of me, just as . . . perhaps I am a greater coward than most men, but I have felt that same thing in the War, in an attack, as the first exaltation of excitement and enthusiasm begins to die out and the enemy's barrage comes down upon one. . . ."

Dawle remembered the feeling well enough, only he would have said that it was the effect of the rum that was dying out.

"I reached the door . . . and hesitated. If I had gone straight in, all would have been well—my courage would have revived when face to face with actual danger, not just the anticipation of it. But I hesitated. Then I thought I heard the sound of a voice, and suddenly . . ."

"In the room, sir?" asked Dawle eagerly.

"I thought so, but I don't know. I'm deaf in one ear —you may remember, Dawle, I was nearly blown up in the big mine explosion at Neuville and it burst the drum of my left ear. I can't locate sounds. I may have been wrong; the sound may have come from somewhere else—from this room perhaps. But it startled me. I suddenly realized what I was doing. There was I, a stranger—worse than a stranger, an unwelcome, uninvited visitor in this man's house, at dead of night, visiting his wife clandestinely, not openly; admitted to her room secretly, through a window. How could I show myself to him? Worse still, how could I show myself to others . . . to his guests, perhaps? Think of my position, think of the scandal; the harm it would do, not only to me personally, but to my order . . . and to her."

It did not, thought Dawle, take much imagination to realize all that; the wonder was that it had not occurred sooner to Father Speyd. But then "the padre" had always been an impetuous "act first, think afterwards" type—perhaps that was why the men had loved him so much—he was always in trouble, generally on their behalf.

"I turned to go back . . . and the same thing happened again. I dared not go back to her and tell her that I had failed her, that I had done nothing, that she must go on bearing it, putting up with it all. I was a coward, Dawle; I dared do neither one thing nor the other. Then the evil one spoke to me, as he always will when we are afraid; he persuaded me to lie, to deceive —the easy way, the fatal way. I went back . . . not at once, I stood for a time in the hall, thinking . . . I went back and told her that she had nothing more to fear, that all would be well. I hardly know now what I meant, but I wanted to get away, to be alone, to have time to think, to plan. I left her, by the same way as I had come, and returned home. All that night I spent on my knees trying to pray, to think . . . but I could not; prayer would not come; how could it, to a man who in his heart had sinned as I was sinning?"

Father Speyd rose to his feet, his thin figure seeming to tower above the others as they sat, waiting. Restlessly he paced the room, his hands still twining, torturing each other.

"In the morning, the blow fell. I got her message, asking me to come, just as I had finished mass I came straight out, as I was, in the car she had sent for me. I thought then, I really thought . . . as I told you . . . that he had killed himself because of what I had said to him the previous morning. I believed that God had answered our prayers; that the way out had been found by His ordering. Then, by degrees, I began to realize, to guess. There was talk—it reached us even in our seclusion. No more than a rumor, a suspicion. Then you came and told me . . . and everything tumbled about my ears. I thought and thought, wondering what I should do. I felt that I must see her, hear what she thought, what she knew. I came out tonight and found . . . oh, my God, it is terrible . . . I found that she believed *that I had killed him!*"

Father Speyd paced feverishly up and down the room, his words rushing from him now in a ceaseless torrent.

"Nothing I can say will dissuade her, will make her believe, understand . . . she smiles at me and tells me that I have saved her . . . that I . . . she speaks as if

I were some knight, some heroic creature of old who has saved her from some dragon . . . saved her . . . won her . . . with my sword, by killing . . . I, a priest, bound by vows to ways of peace and . . . and chastity. . . ."

This wasn't getting them any farther, thought Dawle, all this talk, much as he sympathized with the wretched man's distress. There were facts to be found out yet.

"Sit down a minute, sir," he said; "you'll be getting yourself ill again. That's better. Now, I just want to know one or two things about Saturday night. You say that you saw Mr. Gerald Sterron coming away from the study, and you think it was about ten o'clock, though you're not sure. Did you notice anything special about him?"

"Special? In what way?" Father Speyd stared at his interlocutor.

"Was he doing anything special, like . . . well, I don't want to suggest an answer to you, but I just want a check on a fact I already know. Was he, for instance, blowing his nose?"

"I don't think so. I don't remember it."

"Or carrying anything?"

"I didn't notice it. I'm not . . . I'm afraid I'm not a very observant man."

"Not a paper? Or a book? Or a cigarette? Was he smoking, did you notice?"

To all these questions Speyd shook his head. He could say neither yes nor no; he had not noticed. Dawle changed his ground.

"These voices that you think you heard, sir; did you hear what they said?"

Again Speyd shook his head.

"I could not distinguish any words, nor even that there were two voices. As I told you, the sound may not even have come from the study. It was very faint. It just arrested my attention and made me think."

That was no good.

"And you didn't see any one else, either in the hall or anywhere else?"

"Only Mrs. Sterron."

"Not Willing, the butler?"

"No, no one."

"How long do you think you were standing in the hall, thinking, after you heard the voice?"

"It's difficult to say. About five minutes I should think."

Willing had gone to the study just after Mr. Gerald Sterron left it. He had shut one of the windows and received his orders; that, no doubt, was the voice that Father Speyd had heard. It sounded possible enough, though Dawle realized that he had only got Speyd's word for it, so far. Oh, and that finger-print.

"When you stood outside the study door, sir, did you touch it at all?"

Speyd thought.

"Yes, I think I actually had my hand on the handle at one time, as I hesitated."

"Touched it anywhere else, sir?"

Father Speyd looked puzzled.

"How? In what way?"

"Just go up to that door, sir," said Dawle, "and try to repeat what you did that night—how you stood."

Speyd walked slowly up to the door and hesitated. Then he touched the handle with his left hand, his head bent forward, as if he was listening; his right hand, as if unconsciously, rose and pressed against the upper panel.

Dawle nodded slowly.

"Thank you, sir; that'll do," he said.

"Now if you'll wait here with Sergeant Gable, he'll read over what he's got down and you can sign it—if you're satisfied, that is. I'll just go and have a word with Mrs. Sterron."

But Dawle had no word with Mrs. Sterron that night. On entering the sitting-room, he found Inspector Lott sitting at the writing-table running over his notes. He was alone.

"Where's the lady?" asked Dawle in surprise.

"Gone to bed, Mr. Dawle. She gave me some high-falutin stuff and a few facts and then said she was tired and was going to bed. If I wanted any more, I'd have to come and get it in the morning. Well, I think I've got all I want, but if you want any more, you'll have to go and get it yourself, Super. I don't quite know where I am with that dame; I'd be frightened to go and tackle her where she is now. But you're a married man; don't let me stop you."

XXII. ANTI-CLIMAX

SHE talked a good deal of nonsense, but of two things I'm certain, Mr. Dawle. She believes that Speyd killed her husband—and she's in love with him!"

The two police officers had forgathered for an informal conference on the morning after their discovery of the priest at Ferris Court. Neither of them was feeling at all cheerful; Superintendent Dawle was too much attached to Father Speyd to relish having to regard him as a possible murderer, whilst Lott was savage at the thought that all his work in Birmingham had gone for nothing.

"You see, Super.," he said, "this business destroys the premise that I was working on. When I first saw Mrs. Sterron at Ferris, she denied that there was anything between her and Venning, but when I mentioned the footmark in her sitting-room she gave herself away completely—or so I thought. At that time we thought . . . we had jumped to the conclusion . . . that that footmark was made by Venning. If there was something up between Venning and Mrs. Sterron there was a pretty strong motive for Venning killing the husband; that's the premise I've been working on. But now it turns out that it wasn't Venning at all that she was letting into her room, but this Speyd! Bang goes my premise!"

"Hold hard a minute," said Dawle, whose mind worked less quickly than his companion's. "You say she believes he killed her husband—and still loves him. Or perhaps that's *why* she loves him—or thinks she does. But he says he was only out in the hall, thinking, for about five minutes, and then went back to her and told her everything was all right. How can she think that in five minutes he killed her husband and hung him up and all the rest of it? It isn't possible."

"You've only got his word for it that he *was* only five minutes in the hall—thinking," replied Lott.

"Yes, but the time's all wrong. This was at ten o'clock, Sterron was still alive at 10.45!"

"Same thing again. You've only got his word for it that he went to the study at ten o'clock. It's perfectly possible that he saw Gerald Sterron coming out of it at ten, but then he may have waited, not a minute or two, as he told you, but three-quarters of an hour or more! Much more likely; give the house time to quiet down."

"You think he did do it?"

"Don't know. But you seem to have jumped to the conclusion that he didn't. If he did do it, then she's damn good reason for thinking he did."

The Superintendent frowned, in deep thought.

"Perhaps we could find out what time he got back to the Community House," he said. "If his story's true —as to time, that's to say—he must have got back here by eleven. That would clear him."

"You can try," said Lott skeptically. "But if he's been sneaking in and out for clandestine meetings with a woman, it isn't likely that he let any of his mates hear him."

"Well, we must do something. What do you suggest?" asked the harassed Superintendent.

"You're keeping an eye on him, I suppose? He may

give himself away again. You can have a talk to her, of course, but I doubt if you'll get anything out of it. She's all for the quick impression. She's a poser. You can't tell when she's telling the truth and when she isn't. I tried to trip her up, but she's too sharp—she's no fool, that woman."

"Well, I'll have to let it stand over this morning, anyhow," said Dawle. "I've got this Corrupt Practices prosecution to work up; I promised the Treasury solicitor I'd send it up by the two o'clock train; he wants to work at it over the week-end."

"I tell you what, Super.; I'll just run out to Ferris and have a talk to Willing and the maids. In the light of what we know now something may turn up. Something's got to if we're to hang Sterron's murderer; there's precious little to go on so far."

All through the morning Dawle worked at his case, assembling statements, marshaling exhibits, going over link by link the chain of evidence that was to send an unfaithful public servant to prison for five years. By half-past one it was, so far as he could make it, complete. He heaved a sigh of relief. At last he could get home for some dinner and a pipe; he had only to get the thing off to the train now. He locked up his office and was passing through the charge-room when the outer door opened and two gentlemen walked in.

"Ah, Superintendent, we're lucky to catch you," said the foremost. "Can you spare us ten minutes of your valuable time?"

Dawle groaned. That meant half an hour at least— and no dinner. Still, something might come of this.

"Of course, Mr. Halfcastle," he said, reopening his

office. "Will you step inside, sir. Good morning, Mr. Sterron."

Both visitors were dressed in formal clothes, Mr. Halfcastle in the staid black and gray of his profession and Mr. Sterron in a double-breasted suit of lighter gray. Though he wore a black tie and there were, Dawle thought, lines of worry round his mouth, Gerald Sterron still did not look like a mourner; there was always a twinkle lurking not far behind his eyes.

The solicitor cleared his throat, hitched forward his chair, and began a task that he knew was not going to be easy.

"I traveled down with Mr. Sterron this morning. I had hoped to have a little talk with you in any case before I left, Superintendent, but after hearing from Mrs. Sterron of what occurred last night, I thought it best . . . Mr. Sterron and I, in consultation, thought it best to come over at once and . . . er . . . ascertain how matters stood."

Mr. Halfcastle glanced enquiringly at Dawle, but the Superintendent remained impassive.

"We understand, Superintendent, that, by the use of, shall we say, moral force, you and two other police officers obtained entry to the house, interrupted a conversation between Mrs. Sterron and Father Speyd, who is her . . . spiritual mentor, and obtained from Mrs. Sterron, by means which appear to have been, at the very least, aggressive, a statement of which Mrs. Sterron tells me she has, in her present condition of mental distress, very little recollection and for which, it must be clear to you, she can have little or no responsibility. I know, of course, that you were doing what you conceived to be your duty," Mr. Halfcastle was warming to his theme, "but I am bound to say that your action appears to me to have been very high-handed, if not actually . . . er . . . questionable."

Gerald Sterron, seeing the policeman still sitting stolidly silent under this attack, suddenly leant forward and asked:

"Did you know I was up in town last night?"

"The butler told me that, sir, when I called last night."

"Sure you didn't know before you called? I only ask because it was a lucky coincidence; otherwise, somebody might have got a thickish ear last night."

"My dear sir; my dear sir," protested Mr. Half-castle.

"Oh, don't mind me," continued Gerald. "I'm more or less a colonial; I don't know the ropes in England, but in Shanghai an Englishman's home is still his castle —even the Japs recognize that."

"That is still the case in England, sir," said Dawle quietly, "but the law gives certain rights of entry to its officers in the execution of their duty."

"I thought you had to have a warrant for that kind of thing," said Gerald. "Did you have a warrant?"

"No, sir. A warrant is procured whenever possible, but in a case of a serious nature, such as this, the police are empowered both to arrest and to search in an emergency without a warrant; they are liable, of course, to be called upon to justify their action."

Superintendent Dawle's drab little office remained in appearance as drab as ever; yet there was a feeling of tension in the room now that made the scene almost dramatic. Mr. Halfcastle, matter-of-fact solicitor, did not like drama.

"I think perhaps we are tending a little bit from the point," he said. "I felt bound, Superintendent, to make some protest against the manner in which this statement was taken, but if you agree with me that, in Mrs. Sterron's present condition, it cannot be taken seriously, then perhaps not much harm has been done. It would, of course, be possible, if that statement were produced, to bring medical evidence to the effect that Mrs. Sterron was *non compos mentis* at the time."

Superintendent Dawle tapped the table softly with the palm of his large hand.

"I don't quite know on what grounds you say that, sir," he said, "but you must remember that it was not only Mrs. Sterron who made a statement last night; Father Speyd also made one, in my presence."

Gerald Sterron gave a short laugh.

"Oh, come now, Superintendent," he said; "you're not going to tell me that you pay any attention to what that fellow says; why, he's not all there, in my opinion. You heard the way he talked on Sunday morning; a lot of hysterical nonsense that a schoolgirl would be ashamed of."

"Father Speyd's statement was confirmed by certain known facts, sir," said Dawle calmly.

"What was his statement?" rapped out Sterron.

Dawle remained silent for a time, then said slowly:

"I'm not at liberty to disclose the exact nature of the statement, sir, but it was to a certain extent in the nature of a confession."

"Eh? What?"

"Confession?"

The two questions came simultaneously. Gerald's was followed at once by a further remark.

"You don't mean he confessed to killing Herbert? Why, Superintendent, how could a scarecrow of a fellow like Speyd strangle a great hulking man like my brother? You're not talking sense."

Superintendent Dawle eyed Gerald Sterron thoughtfully.

"That's a point, sir," he said slowly. "That's quite a point."

Mr. Halfcastle, who had long since regretted having brought Gerald Sterron with him, tried now to resume control of the interview.

"I quite understand, Superintendent," he said, "that you cannot reveal the exact nature of the statement or the lines upon which you are working, but I must remind you that the deceased gentleman's family is still completely in the dark as to what is happening. They were under the impression, as I think every one else was at the luncheon adjournment of the inquest, that a verdict of suicide in some form was inevitable; the inquest, however, was, without further evidence, adjourned indefinitely, and since then a number of enquiries and half-statements and suggestions have been made, all of a nature very distressing to my clients, but all so vague as to provide no basis upon which their advisers can form a judgment of the situation. I must really beg of you to try and appreciate the extremely trying and anxious position in which my clients are placed. Can you not be more definite?"

Dawle remained unmoved by this oration.

"I will have to obtain instructions about that from the Chief Constable," he said formally.

"And this alleged statement of Mrs. Sterron's; you will, of course, let me have a copy of it?"

"I will take the Chief Constable's instructions upon that point, too, sir," replied Dawle, displaying a degree of subordination that would have surprised Major Threngood.

"I take it, of course, that it was a properly signed and witnessed statement?"

This, as Dawle well knew, was thin ice.

"No, sir," he said. "There were only three of us present. I myself took the Reverend Speyd's statement and Sergeant Gable wrote it down; it was properly signed and witnessed. But Inspector Lott had to take Mrs. Sterron's statement alone and it was not signed, Mrs. Sterron expressing a wish to retire for the night before it was really completed. I might, of course, have taken the two statements one after the other, but it would have been a very long business. I was anxious not to cause Mrs. Sterron more inconvenience and distress than was avoidable, so I did not press the matter. The statement will not, of course, be available as evidence."

Dawle did not explain that his real reason for taking the two statements simultaneously was the good old-fashioned one of striking while the iron's hot—and before the witness has time to calm down and think.

Mr. Halfcastle made a grimace.

"I'm bound to repeat, Superintendent," he said, "that I consider the whole procedure to be open to question; I must reserve the right to raise it at a later stage if this statement is produced in any form."

That, of course, might be some satisfaction to his legal mind, but Mr. Halfcastle knew very well that this interview wasn't doing any good; he was learning nothing and he—with Gerald Sterron's help—was running some risk of antagonizing the police. He rose to his feet.

"I am obliged to you for giving me your attention," he said stiffly.

Gerald Sterron, who had listened to the legal fencing with amusement mingled with impatience, smiled and held out his hand.

"No ill-will, Superintendent?" he asked.

The Superintendent's hesitation was only momentary.

"Not on my side, sir," he said, as he took the other's hand. "We have our duty to do and it's often very unpleasant."

"Come along, then, Halfcastle," said Gerald, leading the way out of the room. "You must be starving."

As the solicitor turned to go, Dawle raised his hand slightly.

"Just a moment, sir," he said. "I was wanting to ask you a question."

Going to a cupboard, he unlocked it and brought out one of the correspondence files taken from Ferris Court. Opening it, he took a folded paper from the top.

"I found this letter folded up between the sheets of another, sir," he said. "I wondered . . ."

Gerald Sterron reappeared in the doorway.

"Coming?" he asked.

"Just a minute, Mr. Sterron," said the solicitor.

"Something private?"

"Only a small legal point, sir," replied Dawle blandly.

Gerald hesitated, then pulled a case from his pocket and extracted a cigarette.

"Well, don't be all night," he said. "I'll wait for you in the car."

As soon as he had gone, Dawle shut the door.

"Did Captain Sterron have dealings with more than one firm of solicitors, sir?" he asked.

"Not that I know of. Why?"

Superintendent Dawle tapped the still folded letter against his thumb.

"This is from a firm of solicitors, I believe, sir," he said. "It seems to refer to some further correspondence, but I can't find anything else from them. I wondered whether you could throw any light on it."

Mr. Halfcastle held out his hand.

"I can tell you that better when I see what it is," he said.

Opening the letter he adjusted a pair of pince-nez. The letter was headed:

"Clingham, Bland & Co. 55A, Jasper Street, W.C.2," and ran as follows:

23rd July, 1932.

Dear Sir,

Your letter of 21st inst. to hand. Your instructions have been carefully noted and the matter will be put in hand at once. We fully appreciate the necessity for observing the greatest care and discretion; any reports or subsequent letters which we may send to you will be marked "Confidential," and there is no reason to anticipate that the enquiry will come to the knowledge of any one but yourself.

Assuring you of our appreciation of the confidence which you are placing in us,

We are, Sir,

Your obedient servants,

CLINGHAM, BLAND & Co.

Captain Herbert Sterron.

Mr. Halfcastle's expression, as he read, grew steadily more rigid, until, as he handed the letter back to Dawle, it was positively grim.

"You know who these people are?" he asked.

"No, sir, except that they are solicitors."

"They are solicitors of a reputation . . . I should say that they are a firm which specializes in one subject, Superintendent . . . divorce!"

XXIII. A GAME OF LAWN TENNIS

"SO he knew about it after all, did he?"

Inspector Lott had returned from Ferris Court, none the wiser than when he went. The tiresome need for "discretion" had made his task of questioning the servants about Father Speyd and their mistress an almost hopeless one. Even as it was, he did not see how intelligent people could fail to see what he was driving at; there was almost certain to be "talk"—and in return for that he had gained nothing. Now he was listening to Superintendent Dawle's description of the visit of Mr. Halfcastle and Mr. Gerald Sterron and particularly of the solicitor's revelation about the letter.

"I found the damn thing yesterday when I was going through his files," explained the Superintendent. "I meant to go up and see these people this morning, but last night's show put it out of my head. And, in any case, I had to get that stuff up to the Treasury solicitor. Now, of course, it's Saturday afternoon and there'll be nothing doing for another day and a half."

"I'm not sure that that's such a bad thing," said Lott. "Personally, I'm all for having a day off and starting afresh on Monday. I'm feeling a bit addled about it."

"Does Scotland Yard take the week-end off?" enquired Superintendent Dawle innocently.

"It does indeed, Mr. Dawle; and every other Thursday and a week at Easter and three months in the summer. Our brains are fine, highly-tested bits of mechanism; we have to take care of them."

Dawle laughed.

"Well, off you go, my lad," he said. "I daresay we can hold the fort till Monday."

Inspector Lott looked slightly hurt; his vanity would have preferred a remonstrance.

"Half a minute, Super.," he protested. "We must have some sort of a plan. And I'd like to know what you're thinking about this priest business now; has this letter made any difference to you?"

"I don't know yet what the letter's about," said Dawle, non-committally. "But Mr. Sterron raised a point this morning that interested me. He said: 'How could a scarecrow of a fellow like Father Speyd strangle a big chap like Captain Sterron?' Anything strike you about that?"

Lott gave the matter a minute's thought.

"Well, it is a bit of a teaser," he said. "Of course it wasn't a case of strangling; he smothered him, didn't he? But even that must take a bit of doing."

"Ye-es," said Dawle slowly, crossing one blue-clad leg over the other. "You haven't quite got my point, but it is a bit of a puzzle how that smothering was done without any noise or any sign of a struggle."

"Or any marks of violence," added Lott. "I suppose he wasn't chloroformed?"

"Wasn't any smell of it when we went in next morning, though I suppose it might have cleared off. But in any case, chloroforming's not so easy to do to a big man without his kicking and struggling a good deal before he goes off. It *is* a bit of a puzzle, Lott. I suppose he *was* smothered? I'm beginning to get a bit suspicious of these expert witnesses."

Lott stared at him.

"Good lord," he said; "that's a nasty idea. One does come to rely on them, doesn't one? Bit of a joke if it turned out that he hanged himself after all."

"Not my idea of a joke," said Dawle solemnly.

Lott knew enough of his companion by now not to apply his sharp tongue to this obvious opportunity.

"I don't think it would be a bad thing," he said, "if we were to get some doctor on to this subject of how the smothering was done without any noise or marks. I wish I'd been here when Sir Hulbert did his P.M.; I'd have asked him."

Dawle sat puffing at his pipe for some time. His rugged face looked almost stupid when he was thinking. It was one of his greatest assets as a police officer—once his superiors had got to know it.

"I tell you whose opinion I'd like as much as any," he said, "and that's that Sir James Hamsted. Impressed me a lot, that gentleman did. Been a doctor, and been a coroner, and now a big bug at the Home Office. I'd like to know what he's got to say about it."

Inspector Lott looked at his watch. It was nearly time to go, if he was to catch the train to London that he had set his heart on. He was longing to be back in London. The country was all very well for a few days, but to a Londoner it is intolerably dull and lonely after a week. Lott missed the rattle and rush of the streets, the glitter of lights on wet pavements, the voices and laughter of the people—the millions of people who were his neighbors in London.

"How would this do, Super.?" he asked. "Suppose

I run up to town this afternoon, see my boss tonight or tomorrow, have a word with your Sir James, and on Monday morning go down W.C. and find out what that letter's about? What's the name? Clingham and Bland? I fancy I've heard of them and if there's anything fishy they'll know about it at the yard. How's that suit your book?".

Superintendent Dawle was annoyed. He knew well enough that this was the sensible plan; that the C.I.D. man could work the London end of the business better than he could, leaving him free to attend to his routine duties and anything that might crop up at Ferris. Yet he was annoyed—because he had been looking forward to a day in London himself. For the life of him, however, he could not think of any good reason to give for turning down the suggestion. He sniffed loudly and knocked out his pipe.

"All right, my lad," he said, "you cut off to the city lights and I'll stay and prod round the local ponds."

Lott felt slightly ashamed of his success; the Super. was an unselfish old cuss—and not half such a fool as he looked. But there was no time to be lost if he was to catch that train, so with a friendly farewell he made off.

Superintendent Dawle had one consolation, which he had kept up his sleeve in case his trip to London did not come off. There was one person who might be able to tell him something about the correspondence with Clingham and Bland, and that was the pretty young secretary up at Ferris Court; he was not at all averse to having another little chat with her. The heat of the day was over now and a run in the car would be quite pleasant.

Within half an hour he was at Ferris. Leaving his car

outside the gates, Dawle walked up to the house and
rang the bell. Henry, who answered it, informed him
that he thought Miss Nawten was out but he would
enquire. He disappeared, leaving Dawle standing by
the open front door; hardly had he done so when Grace
Nawten herself came down the front stairs. Seeing the
police officer she checked involuntarily, then came forward with her friendly smile.

"Are you looking for some one, Superintendent?"
she asked.

"I was looking for you, miss, if the truth be told,"
replied Dawle, feeling a glow of pleasure at the sight
of the pretty face and the sound of the charming voice.

"Come along, then. I was just going for a walk, but
we can go and sit in the pigeon-house. It's lovely there
now."

This was what Dawle had hoped. He had already
spent a pleasant half-hour in the pigeon-house with the
same companion.

"D'you mind if we go through the shrubbery?" asked
the girl. "I don't . . ."

She stopped as the sound of a man whistling and of
feet on the stairs was heard.

"Hallo, Grace," called a voice. "Are you coming
to make a four?"

Dawle, who was outside the front door and invisible
to the speaker, saw the girl's face flush, as if with annoyance.

"No, Mr. Sterron, I'm not," she replied shortly, and
shutting the front door joined Dawle on the drive. For
a minute she walked beside him in silence.

"Mrs. Sterron's furious with me for not making a
fourth at tennis," she said at last. "They say it's no

good going on living in mourning for ever and they must get some exercise, but I think it's *beastly!*" The girl's eyes flashed and her voice conveyed her feelings as much as her words.

"Who are 'they'?" asked Dawle.

"Mr. Sterron asked Sir Carle Venning to come over and play with him this evening. That's not so bad, I suppose, but then Mrs. Sterron suddenly said she wanted to play, and asked me to, and I said I didn't want to, and she said I should spoil their game, and I said I didn't care if I did, and she was furious. . . ." The words poured out in a torrent. Evidently it was a relief to have some one to whom they could be unburdened.

"We shall see the tennis-court from the pigeon-house, but if we don't talk too loud they won't hear us. Sound carries up, not down."

They emerged from the comparative gloom of the overgrown shrubberies into the warmth and dazzle of the evening sun as it struck the graveled space in front of the pigeon-house. Down the main terrace steps from the house came Gerald Sterron, dressed in flannels, with a tennis racket in one hand and a box of balls under his arm. Reaching the court, he raised the net and emptying the box of balls at one end began to practice service. His short, sturdy figure looked unsuited to the graceful game, and Dawle was too little an expert to judge whether the hard, curling strokes were good or not.

Presently the sound of a car was heard—and ceased. A minute later a tall, erect figure appeared from the lower end of the garden. Gerald Sterron went across to greet his guest. Their voices came clearly up to the two sitting in the pigeon-house above them.

"Good of you to come," said Gerald. "I'm dying for some exercise. Cooped up all day in a house with the blinds down—metaphorically—it's no joke in this weather."

"Of course; quite understand that. I ought to have called, but . . . well, I never know whether one'll be welcome or not."

Sir Carle Venning was evidently less fluent with a man than he was reputed to be with women.

The two men peeled off their coats and scarves and the game began, the monotonous plop-plop of the ball and an occasional calling of score being the only sounds to reach the hut. Dawle turned to the business in hand.

"I want to ask you about some correspondence Captain Sterron had with some people—solicitors, I believe —called Clingham and Bland."

Grace Nawten raised her pretty eyebrows.

"Clingham and Bland? Never heard of them," she said.

"It's quite a recent correspondence. Are you quite sure, miss?"

"Quite. What was it about?"

"That's just what I don't know, miss. I only found just the one letter and it didn't say much; it referred to some instructions and mentioned the word 'enquiry.' It was marked 'Confidential.' "

Miss Nawten turned her head sharply.

"Then I probably shouldn't have seen it," she said. "I opened all Captain Sterron's letters except ones in obviously private envelopes and ones marked confidential. Sometimes I was given them to answer or deal with in some way, but I don't know Clingham and Bland."

That was unlucky, though it was only what might have been expected. Dawle looked down towards the tennis-court and his eyes were caught and held by the flying ball. Plop-plop-plop-plop, it flew from one side to the other. The agility of the big-framed Venning seemed to Dawle marvelous; he dashed from one side of the court to the other, striking, leaping, sliding. By comparison, Gerald Sterron on the other side seemed positively lethargic.

"Mr. Sterron doesn't seem to get about much, miss," he said. "I suppose he's getting old."

Grace Nawten laughed quietly.

"You don't know much about lawn tennis," she said.

Dawle looked at her with interest.

"I don't, miss, but what do you mean?"

"Watch them."

Dawle watched and saw at first the same thing; then he began to realize that many of the rallies seemed to end in Carle Venning just failing to reach the ball, or hitting it into the net, or out—Dawle knew just enough about the game for that.

"You mean . . . that Mr. Sterron wins points without running about, miss?"

He doesn't have to run about. He makes his opponent run about. It's all a matter of placing. Of course, Mr. Sterron couldn't do it against a really good player; he's not active enough himself. But Sir Carle's not a good player; he's only a good athlete—and he doesn't like it."

Dawle could see now that the baronet's face was not only flushed with heat, but that his mouth was set in a hard line, while a furrow cut his forehead above the nose. In the middle of a long rally he suddenly missed the ball altogether and Dawle, following his eyes, saw Griselda Sterron coming down the broad steps of the terrace. She was dressed in a gray foulard frock and a broad-brimmed hat of the same color, but an orange sunshade gave a touch of brilliant color—and effect— to her appearance.

Sir Carle walked quickly across the court and took her hand. Dawle could not hear the words, but there seemed no awkwardness or hesitation now. Gerald Sterron went slowly across to a chair and, dropping into it, lit a cigarette. The two others talked together in low voices for a time, then walked across to where he sat.

"You're not going to play, Mrs. Sterron?" asked the baronet in a louder voice.

"No, Carle. I can't—not now. People might think it heartless of me."

Dawle turned to his companion with a look of enquiry.

"I thought she wanted to?"

Grace Nawten's lip curled.

"She did, but you don't catch her telling him that she doesn't always get what she wants."

The Superintendent looked at his companion with renewed interest.

"I take it you're not altogether fond of Mrs. Sterron?" he said.

Grace shrugged her shoulders but did not answer.

"You told my colleague, Inspector Lott, that he could find out for himself something that he asked you; you wouldn't care to give me a different answer, miss?"

Grace Nawten looked calmly at the Superintendent.

"I think you are finding out for yourself," she said.

"That's all very well, miss, but if you know anything

you ought to tell us. You said last time you wanted us to catch the man that killed Captain Sterron; you don't want to make us miss him, do you?"

The girl turned her head away and looked out over the garden.

"I shan't let you miss him," she said in a low voice.

"You don't know who he is?"

Miss Nawten turned back towards the Superintendent.

"No, I don't know," she said. "But I can use my brains, Superintendent, and I'm sure you can use yours."

Dawle turned away with a frown. As he did so he saw Carle Venning dash across the court to make a spectacular return; Gerald Sterron took the return quietly on the volley and lobbed it just over the net on the other side of the court; Venning dashed for it, got to it, and sent it a foot out of the court. Savage with anger he struck his racket violently against the post and the fragile frame broke.

"Naughty temper!"

Griselda's clear laugh rose to the two watchers in the pigeon-house. Venning, his sudden temper as quickly gone, looked shamefacedly at his broken racket.

"Sorry, Sterron," he said. "No business to do that."

"I'll get you another," said Gerald calmly. "No, don't you move. Talk to Griselda. I'll bring some drinks."

He slipped on his gray flannel jacket and walked slowly up the steps. Venning flung himself on the grass beside Griselda's chair and, looking up, said something which Dawle could not hear. Griselda bent down and passed her fingers gently over his hair and forehead.

"You're hot," she said. "You mustn't sit in the shade. Carry my chair into the sun."

Carle Venning sprang to his feet and with a laugh picked up chair and lady and carried them bodily across the court to the sunny side.

Dawle's eyes widened to a stare.

"My Lord!" he exclaimed. "Look at that!"

XXIV. INSPECTOR LOTT'S
WEEK-END

AS Inspector Lott traveled to London he went over in his mind the report that he was to make to his chief at headquarters. Superintendent Wylde himself would probably want to hear about this case, possibly even the Assistant-Commissioner. Though senior, neither of these was really so formidable as Chief Inspector Hazzard, under whom Lott usually worked. On the whole, Lott hoped that it would be Superintendent Wylde, whose criticism would be tempered by both understanding and wisdom.

Lott knew that he would need a bit of both; on the face of it, he had a very barren performance to report. In four days of hard work—the detective could credit himself with that quality—he had persistently followed up a theory that was based partly upon rumor and partly upon a hasty judgment of his own which had proved mistaken—he had jumped to the conclusion that Mrs. Sterron was carrying on an intrigue with Sir Carle Venning because he had seen her flinch at the mention of the man's footprint in her sitting-room; now it turned out that it was not Sir Carle's footprint at all, but Father Speyd's.

On the basis of that conclusion, Lott had spent two days in Birmingham, with the sole result that he had proved it impossible for his quarry to have been at Ferris at the time that the murder had been committed.

That meant "opportunity" gone, and now "motive" had been blown sky-high, too; it was not Venning but Speyd who was the subject of Mrs. Sterron's passion and the object of Captain Sterron's jealousy. And that discovery was to the credit, not of himself, but of the despised local constabulary. Truly, Detective-Inspector Lott, C.I.D., would not be a popular figure at headquarters! However, it was no good anticipating trouble and no good going to look for it on a Saturday evening. Here he was, back in his beloved London; he would have an enjoyable evening and fortify himself against the hazards of the morrow.

With this end in view, he dug out a colleague with similar misogynous propensities to his own, and took him off to a Corner House for a meal, after which the pair found a couple of rather expensive seats at the "Kingdom," where an American underworld film was "showing." It was a busman's holiday for the two detectives, but it made them laugh; the way in which police and criminals sprayed each other with bullets in a crowded restaurant with nothing but a slung arm and a bloody coxcomb to show for their trouble always tickled the English professionals, and the inevitable triumph of the wrongdoer in "God's Own Country" gave them a comfortable sense of the superiority of their own.

It was a matter of some annoyance to them that this underworld piece was half over when they arrived, a wretched theatreland film, full of girls and glamour, being the *pièce de résistance*. However, it was too late and too expensive to go elsewhere and the two womenhaters sat on to grumble and grouse, to their own satisfaction and the annoyance of their neighbors. After a time, Lott fell silent; one of the lightly-clad chorus girls had reminded him of Rose Wilters and he soon found himself looking out for her reappearance with something more than curiosity. The music was catchy and Lott's hand automatically beat against his knee; the scent of a girl sitting on his right tickled, quite unconsciously, his senses; suddenly he felt an almost overmastering wish that his companion was not of his own sex, not a stolid, solid policeman, of little imagination and still less charm. Abruptly he rose to his feet.

"Oh, come on," he exclaimed. "I can't stand this leg-wagging rot any more."

He struggled roughly out of the line of seats, careless of the annoyance and protests he was arousing. Perversely, he was irritated by the congratulations of his friend upon his good sense in quitting such a "nauseating performance." He declined an offer of bun and coffee at a Y.M.C.A. hostel and, jumping on to a bus, made his way home to Pimlico and solitude.

The following, Sunday, morning, Lott made his way early to New Scotland Yard and found Superintendent Wylde on duty and anxious to hear his story. Its reception was rather less frigid than the detective had feared; Superintendent Wylde probably shared Lott's own views about it but he did not voice them, and contented himself with the constructive suggestion that the time had come to forget about "delicacy" and to question everybody connected with the case much more frankly and searchingly about their doings, their knowledge of each other, and their thoughts. It was time, in fact, that the velvet glove came off. Superintendent Wylde hinted that if the Chief Constable proved obstructive in this respect he would bring some pressure to bear through the Home Office and would, if necessary, send Chief Inspector Hazzard down to apply any extra drive that might be required. This last, Lott realized, was a pretty definite hint to himself.

So much for Scotland Yard; there was one more bit of duty to be done and then he could have the rest of Sunday to himself. At half-past twelve—time enough for the most comprehensive service to be over—Lott rang the bell of 355, Cromwell Road. He found Sir James Hamsted, not in the gloomy library where Superintendent Dawle had taken tea with the ex-coroner, but in a large room at the back of the house which proved to be the converted top of the old stables-garage underneath. The room was lit only from above and the walls were covered with paintings and drawings of an obviously high order. Sir James himself was standing beside a large table in the center of the room, engaged in cataloguing a portfolioful of dry-point etchings.

"Yes, I've heard of you, Inspector," he said, as Lott introduced himself. "You were on that case at Quenborough, weren't you, where all the aldermen started killing each other? Very intriguing it must have been."

"I was, sir, but it's one of the last cases I want to be remembered by. I was on the wrong line and let a man shoot himself under my nose."

"Well, that's sometimes done on purpose, isn't it? The 'letting,' I mean. Now, then, how can I be of assistance to you? Take a chair. You won't mind if I go on fiddling with these things? I do not get much time during the week for my hobby. I shall be able to attend to you while I examine them."

Sir James picked up a magnifying-glass through

which he closely examined the fine lines of the print in his other hand.

"Perfect," he murmured. "Undoubtedly first state. Go on, Inspector."

Automatically, Lott pulled out his note-book and turned over the pages.

"We haven't made much progress with this case, sir," he said. "There's one particular point the Superintendent wanted me to consult you about, but before we get to that I'd like to ask you whether anything else has occurred to you that might throw any light on the matter?"

Sir James Hamsted shook his head.

"I have given the matter very careful consideration," he said, "and beyond the fact of hearing footsteps which I have already mentioned to Superintendent Dawle, I have nothing to add to my original statement. By the way, have you been able to identify those footsteps?"

"Yes, sir," said Lott. "They were made by the local constable going his rounds."

Sir James raised his eyebrows. Evidently the same thought had occurred to him as had originally struck Lott, but he was not the type to criticize an official unasked.

"That must have been a disappointment for the Superintendent," was all he said.

"It wasn't altogether that, sir. It turned out to be a very important point indeed, because it enabled us to fix one end of the time limit."

Lott explained about Constable Bunning having seen that the study window was still empty and unclosed at 10.45. Sir James listened with great interest, his magnifying-glass for the time being forgotten.

"That is, indeed, an important point," he said, "and as the medical evidence places the other limit at 11 P.M., or midnight at the very latest, Mr. Gerald Sterron and I are clear of suspicion—we provide each other with a mutual alibi. Unless, that is, you suspect us of collusion," Sir James added with a smile.

Lott nodded.

"There is that possibility, sir," he said calmly, "but as far as you yourself are concerned, we are unable to discover any possible motive."

Sir James bowed.

"Have you thought of notoriety?" he asked.

"Notoriety, sir?"

"Yes, the craving for notoriety—in my experience one of the strongest human motives for crime."

Lott smiled.

"I know there is such a thing, sir, but it hadn't occurred to me to apply it to a gentleman like yourself."

Sir James shook his handsome white head.

"You are wrong," he said. "There is no one who can be excluded from that possibility, least of all a man or woman who has led a comparatively humdrum life, as I have. Still, I am prepared to assure you that I am not guilty of this crime. And that practically excludes Mr. Gerald Sterron, though I imagine that he may have a better motive than I; he may benefit in some direct way by his brother's death."

"He succeeds to the property, sir."

Sir James shot a quick glance at the detective, then picked up print and glass again.

"But it's of no benefit to him, unfortunately," continued Lott, unconsciously applying the word to the police point of view rather than the legatee's. "The estate's so tied up—mortgages and sinking fund and things—that he'll not benefit for another twenty years and may actually lose over it, what with death duties and the cost of keeping the place up. So I'm afraid we shall have to wash out the collusion idea, sir."

"Then how can I help you?"

Lott put away the note-book that he had not needed.

"It's rather unofficial this, really, sir," he said. "The fact is, Superintendent Dawle's sets a good deal of store by your opinion; your having been a doctor and a coroner—and your spotting that about the cause of death. We've got our police surgeons, of course, and our H.O. experts, but Mr. Dawle sent me up to ask you how a man could smother another man without a pretty good rough and tumble and marks of violence and so on. Captain Sterron was a big man and yet he was first smothered and then hanged without there being a mark on him. How was it done, sir?"

Sir James Hamsted put down his magnifying-glass and pulled a chair up close to Lott's. Taking off his glasses, he polished them carefully.

"This must remain an unofficial opinion, you understand, Inspector," he said. "I am not a practicing doctor and if you want evidence for the court, you must go to an expert. But I'm quite ready to give you my opinion for what it's worth. The only ways in which a big man like Captain Sterron could be smothered without a violent struggle and noise would be if he were rendered unconscious either by a blow—by stunning—or by blocking the air passages. I gather that stunning can be eliminated—Sir Hulbert Lemuel would have found traces of that, even if it were done by a sandbag. Blocking the air passages with a cushion would prevent his crying out, but it would not prevent him drumming on the floor with his heels—a natural reaction—unless it were done by an even bigger and stronger man, who might in some way lock his victim's legs with one of his own. . . . I don't know; it might be done. A more effective method would be to drench the cushion with some anesthetic—not chloroform, that would be too slow in its effect—more probably ethyl chloride . . . two or three breaths of that would cause complete unconsciousness."

"What about smell, sir? Wouldn't that hang about? Would it be clear eight or ten hours later?"

Sir James shook his head slowly.

"Not unless there was a draught to carry it away. Leaving doors and windows open might do it—or an electric fan would certainly do it . . . in an hour or two."

"I must look into that, sir," said Lott. "The doors and the windows were shut."

"Then even an electric fan would not do it. Of course, there is a third possibility—incapacitation by a blow on some nerve center—the solar plexus, for instance, or the side of the neck, where the vagus—the nerve supply—runs down the carotid. But there again, both of those would leave a bruise."

"It's a puzzle, sir," said the detective.

For a time the two men continued to discuss the case and then the detective, seeing Sir James's eye begin to wander back to his engravings, rose to his feet.

"You've got some treasures here, Sir James," he said, picking up his hat.

"You are interested in painting? Take a look round, Inspector; I like to share my pleasure."

Lott walked slowly round the room, stopping presently in front of a pleasant oil-color landscape.

"That's awfully like a Bonington, sir," he said.

"It is a Bonington. You're a connoisseur, Inspector."

Lott flushed with pleasure.

"Not that, sir, but I go round the galleries when I can. I wonder you don't have the name on the frame. People like to know what they're looking at."

Sir James laughed.

"If I did that," he said, "some of my friends and acquaintances would know more than I want them to. I've collected all these paintings and drawings, Inspector—every one of them—and there are some good things here. And yet I am far from being a rich man; the salary of an inspector under the Home Office is not princely, whatever the papers may say at Budget time. All these I have picked up for modest sums, by keeping my eyes open and using my judgment. Of course I have made mistakes—the greatest art expert in the world may do that; but as I never pay a big price, I never suffer a serious loss if my judgment proves wrong. On the other hand, I frequently pick up a real treasure that is unrecognized as such by its owner, and if he is willing to part with it at my price, why should I enlighten him? You will see, though, that having paid a modest sum for a painting, I cannot proceed to label it Bonington or Constable; if its owner happened to see it here so labeled, he might think—quite unjustly, in my view—that I had cheated him. So I leave them as I found them—save for cleaning or restoration—and then no one is any the worse—ignorance remains bliss."

This dissertation upon the ethics of art collection was

rather beyond Lott's province; besides, he wanted his dinner, so he took his leave.

As he quitted Sir James's house, the sun was shining with a power that made the thought of town, even to such a confirmed Londoner as Lott, anything but agreeable. Wondering what to do with his afternoon, his mind first turned to a bicycle run with one of his friends, but remembering his unfortunate experience of the night before, he resolutely took himself down to Balham, extracted a married sister and her brood from their Sunday quarrels, and took the whole lot off to Richmond for an afternoon on the river. For the first time in his experience he actually found himself regarding the high-spirited rampagings of the children with something warmer than avuncular tolerance; was there, after all, something to be said for family life? Was it conceivable that he might himself . . . he glanced at his matronly sister and the very thought of her receiving a certain Rose, utility dancer, as a sister-in-law made him chuckle and shiver in one breath. The afternoon passed in placid meandering and lazy conversation, with occasional spells of unwonted dreaming—generally broken by some childish misdeed or catastrophe. A cheery supper in the comfortable suburban "semi-detached" ended the evening on a much more cheerful note than its predecessor.

On the following morning the detective presented himself at a not too unreasonably early hour at the offices of Clingham and Bland, solicitors. He sent in his professional card and within five minutes was received by the senior partner. Mr. Bland was a tall, military-looking man, with fair hair and a clipped mustache. He took great pride in his unlegal appearance, but the general effect was marred by a pair of watery eyes that no amount of training could persuade to remain firmly fixed upon their objective.

"Very good of you to see me, sir," said Lott, with a formal politeness that he did not feel. "I have called about some correspondence which has lately passed between your firm and the late Captain Herbert Sterron."

Mr. Bland maintained a dignified silence. He knew this gambit and the reply to it.

"The correspondence in our possession is incomplete," continued the detective with truthful perversion of the truth; "I have to ask if you will allow us to have copies of the whole correspondence, or at any rate, to let me see it and to amplify verbally."

Mr. Bland raised his eyebrows.

"I am afraid that is quite out of the question, Inspector," he said. "Our dealings with our clients are strictly confidential and cannot on any account be divulged, except by order of the court."

Lott had expected this and was prepared for it. Before starting out that morning, he had looked in at Scotland Yard and made one or two enquiries about Messrs. Clingham and Bland; to his delight he had discovered that they were well known to the police and were unlikely to put up a prolonged resistance to any not too preposterous request for information. In the course of building up their present lucrative business the firm had from time to time employed methods which brought them to the shady side of the law. Only a year ago they had been caught out manufacturing evidence in support of a client's petition for divorce and had escaped prosecution only through a more than usually scandalous bit of political wire-pulling. Messrs. Clingham and Bland knew well enough that the police "had it in for them" and they were unlikely to provoke a hostility that was best left dormant. All this Lott knew and his immediate reception by the senior partner had only confirmed his anticipations.

"I must remind you, sir," he said, "that this is a murder case, and that any attempt to withhold information may have serious consequences."

Mr. Bland's watery eyes flickered uncomfortably from side to side; his lawyer's mind longed earnestly to combat this provocative assertion, but his business instincts advised him to yield.

"I think the best thing would be, Inspector, for you to tell me just what you want to know."

This was good enough for the present. It should be easy to tell whether the solicitor was speaking the truth; he would hardly dare to do otherwise.

"You were undertaking some enquiry for Captain Sterron," said the detective. "Will you please let me know the nature of that enquiry?"

Mr. Bland tapped the blotting paper in front of him restlessly. This was very irregular, very unprofessional —but what could he do?

"The enquiry was in connection with divorce proceedings which Captain Sterron was contemplating," he said grudgingly.

Ah! So he was.

"Any particular personnel involved?"

"Er—yes. There was a certain party whom Captain Sterron proposed to cite as co-respondent."

"Name, sir, please?" said Lott, taking out his notebook.

But that was rather too abrupt.

"Really, Inspector, I cannot feel myself justified in divulging such a very confidential piece of information. There is such a thing as libel, you know. We have to guard our own interests—and our reputation."

Inspector Lott's eyes gleamed behind their convex glasses.

"Reputation did you say, sir?" he asked innocently.

Mr. Bland blushed, but he was not done yet.

"I shall have to consult my partner, definitely, before I divulge the name," he said firmly.

All right; it would come in time—and in any case Lott knew it.

"May I ask how far successful your enquiries have been, sir?" he asked.

"Very successful—in the short time since our instructions were received."

"Completely successful? Evidence in support?"

"Well, no, not complete. But we have every hope . . ." began Mr. Bland unctuously, but checked himself. "That is to say, the case, of course, is now closed —in an incomplete condition—through no fault of our own."

Damned ghouls, thought Lott; who could say that the fault was *not* theirs—hounding men and women to desperation?

"You had not definite proof of infidelity, I take it, sir?"

"Not definite, no. Clandestine meetings, a late meal at a hotel, a visit to a questionable dance resort at Maidenhead, but no absolutely . . . er . . . intimate occasion."

Lott stared. Dance resort? Father Speyd?

"Who are you talking about?" he asked brusquely.

Mr. Bland stared back—but his eyes dropped.

"My partner . . ." he began.

"Come, sir, this is no occasion for beating about the bush," said Lott sharply. "I've got to have this name or I shall have to report to Scotland Yard that you are obstructing the enquiry."

Mr. Bland flushed angrily, opened his mouth to retort . . . then shrugged his shoulders and said:

"I am referring, of course, to Sir Carle Venning."

Venning? After all, Venning! Lott felt his blood stir; a little quiver of excitement passed through him.

"Did Captain Sterron himself know how far the case had gone?" he asked.

"Certainly. We reported to him regularly."

Where were those reports? Destroyed, presumably, and this one letter overlooked.

"And did the other two—Mrs. Sterron and Sir Carle —know that he knew?"

"That I cannot say."

Lott thought for a minute. Why, he wondered, had Herbert Sterron started this "enquiry"—this loathsome business of spying upon his wife? There was nothing that he had so far heard to justify such extreme action— nothing but hate, jealousy, or . . .

"What was Captain Sterron's idea in starting these proceedings?" he asked.

Mr. Bland's hard-worked eyebrows went up again— this time in genuine surprise.

"Idea?" he asked. "The usual idea, I suppose."

"Jealousy of his wife?"

The solicitor laughed.

"Oh, dear, no," he said. "Jealousy is very seldom the

reason for getting a divorce. Freedom is what our clients want—freedom to go elsewhere."

"You mean . . . remarriage?"

"Why, of course," replied Mr. Bland.

This was a new idea to Lott. For some reason it had not occurred to him.

"Had he any particular lady in mind?" he asked. "Do you know who she was?"

Mr. Bland gave vent to his slightly salacious laugh.

"I was not in Captain Sterron's confidence to that extent," he said, "but I can't believe that you would have very far to look."

XXV. THE CIGARETTE CASE

MAJOR THRENGOOD sat in Superintendent Dawle's office in Hylam, gloomily sucking an empty pipe. He and Dawle had been listening for the last hour to Inspector Lott's account of his visit to London, including his interviews with Sir James Hamsted and Mr. Bland; listening, too, to a discreet version of the advice given to the detective by Superintendent Wylde, C.I.D.

"All very well for your people at the Yard to talk like that," said the Chief Constable; "they can sit there behind an entanglement of red tape and no one can get at them, but we've got to live with these people we're told to be 'less delicate' with."

"Not 'told to,' sir; only a suggestion," murmured Lott.

"Oh, yes, I know these official suggestions; I've had some." Major Threngood dug into his pouch with stubborn fingers. "A nice job for the County Police—to try and turn inside out a man who's not only High Sheriff, but a Deputy Lieutenant . . . and trying his best to be Lord Lieutenant of the County! And if it goes any farther . . . my lord, think of the county having to prosecute its own High Sheriff!"

"Yes, sir; that does make it rather difficult," said Lott sympathetically, "but that's the very point that makes the motive so strong—now that we know that Captain Sterron was trying to make a co-respondent of him."

"What is? What d'ye mean?"

"Why, sir, if he wants to be Lord Lieutenant, he can't possibly afford to be cited as a co-respondent; it would spoil his chances altogether."

"I should think it would," said Major Threngood grimly, "and quite right, too. Why can't he leave the woman alone, then? You don't mean to say any one's going to commit a murder in order to avoid being cited as a co-respondent?"

"It's difficult for me to say that, sir," replied Lott primly. "I have no personal experience of the temptation. But I've always heard that some men, when they fall in love with a woman, can't control themselves till they've got her. From what I've heard of Sir Carle's past career he's lived a pretty free life and generally had what he wanted; he's not the man, I should say, to be stopped by a scruple—or by fear."

The Chief Constable sat for some time in silence, frowning at a pipe that had gone out again. At last he rose to his feet.

"Well, you must do what you think fit," he said. "I've called you in and I'm prepared to follow your advice, much as I dislike it. You and Dawle settle it between you."

He walked to the door and Superintendent Dawle respectfully followed him to his car and saw him off. Returning to the office he sank down in the chair vacated by his chief.

"Well, there you are," he said. "You've got a free hand. What do you propose to do?"

"Go out and see Venning and put him through every minute of his time on Saturday night. I know a lot more now than I did when I last interviewed him, and I can

check almost everything he says—and ask some damned
awkward questions into the bargain. If he's faking, I
shall catch him out. I'll get it down in writing if I can;
can I have Gable?"

"Certainly. But it's no good going tonight; he's gone
out to dinner with some people the other side of Lambon; my man's telephoned through. He'll keep an eye
on him all night till tomorrow."

Lott shifted impatiently in his chair. The Superintendent smiled.

"You're very keen on him again," he said. "I thought
you'd switched on to Father Speyd."

"So I had when I thought it was he who Mrs. Sterron was carrying on with. But this business of Clingham
and Bland switches it all back to Venning again. I've always felt that fellow was a wrong 'un; he's lied to me
already about Saturday night and now he's tried to cover
it up—getting at those girls and the commissionaire."

"And Captain Bowys?"

"Oh, he's probably in it, too, or else he's been bribed
to hold his tongue. You've only got to look at him to
see that he'd do anything for money."

"But I thought Venning had got a complete alibi?"

"So he has between half-past eleven and one—he was
undoubtedly at Birmingham between those hours and
that means he can't have been at Ferris between half-
past ten and two; half-past ten is too early, we know,
but what about after two? I'm dashed suspicious about
these medical time limits; I've read of cases where time
of death has been faked—heating the body and that sort
of thing; it may have been done here and if I can catch
Venning tripping at all, I'm going to get all the doctors

in England, if necessary, on to how the faking was done."

Superintendent Dawle smiled.

"He's certainly had the better of you so far," he said. "I thought you'd been into that alibi so thoroughly that he was clear."

Lott stuck out his chin.

"So did I," he said, "and I expect Venning does, too, but he's not. I'm on the right line and I'm going to hang on till I've pulled his alibi to pieces. As my chief says: 'It's dogged as does it.' "

Dawle laughed.

"Well, I like to see you keen again, my lad," he said, "and mayhap I may be able to help you a bit. I've been doing a bit of quiet thinking while you've been gallivanting round London. Stand up, young fellow."

Lott, looking rather mystified, stood up.

"Now take your coat off."

The detective did so.

"Now, turn round."

"Here, Super., what are you getting at? Is this where I get kicked?"

"Turn round and you'll see."

Lott did so, displaying exaggerated signs of nervousness as to his defenseless posterior.

"All right," said Dawle. "You'll do nicely. I shan't kick you this time. Now you can put your coat on."

"Is that all that happens?"

There was disappointment in the detective's voice.

"No, it isn't; now we're going out to Ferris Court to try a little experiment."

Lott pricked up his ears.

"Ah, that's better," he said. "What is it?"

"You'll see when we get there. It's a shade too early to go yet. We'll just run round to my house and get a bite of something to eat."

It was nine o'clock—past lighting-up time—when the two police officers reached Ferris. Leaving their car outside the gates they walked up to the house. The front door was opened to them by Willing, who appeared anything but pleased to see them.

"We shan't disturb any one, Willing," said Dawle. "Just want to have a look at the study a minute."

"I will enquire from Mrs. Sterron . . ." began the butler, but Dawle interrupted him by walking across the hall to the study door. The hall was lit by a large chandelier hanging from the ceiling high up at the top of the house. Dawle looked at it, then at a switch on the wall near the foot of the staircase.

"That switch operate the chandelier?" he asked.

"Yes, sir."

The Superintendent walked across the hall and turned up the switch; darkness descended almost like a blow. A single pendant in the passage leading to the sitting-room and a light on the landing at the top of the stairs alone lit the hall now and their light was both distant and dim. Dawle switched on the current again.

"Can this be turned on or off from upstairs?" he asked.

"No, sir; it's only a one-way switch. The installation in the house is old-fashioned, I've heard the Captain say; there's no two-way switches nor yet any control switch."

Dawle nodded.

"I see," he said. "Thank you, Willing; we needn't

bother you any more. We'll seal up when we've finished."

The butler hovered, unwilling to leave intruders at large in his house.

"I'd be glad to know when we're going to be allowed back into that room," he said. "It must be getting into an awful state—dust and what not."

"It won't be very long now, I think, Willing," replied Dawle, calmly, examining the seals and then tearing loose the tapes. The door, its lock still unrepaired, swung open at a touch. Turning on the light the two police officers entered the room and shut the door behind them, securing it with a chair.

"It's wonderful how dust collects, even in the country," said Lott, running his finger over the surface of the study table. Superintendent Dawle, however, was not attending to him. He was gazing at the bottom of the door.

"Don't fit very well, do it?" he murmured, stroking his chin.

"What doesn't?"

"That door—look at the bottom of it."

Lott did so, then stared at his companion.

"You're not thinking the door was locked on the outside and the key slipped underneath?" he asked.

Dawle shook his head.

"It couldn't have slipped itself back into the lock on the inside. I specially asked Hamsted about that. No, I wasn't thinking of the key. But that can wait."

He turned towards the big sofa by the farther window.

"That's where we laid the body," he said. He placed his hand on the seat and pressed on its well-sprung and cushioned surface. "It lay there for a matter of an hour or so, I suppose," he said. "Anything strike you, Lott?"

The detective, who had been looking completely mystified, shook his head. Dawle drew from his breast pocket a white handkerchief, folded into a fairly thick packet. Unfolding it, he produced a silver cigarette case.

"That's what the Captain was wearing in his hip pocket the night he was killed," he said. "Now, Lott, I happen to have noticed that your tailor supplied you with a hip pocket, though it doesn't look as if it was ever used."

Lott slipped his hand behind his back and felt the button above his hip.

"Well, so there is!" he exclaimed. "D'you know, I don't believe I ever noticed that before. Was that what you made me take my coat off for?"

"Yes, my dear Watson, it was," replied the Superintendent with a grin.

"Well, I'm bothered." The C.I.D. man looked none too pleased with the rôle for which he had been cast. "I've never used it, anyhow."

"Well, you're going to now. Slip this into it." Dawle handed the cigarette case to Lott. It was a slim affair and slipped easily into even the tight, unused hip pocket of the detective.

"Now lie on that sofa—on your back—flat. That's it. D'you feel anything?"

"What? From this case?"

"M'm."

"Not a thing, but the cushions are so soft."

"Well, you lie there for five minutes and see if that makes any difference."

The five minutes stretched into ten and still Lott reported complete freedom from discomfort.

"Well, perhaps it's made a mark, anyhow. You'll have to slip your pants down and let me have a look, my lad."

Lott blushed but did as he was told. The case had made no mark whatever on his flesh.

"Yes, but I'm alive; the other fellow was dead," he said.

"Quite, and that's why the flesh didn't go back to normal when the pressure stopped—no blood flow to push it back. I asked Tanwort about that," said Dawle. "But if it was going to make that depression surely it would have made some mark now, wouldn't it?"

"Well, it hasn't."

"No, that's just the point. Now just you go and lay yourself down flat on the floor behind the writing-table —by the wall, where there's no carpet."

Lott, his face showing every sign of growing interest, did as he was told. In a minute he said:

"Yes, I can feel it now, Super."

"Well, lay there a bit."

After five minutes:

"It's damned hard."

And after ten:

"I've had enough of this; it's pressing on the bone. Can I get up?"

"Yes; up you get."

Without waiting to be told, the detective slipped down his trousers and pulled up his shirt. An angry red mark showed where the case had pressed into his flesh— a slight depression even was visible. Dawle rubbed his hands together with a chuckle.

"Not so bad," he said. "Not so bad."

Lott's eyes were glittering with excitement.

"What's this mean, Super.?" he asked eagerly. "Have you worked it out?"

"Roughly. Of course, I wasn't sure. Only came to me last night and I went round and talked to Tanwort this morning. What it means, as I figure it, is that the body was laying on the floor for a considerable time before it was strung up!"

Lott stared.

"Then . . . then . . . that means . . . the fellow came back . . . and strung up the body afterwards?"

"Looks like it."

"Then it may have been . . . when your constable saw that window still open . . . and the light on . . . the body may have been lying on the floor then?"

Dawle nodded.

"May have been," he agreed. "No proof that it was, of course."

"But, then, the alibi . . . this alters the whole alibi! Don't you see that, Super.? The 10.45 alibi . . . the time we thought Sterron must have been alive . . . and when it wasn't possible—after that—for Venning to be here! Why, it's vital!"

"Yes. I do see some of that," said Dawle dryly.

"I beg your pardon, sir, of course you do. But this means so much. If that 10.45 business is a washout, if he may have been dead then, why, Venning could have been here between ten and half-past—I've proved that. Suppose he killed him then, and came back after two to hang him up? Great Scott, sir, I believe that's how it was done!"

Dawle nodded.

"Yes," he said. "I think that's how it was done."

Suddenly Lott's face fell.

"But, Super., what about the staining—hypostasis, the doctors call it? If he'd been lying on his back, wouldn't his back have been marked? Stains begin to show pretty soon after death. If he was lying down a long time—it must have been two o'clock before Venning got back here—wouldn't the stains have shown on his back? They always come in the lowest parts—where the blood settles. And where his back rested on the ground—his shoulder blades and buttocks—would have remained white—it would have been obvious!"

Dawle shook his head.

"No, it wouldn't," he said. "I asked Dr. Tanwort about that. It takes a long time for blood to congeal to that extent; if he was strung up at two o'clock the blood would still have been fluid enough to move down into the legs and hands, as we saw it. The back would become normal again."

"Then it's on?"

"I think so."

Lott sprang to his feet.

"I'm going to get at that chap Venning straight away —dinner-party or no dinner-party," he exclaimed.

Dawle laid a hand on his arm.

"Hold on, my lad, hold on. What about finding out a bit more first? What about knowing the time he was strung up?"

"How can we find that out?"

"I don't say we can, but we can have a try."

Dawle moved across to the bell and pressed his thumb against it. Then, before it could be answered, he crossed to the door, removed the chair, and turned out all the lights except the reading lamp on the writing-table. After an appreciable interval the butler appeared.

"You rang, sir?" he asked, with an expression of slight surprise, suggesting that if that were so it was a piece of damned impertinence. Superintendent Dawle, however, was not interested in Willing's expression.

"Ask Mr. Gerald Sterron if he can kindly spare me five minutes . . . in here," he said.

XXVI. DOGGED DOES IT

GERALD STERRON appeared almost at once; being a business man, he did not believe in keeping people waiting when it was not necessary. He was in evening dress and smoking his inevitable cigarette.

"Good evening, Superintendent. I didn't know you were here," he said. "You're rather gloomy, aren't you?"

He reached his hand out towards the switch, but Dawle checked him.

"Don't turn any more on for the moment, sir," he said. "I'm sorry to worry you at this time of night, but there's been an important new development in the case and we'd be glad of your help."

Gerald dusted the corner of the writing-table with his handkerchief and sat on it.

"Anything I can do, of course. But I'm afraid I've told you all I know," he said.

"I'm sure you have, sir, so far as we've asked you, but this is a new point. There's an idea now that your brother's death occurred at a much later hour than was at first thought—perhaps as late as two o'clock. Do you think that's possible, sir?"

Gerald flicked the ash from his cigarette into an empty tray.

"How can I answer that, Superintendent?" he asked. "That's a medical question, isn't it?"

"Partly, sir, but not altogether. You were up very

late that night; did you hear or see anything suspicious—round about two o'clock?"

Gerald Sterron stared thoughtfully at Dawle.

"I should have told you if I had," he said. "Where does this new idea come from? It's a bit . . . revolutionary, isn't it?"

Dawle paid no heed to the question.

"Perhaps you'd tell me again about the end of your game with Sir James Hamsted," he said.

Sterron stubbed out his cigarette, chose another, and lit it. As he blew out the match with the exhalation of a first lungful, he glanced at Inspector Lott with a sly smile.

"What *is* your Number One getting at?" he asked. "Am I to be caught tripping?" Then with a quick change to seriousness he turned to Dawle. "Superintendent, I told you the first time you questioned me all that I've got to tell. I'll go over it again, of course, if you want me to, but I've got nothing new for you. Sir James and I played chess from ten o'clock, or thereabouts, till two; I think just after two, but within five minutes of it, one way or the other. Then we went straight to bed. We heard nothing at all suspicious; at least, I didn't; I don't know about Sir James. That really *is* all I can tell you; I wish to God I could help you more."

Superintendent Dawle rose to his feet.

"Well, perhaps you'll be able to yet, sir. Would you mind stepping out into the hall a minute?"

Looking mildly mystified, Gerald Sterron slipped off the writing-table. Lott, hardly less so, followed his senior and his hand had gone automatically to the electric switch by the door when he felt it sharply knocked away.

Superintendent Dawle, his face expressionless, shut the door as Lott emerged into the hall.

"Now, sir," continued the Superintendent, "you say you went straight up to bed. You didn't go in to say good night to your brother before you went up?"

Gerald stared.

"No, I didn't," he said. "Naturally, I thought he'd gone to bed long ago."

"You didn't try the door?"

"No, I'm afraid I didn't."

"Right, sir. Now, do you mind going to the library and coming out and doing everything you did that night when you went up to bed."

Gerald scratched his head, a puzzled smile on his face.

"Tall order, isn't it? I can't remember where I put each foot a week or more ago."

"No, sir, of course not, but you can do the main things; if you went and tried the front door, for instance, you would remember that."

"I didn't do that, Superintendent. I was a guest in the house just as Sir James Hamsted was."

"You were the last of the family to go to bed, sir—at least, I understand you thought you were. There would be one or two things to do before you went to bed, wouldn't there?"

"You fill me with alarm, Superintendent. What ought I to have done that I didn't do?"

"If I may suggest, sir, you go and do what I said."

Gerald shrugged his shoulders and turned towards the library passage. Walking down it, he disappeared into the library; a moment later he reappeared, yawning heavily.

"Capital game, Sir James," he said. "You made a great fight. I hope I haven't kept you up too late."

By this time he was at the foot of the stairs. He had taken a step or two when he checked and looked round at the Superintendent.

"Did you mean the lights?" he asked.

"I don't know what you did, sir; that's what I'm asking you."

Gerald switched off the big chandelier; the hall was once again plunged into comparative darkness, the single light in the passage and the light on the landing above alone illuminating it. Gerald moved on up the staircase.

"I let Sir James get up to the landing before I did that," he said. "It's rather dark at the corner."

"I thought you might have, sir. But what about the passage light; did you leave that on?"

Gerald hesitated.

"No," he said. "No, I turned that out, too, as we came along to the hall."

"Then would you mind coming down and doing it all again, sir, please?"

Gerald gave a gesture of some impatience but did as he was asked, first switching on the chandelier again. Coming down the library passage he turned out the light, then the big chandelier; complete darkness blotted out the lower part of the hall.

"Now, sir, look round," exclaimed Dawle sharply.

A sound like a sharp intake of breath came from the stairs; then Gerald's voice:

"What d'you mean?"

Superintendent Dawle took three quick steps up to where the merchant was standing.

"What about the study door, sir?"

Lott, in the darkness below, turned sharply and looked behind him. Under the study door a band of dull-red light was shining. Was that what the Superintendent had meant?

"Was it like that on Saturday?"

"No, of course not; it wasn't on."

"Wasn't it? I thought you told me, sir, that you found it on in the morning?"

"My God!" The exclamation, low though it was, sounded startlingly clear in the darkness.

"It can't have been, Superintendent. My brother must have turned it off."

"And sat in the darkness?"

There was a pause. Suddenly the chandelier light went on. Dawle took his hand off the switch.

"You don't really think that, sir?"

Gerald, blinking in the sudden light, looked quite bewildered.

"I don't know what to think, Superintendent. What does it mean?"

"Come back into the study, sir. We can talk quieter there."

The three men trooped back into the dimly-lit study. Dawle shut the door.

"I told you, sir, that it's now thought that your brother's death took place quite late. If this study light was out when you went up to bed and on when you came down in the morning—what does that mean?"

Gerald stared.

"You mean . . . that some one turned it on after I went to bed?"

Dawle nodded.

"Looks like it, sir."

The Superintendent turned to his junior.

"That fit in with your ideas, Lott?"

"About the alibi? Yes, he could have got here soon after two—not before."

"He? Who?"

Sterron was staring at the two officers in turn.

"There's an idea, sir," said Dawle, "that Sir Carle Venning may have come into the house on his way back from Birmingham that night. He left Birmingham at one; he got home at half-past two."

"Venning?" There was consternation on Gerald's face. "It's impossible. How could he have got into the house?"

"I'm afraid, sir, that he may have been admitted."

Gerald's stare of astonishment changed to horror.

"Good God!" he muttered. "You don't mean . . . you don't mean . . . ?"

Dawle nodded.

"Yes, sir, I'm afraid so. Through the sitting-room window."

"But you said that it was Speyd—that priest—who was . . . admitted."

"Yes, sir, I did say that."

Gerald passed his hand over his forehead.

"I can't make head or tail of it," he said. "They weren't both here, were they?"

"Let's leave that a moment, sir, and follow up this idea of the light in here being out at two o'clock. You agree that it must have been, eh?"

"I suppose it must," said Gerald. "I should have seen if it was . . . like it was just now."

"Then if the light was off then, when was it turned off, and who by?"

Sterron shook his head.

"I can't make it out. My brother must have gone to sleep."

"Asleep, sir, or . . . dead."

"Dead! D'you mean . . . *before* I went to bed?"
Dawle nodded.

"Yes, sir. The murderer came back after two o'clock to finish the work that he had done before."

Gerald Sterron, his face tense and drawn, stared at the Superintendent.

"When?" he whispered. "When had he . . . done it?"

"At about ten o'clock, sir."

"But you said . . . you said it was much later . . . you said . . ."

"Oh, yes, sir; I said all that . . . but your brother was killed—and this light turned out—at about ten o'clock . . . at about the time you came in to see him again . . . after smoking that cigarette in the anteroom."

Slowly Gerald Sterron slipped down from the writing-table on which he had been sitting. His face was deathly white.

"What do you mean? How can . . . why, the light was still on at a quarter to eleven . . . long after my game with Sir James had begun."

Dawle's face changed. A look of astonishment came over it.

"Why, so it was, sir! So it was, wasn't it, Lott?"

The detective nodded, his face a picture of bewilderment. Dawle turned back to Gerald.

"And how, sir," he asked in a quiet voice, "did you know it was still on at a quarter to eleven?"

There was silence.

Gerald Sterron opened his mouth to speak, but only a stifled croak passed his dry lips. He turned towards the door, but Dawle seized him by the arm.

"No, sir," he said, "not till you've answered my question."

Sterron stopped.

"Take your hand off my arm," he said sharply, his self-possession suddenly recovered. Dawle shook his head. The next moment he felt his own arm seized in a grip like a vise; with a sudden jerk it was twisted behind his back, causing him to release his own grip. A sudden intolerable pressure wrenched him almost from his feet; a loud snap resounded through the room and he staggered backward against the table with his arm hanging limply at his side, pain and nausea combining to make him almost unconscious.

The breaking of Dawle's arm had been the work of a few seconds; Lott, taken for a moment by surprise, sprang forward to help his chief but, as Dawle staggered back, Sterron turned and, raising his right arm, struck the detective a horizontal blow on the neck. Lott dropped as if he had been poleaxed. Instantly Sterron dashed to the door, pulled it open and disappeared into the hall. Through a crimson haze Dawle watched him go, struggling to overcome the faintness which was surging over him. He took a few staggering steps across the room, when the door opened again and Grace Nawten appeared, her eyes gleaming with excitement.

"He's made for the garage," she exclaimed. "Quick, take this; I'll lead you."

She thrust a small Colt automatic into Dawle's hand and, catching hold of his arm, almost thrust him out of the room. The movement seemed to do Dawle good; though the awful pain in his broken arm continued, the sickness and dizziness cleared off. Guided by Grace Nawten, he blundered through a swing door into the servants' quarters, down a stone-flagged passage, oblivious of startled maids crowding in the doorways on each side, and out through the back door into the night.

As he emerged, the roar of an accelerated engine came from across the courtyard.

"Look out; he's off!" exclaimed the girl beside him, flashing a torch towards the garage door. "Shoot! Shoot!"

The beam of powerful headlights suddenly shot out from the garage opposite and a car rolled out into the yard. The headlights, swinging round for the turn, caught Dawle in their glare and blinded him.

"Stop!" he roared, raising his pistol. As he spoke a shot rang through the night and a bullet flattened itself against the wall behind him; simultaneously Dawle jerked at his own unfamiliar weapon, there was a crash, and the car plunged violently to one side into the wall of the house. Quick as lightning Grace Nawten ran to the back of it and flashed her torch on to the man crouched over the steering-wheel.

"Quick, quick, before he shoots again!" she cried shrilly.

But Gerald Sterron did not move.

XXVII. THE COUNTY WINS

"WHAT the devil's going on here?"

Superintendent Dawle turned from his examination of the wounded man. Some one had switched on a light which projected from above the back door and by its light he saw the massive figure of the High Sheriff. Behind Sir Carle stood Griselda Sterron, her eyes staring with mingled fear and excitement.

"He's badly hurt, sir. We must carry him inside and get the doctor out."

"But what's happened? What was all that shooting?"

"Never mind that now, sir," replied Dawle calmly. "We must see to him first. Will you lend a hand, please; my arm's broken. Perhaps Mrs. Sterron will see about a bed?"

With a last look of horrified curiosity, Griselda disappeared into the house. In her place appeared Lott, white and shaken but making a great effort to get to the sound of battle. Willing's head appeared nervously round the door, while maids peeped out of upper windows.

"Get an overcoat and two broom handles, Willing," said Dawle sharply. "I don't suppose you've got a stretcher, have you?"

Sir Carle Venning had been examining the wounded man by the light of the torch which Grace Nawten was holding for him.

"He's badly hit, Superintendent," he muttered. "Stomach, it looks like."

A smothered groan came from the huddled figure. Sir Carle nodded significantly at Dawle.

"We must lift him carefully," he said, as Willing and Henry appeared with an improvised stretcher. "Don't straighten his legs, let him keep them bent up. Easy. That's the way. Now lift."

The little procession made its way into the house, through the hall, and upstairs to Gerald Sterron's room. The wounded man's eyes were open and he was clearly conscious but in great pain. When he was safely deposited on the bed, Venning bent over him.

"The doctor'll be here soon, Sterron," he said distinctly, "but if you'll let me, I'll have a look at you. I may be able to help; you mustn't lose too much blood. I've done a lot of doctoring one time and another, knocking about the world."

Sterron smiled faintly.

"I'm done," he whispered. "Good of you, though. Yes, please."

Carefully cutting away the clothing, Venning exposed the abdomen, disclosing a jagged wound in the right side, from which dark blood was oozing.

"I'll just bandage that up," he said quietly.

Though his hands were big and rough, they moved with surprising deftness as he applied the lint and bandages which Grace Nawten had brought him. Having made the wounded man as comfortable as possible, he beckoned to Superintendent Dawle to follow him out of the room, leaving Lott and Miss Nawten in charge.

"He's for it," he said when they were out in the passage. "Liver smashed, internal hemorrhage. What were you using, Dawle; soft-nosed bullet?"

"No, sir, I don't think so. It was a small automatic

that M . . . that some one pushed into my hand. Nickel bullet, I should have thought."

"Well, it's made the hell of a mess. Must have turned over."

"It hit the windscreen first, sir—smashed it."

"Ah, that's it—ricco'ed. Well, he'll not live many hours, poor devil."

"Best thing for him, sir, perhaps."

"Ah, that's it, is it?" said Venning, eyeing the Superintendent keenly. "Well, it's not my business."

"Is he—fully conscious, sir?"

"Yes, quite."

"Then I'd better charge him. I wonder if you could do something for my arm, sir, till the doctor comes? It's broken and it hurts pretty bad."

"Yes, of course, I'll fix it in temporary splints. I'll be back in a second."

Sir Carle ran lightly down the stairs and Dawle reentered the bedroom. He looked at Grace Nawten.

"I'll take charge now, miss. Thank you kindly for your help." He glanced significantly at the door and Grace nodded and withdrew. Dawle went up to the bed.

"Gerald Sterron," he said in a low, distinct voice. "I must formally charge you with the murder of Captain Herbert Sterron, here in this house, on the night of Saturday, 27th August. I caution you that you need say nothing now, but that anything you do say will be taken down and may be used in evidence at your trial."

Gerald had winced at the first words but at the last he smiled wanly.

"There'll be no trial, Dawle," he said faintly. "I know that well enough. I'd like to make a statement before I go . . . clear things up. I don't want . . . any one else to get into trouble."

"It's as you wish, sir, but you'd better wait till the doctor comes. It may do you harm to talk."

There was a tap at the door and Sir Carle appeared. He beckoned Dawle outside.

"That damn doctor can't be found," he said. "They think he's at Mrs. Lowood's; not on the 'phone. Car's going up for him, but it'll be half an hour before he gets here."

"Then we'd better have his statement if he really wants to make it," replied Dawle. "He looks to me pretty bad."

"He is; only a matter of an hour or so, I think. Come, I'll do your arm."

Venning had procured some strips of wood broken from grocery boxes and with these and more bandages he soon had Dawle's arm in splints and a sling. The police officer returned to Sterron's bedside.

"It'll be a little time before the doctor can get here, I'm afraid," he said. "If you really want to make a statement, I'll take it, but I warn you again that there's no need for you to."

"I want to. No good waiting. I'm getting weaker."

Dawle nodded and signed to Lott, who had already discovered writing paper and a pen.

"When you're ready, sir. Better have a sip of water first."

Gerald Sterron took a sip from the glass which Dawle held to his lips. His head sank back on the pillows. When he spoke, his voice was faint but distinct.

"I don't want to give more trouble than I can help now you've got me," he said. "I think I'm dying anyhow, but it makes no odds. I'd rather not be tried. I killed Herbert because he told me he was going to divorce Griselda and hinted that he would marry again. I didn't at first believe it, but that same afternoon I saw him making love to Grace Nawten; they were in the pigeon house, and I saw them from this room, through my glasses. It was a fearful blow."

His voice cracked as his throat and lips grew dry. Dawle gave him more water.

"It meant the risk of his having an heir. She's a young, healthy-looking girl and, of course, there was nothing to stop them having children. It meant the end of all my dreams. I'd seen my boy here—I didn't mind so much about myself—but my boy was to come and build up the family again. I thought it was certain, but I was always afraid of his going smash again and selling things. Most of the good stuff is heirloom, but it's difficult to keep an eye on it all. There were small things— miniatures, drawings, and so on—that he might have sold without any one knowing. He fancied himself as a business man, but any crook could have cheated him. When I found out about this . . . remarriage idea it was more than I could stand. He'd had his chance; I was determined to have mine . . . for the boy.

"I thought I could fake a suicide. Herbert used to talk about it at one time—he was a whining fellow. It wasn't difficult to arrange an alibi because everybody in England does things by clockwork. I knew Willing brought the drinks at ten; I arranged for him to see me leave the study. When he'd gone, I went back. I made an excuse to get near Herbert and knocked him out as I did that detective just now . . . it's an old ju-

jutsu trick I learnt from a Jap in Shanghai. You had another, Dawle; I'm sorry."

Dawle managed to produce a wry smile.

"Then I smothered him with a cushion. I tried not to bruise him, and I don't know now how you spotted that he didn't hang himself.

"Then I laid him down behind the sofa, where I hoped no one would see him if they did look in. I had to leave the light burning because I wanted the constable to see it; he's another bit of clockwork; he's been round every night I've been here at the same time, between half-past ten and eleven. I counted on that for an alibi —it would fix the earliest time of death. The whole thing took about ten minutes, but I had arranged to keep Sir James's attention occupied by providing him with a magazine to read—an article on Li Hung Chang, whom we had been discussing at dinner. I had put the clock in the library back and as soon as I returned there I apologized to Sir James for keeping him waiting; that naturally made him look at the clock and note the time which appeared as just before ten, without his realizing that I was calling his attention to it."

Lott, scribbling away as fast as he could go, had seen Superintendent Dawle's look of satisfaction when Sterron spoke of altering the clock.

"We played our game of chess. I'm a much better player than Hamsted, but I let him beat me the night before; it pleased the old boy and came in very useful, as it happened. On Saturday night I kept him at it till two, so as to be sure of an alibi at the other end. You gave me a shock this evening, Dawle, when you said it was now thought that death occurred after two; I thought the damn fool doctors were mucking my alibi."

Gerald smiled bitterly at the thought.

"I saw Hamsted up to bed and turned off the lights. I'm damned if I know whether I noticed the light under the study door, but then, I knew it was on, so it wouldn't have struck me as odd. I had to leave that reading-lamp on all night so that it would be found on in the morning; no one would commit suicide in pitch darkness. I unlocked the back door and then I went into the study and arranged the hanging—he was a fearful weight and I had to use the cord partly to pull him up. I was afraid it would make a mark on the pole, but I couldn't help it."

Again Lott saw his senior's look of pride. The C.I.D. man was playing a salutary second fiddle in this piece.

"After he was up, I got out of the window and, standing on the sill, shut it from the outside. Of course, I couldn't latch it but I was counting on doing that later. I let myself down and dropped; I'm fairly light on my feet and it was no distance. The ground was too hard to mark. Then I went in at the back door and locked it. Of course, I'd locked the study door on the inside when I went in. I put the library clock on again to the right time. That left me only one thing to do and if it hadn't been for that damned old fool Hamsted, I should have done it."

Sterron's bitterness brought a flush of color to his pale cheeks.

"When Willing called me, as I knew he would—he's too stereotyped to act on his own responsibility—I went down with him and we broke the door in. I thought I must cut Herbert down, for the look of the thing, though I'd much rather have left him hanging, for the police to see. Hamsted arrived most opportunely to stop that, but he also stopped me doing what I still had to do. I had meant to tell Willing to draw the curtains of the other window and while he was doing it I was going to latch the window that I'd got out of; that would have made suicide a certainty. But Hamsted stopped that, blast him."

Lott's hand, flying over the paper, was beginning to ache terribly.

"Even so it seemed to go all right at the inquest till that adjournment. What *did* happen there, Dawle?"

"Sir James spotted he'd been smothered, sir. He went to look at the body and found the dental plate was bent and there were bruises on the inside of the lips. That started it."

Gerald Sterron groaned.

"God! And I thought he was an old fool!"

Dawle could sympathize with the man's feelings; if it hadn't been for Sir James Hamsted, Sterron would probably have got away with it.

There was a knock at the door and in response to Dawle's answer Willing came in.

"The doctor's here, sir," he said in a hushed whisper, looking at the man on the bed with mingled horror and interest.

Dawle followed the butler from the room. Outside he met Dr. Tanwort and Mrs. Sterron, followed by Sergeant Gable and a constable. Dawle stopped to tell the police surgeon what had happened and to give Sergeant Gable instructions for guarding the prisoner until he could be moved to hospital. Relieved by Gable, Inspector Lott followed the Superintendent downstairs. In the hall Sir Carle Venning was standing.

"I want to get off home," he said, "but I'd like a word with you fellows first."

Superintendent Dawle did not much care for being called a "fellow," but it would round the case off nicely to get a statement from the High Sheriff tonight.

"Very well, Sir Carle," he said. "Shall we go into the study?"

Inside the study, Venning turned on the Superintendent.

"I want to know what the hell all this shadowing is about," he said roughly. "There's a damn fellow been following me about like a dog wherever I go. He followed me here tonight on a motor-bike."

"That's right, sir," said Dawle calmly. "You've been under observation."

"What for?"

"For not telling us the truth when we first asked for it, is what it amounts to, Sir Carle. You told Inspector Lott here that you came straight home after the theatre on Saturday night; well, you didn't. You had an obvious motive for the murder and we were bound to suspect you—amongst others. Why *did* you tell Inspector Lott that falsehood, sir? It's given us no end of trouble."

Sir Carle looked puzzled.

"I'm dashed if I see why," he said. "I thought the death was put at between ten and twelve o'clock; I was in Birmingham then."

"Yes, but you could have got back here and gone back to Birmingham again . . . but I needn't bother you with the details if you'll tell me why you misled us."

Venning frowned. He was evidently a man of deliberate thought, though his actions were prompt enough once his decision was made.

"This case is over, eh?"

"Practically, sir. There'll be a trial if he lives, of course."

"But if I tell you, will it have to come out in court?"

"I don't see why it should, sir; you're out of it now."

"Well, on that understanding I'll tell you. It's that poor fool Bowys. He's married to a hell of a woman; can't call his soul his own. She made the Lord's own fuss just because he came and stayed with me for a week-end while she went to her mother. If she'd known poor old Frank had been out to supper with a couple of chorus girls he'd never have had a happy day again for the rest of his life. Even as it was, we fitted him up with a false mustache so that no one should spot him. So I said we came straight back after the show. As a matter of fact, we picked up a couple of girls I happened to know, gave 'em supper, had a dance or two, and Frank took one of 'em home. I had to wait for him and that meant we didn't get back till half-past two."

Lott had felt himself go hot all over. He couldn't stand it. He must know.

"I beg your pardon, sir," he interrupted, "but which one?"

"Which one did Frank . . . ? Dulcie. Why . . . what do you know about it?"

Lott, relief flooding his soul, broke into a smile.

"I had supper with them myself a night or two afterwards, Sir Carle," he said.

The baronet stared.

"Well, I'm b . . . !" he exclaimed. "I knew you were making enquiries about Saturday night, and I went in to try and fix a story that'd save poor Frank's last shred of reputation."

"You ran a great risk, sir; I found out everything—except that last little detail you mentioned."

Sir Carle rose to his feet.

"Well, it's time I went to bed," he said, "—and stayed there. England's not a safe place for a respectable bachelor to be about in after dark."

"Just one minute, sir, please," said Lott. "You went to the Pantodrome, I understand; where were you sitting?"

"In the stalls. Why?"

"I questioned almost everybody in the house and no one had seen you."

"Probably not. We were behind most of the time. I know my way about pretty well and Frank wanted to go. We had a talk to some of the girls but most of the time we were in Samuelson's room—the proprietor, you know—interesting fellow, Samuelson."

The proprietor! The one man connected with the theatre whom Lott and Sergeant Mascott had not thought of questioning.

"Thank you, Sir Carle; I think that explains everything."

"Then I'll get along home. And for goodness' sake call off that bloodhound of yours, Superintendent; I'm sick of being followed about wherever I go."

"I can do that now, Sir Carle."

"But what was he up to here tonight, I'd like to know?" asked Dawle as the door closed on the High Sheriff.

"A little courting, Superintendent, I surmise," replied Lott primly.

"Ah. That accounts for his 'waiting,'" said Dawle rather obscurely. "If you're hunting big game you don't bother about chorus girls."

"She's not a chorus girl; she's a dancer!"

Dawle stared at his companion.

"My lad, what's biting you?"

Lott flushed.

"That must be a plucky young lady, that Miss Nawten, Super., from what you tell me," he said by way of changing the conversation.

"She is. I'd like a word with her, but I expect she's gone to bed by now. I'd like to know where she sprang from so prompt. She must have spotted something was up and been waiting with the gun handy. She told me on Saturday she wasn't going to let me miss the man who killed Captain Sterron."

"You think she was in love with him?"

"Looks like it. Why couldn't she have told me what was up between her and the Captain? Though, I suppose, I ought to have guessed something from that legacy. £200 a year's a bit . . ."

The door opened and Dr. Tanwort came in.

"What's this about your arm, Superintendent?" he asked.

"Only that he broke it, sir. How is he?"

"Bad, very bad, though still conscious. Persistent hemorrhage. It's no good trying to move him; I've telephoned for a nurse and now it's only a matter of time and nursing."

"You think he'll live, sir?"

Dr. Tanwort shook his head.

"I doubt it, but we've got to try and save him for you. Now let me look at your arm."

"Sir Carle bandaged it for me, sir."

"Let me look at it."

Dr. Tanwort, when he was working, was much more impressive than when he was talking. His quick fingers ran over the bandaged arm without removing either bandage or boards.

"He's done that well," he said. "We'll leave it alone till we get you into hospital, then when I've set it I can pop you straight into bed."

Dawle's face fell.

"Hospital, sir? There's no call for me to go to hospital."

"Nevertheless, that's where you're going," said the doctor. "Now, then, get along into my car. You can't drive your own and Inspector Lott can sit in the back with you and keep you steady."

"Just a moment, doctor. Sterron tells us he knocked out his brother before he smothered him by hitting him on the side of the neck. Wouldn't that leave a bruise? You didn't find one anywhere, I thought?"

"We didn't—neither I nor Sir Hulbert. Where exactly did he hit him?"

"I can tell you," said Lott, "because he hit me in the same place."

He pointed to the side of his neck, where an angry mark still showed.

"Great Scott! Exactly on the line of the constriction mark made by the ligature!" exclaimed Dr. Tanwort. "And when I took a section out for Sir Hulbert to examine under the microscope, I took it—quite by chance —from the other side of the neck! Come on now, Dawle."

The three men made their way out to the car, which

was soon moving smoothly in the direction of Hylam.

"Damn this arm of mine," muttered Dawle. "I don't want to go to hospital . . . just now."

"Lucky it's you, in a way, and not me, Super.," said Lott. "You go in on the top of the wave, so to speak. When did you get that hunch about Sterron?"

"I've had it all along. At first sight he was the obvious answer; he had both motive and opportunity; but first one thing and then another seemed to put him out of court. What put me on to him again was something he said on Saturday. I told you he came in to my office with the solicitor fellow; we were talking about Father Speyd and he suddenly said: 'How could a weakling like that have strangled a big man like my brother?' Well, how did he know what was in our minds? We'd said nothing about strangling—nor yet about smotheration, of course. For all any one knew, we might have found the Captain had been poisoned. He seemed keen on calling it strangling as if he didn't want us to think of smothering. It was nothing definite, of course, and it sounds far-fetched, but it set me thinking."

Lott nodded.

"Yes, I see it might," he said.

"Then there was the question of his cigarette," continued Dawle. "Willing had told me that when he saw Mr. Gerald Sterron leave the study at ten o'clock he was smoking a cigarette. Father Speyd, on the other hand, said he wasn't—or rather, he said he didn't notice him smoking one. Of course, Speyd might just have been unobservant, but you'd think he'd notice a thing like that. Actually, of course, Speyd saw him leave the room the second time—after he'd killed his brother. If Speyd had opened that door when he had his hand on it he'd have found Captain Sterron dead—laid on his back behind the sofa. He might, of course, have thought the room empty. Of course, I didn't realize all this when Speyd told me; it's come on me gradually as I thought things out—over the week-end. I'm not a quick thinker. In any case, it was only a hint—there was no proof in it. To get proof, I had to catch Sterron tripping —make him give himself away, as he did tonight."

"And very neatly you did it, sir," said Lott admiringly. "But, Mr. Dawle, I can't make out that Mrs. Sterron. Which of the men was she after—Venning or Speyd?"

Dawle shook his head.

"Ah, my lad, we can't expect to understand women. If you ask me, I should say that she'd have gone off with Sir Carle just to get away from her husband, but I believe she was in love with the *padre*. As for him, poor chap, he's taking it pretty badly. He's resigned from his Brotherhood, or whatever it is, says he's disgraced his cloth—though I don't believe he's done anything except have thoughts that lots of us have. He's one of these erratic fellows; it's my belief he'll appear next in a Salvation Army uniform."

They journeyed for a time in silence. Then Dawle smote his knee with his sound hand.

"Dash it!" he said. "I never asked him about that directory!"

"What's that, Super.?"

"Why, the Baronetage that had that red ink marking in it. Did he do that, or did Captain Sterron?"

"Gerald did, I expect, to call attention to Venning as a cause of suicide."

"Or as a murderer?"

"Perhaps he did have that idea—sort of second string to suicide; he seemed ready enough to switch it on to him tonight." Dawle thought a minute. "Yes," he added, "it must have been Gerald, because Gable couldn't find any finger-prints on the directory; he must have worked in gloves throughout."

There was another pause, broken this time by Lott.

"How did that tire mark of Sir Carle's get into the lane at the bottom of the garden, I wonder?" he said.

"He probably parked his car there when he came to play tennis that day," answered Dawle. "He came to that gate when he was up here this Saturday—nearest point to the tennis-court."

"Dash it!" said Lott. "I ought to have thought of that; I set a lot of store by that tire mark, too."

"Natural enough. That's the sort of clew we have to work on." Dawle sat for a time in silence. "Doesn't it seem odd to you, Lott," he continued, "the way one feels about a fellow like this Gerald Sterron. Here he's gone and murdered his brother in as cold-blooded a way as you could find and yet, just because he was clever and cool, one can't help admiring him and feeling a sort of sneaking sympathy for him now he's been caught after all. And you know, Lott, he dashed nearly brought it off. If it hadn't been for Sir James he would have."

Lott sat for a time in gloomy silence.

"No thanks to me, anyhow," he said. "I've been a pretty gloomy failure."

"Nonsense, my lad," said Dawle. "We've worked this together. I told you at the start it was either Gerald Sterron or Sir Carle—bound to be. We settled that you should follow up Sir Carle—because the Chief was nervous about our touching him—and I was to take Sterron. It just happened that my line turned out the right one; that's all. You followed your line like a good 'un; if it had been right you'd have got him."

Lott felt ashamed of his momentary jealousy.

"Thank you, sir," he said, "you're very generous. I wish I could think my chief at the Yard'd be the same."

He heaved an anxious sigh. The car was running through the now deserted streets of Hylam.

"I shall get the sack for this," added the C.I.D. man with a return of his usual twinkle. "They'll degrade me to a county constabulary."

"That'd be promotion, my boy," said Dawle with a laugh. "If you're going to be demoted, it'll be to some borough police force."

Lott sat up.

"That's an idea, Super.," he said. "Borough or city. I'll get them to send me to Birmingham."

"Birmingham? Why Birmingham?"

"Ah, Super.," said Lott with a grin. "Thereby hangs a tale."

The car drew up at the doors of the hospital.

If you enjoyed this book you'll want to know about THE PERENNIAL LIBRARY MYSTERY SERIES

Nicholas Blake

☐	P 456	THE BEAST MUST DIE	$1.95
☐	P 427	THE CORPSE IN THE SNOWMAN	$1.95
☐	P 493	THE DREADFUL HOLLOW	$1.95
☐	P 397	END OF CHAPTER	$1.95
☐	P 398	HEAD OF A TRAVELER	$2.25
☐	P 419	MINUTE FOR MURDER	$1.95
☐	P 520	THE MORNING AFTER DEATH	$1.95
☐	P 521	A PENKNIFE IN MY HEART	$2.25
☐	P 531	THE PRIVATE WOUND	$2.25
☐	P 494	A QUESTION OF PROOF	$1.95
☐	P 495	THE SAD VARIETY	$2.25
☐	P 428	THOU SHELL OF DEATH	$1.95
☐	P 418	THE WHISPER IN THE GLOOM	$1.95
☐	P 399	THE WIDOW'S CRUISE	$1.95
☐	P 400	THE WORM OF DEATH	$2.25

E. C. Bentley

☐	P 440	TRENT'S LAST CASE	$2.50
☐	P 516	TRENT'S OWN CASE	$2.25

Buy them at your local bookstore or use this coupon for ordering:

Gavin Black

☐	P 473	A DRAGON FOR CHRISTMAS	$1.95
☐	P 485	THE EYES AROUND ME	$1.95
☐	P 472	YOU WANT TO DIE, JOHNNY?	$1.95

George Harmon Coxe

☐	P 527	MURDER WITH PICTURES	$2.25

Edmund Crispin

☐	P 506	BURIED FOR PLEASURE	$1.95

Kenneth Fearing

☐	P 500	THE BIG CLOCK	$1.95

Andrew Garve

☐	P 430	THE ASHES OF LODA	$1.50
☐	P 451	THE CUCKOO LINE AFFAIR	$1.95
☐	P 429	A HERO FOR LEANDA	$1.50
☐	P 449	MURDER THROUGH THE LOOKING GLASS	$1.95
☐	P 441	NO TEARS FOR HILDA	$1.95
☐	P 450	THE RIDDLE OF SAMSON	$1.95

Buy them at your local bookstore or use this coupon for ordering:

HARPER & ROW, Mail Order Dept. #PMS, 10 East 53rd St., New York, N.Y. 10022.

Please send me the books I have checked above. I am enclosing $ _____ which includes a postage and handling charge of $1.00 for the first book and 25¢ for each additional book. Send check or money order. No cash or C.O.D.'s please.

Name _____

Address _____

City _____ State _____ Zip _____

Please allow 4 weeks for delivery. USA and Canada only. This offer expires 5/1/82. Please add applicable sales tax.

Michael Gilbert

☐	P 446	BLOOD AND JUDGMENT	$1.95
☐	P 459	THE BODY OF A GIRL	$1.95
☐	P 448	THE DANGER WITHIN	$1.95
☐	P 447	DEATH HAS DEEP ROOTS	$1.95
☐	P 458	FEAR TO TREAD	$1.95

C. W. Grafton

☐	P 519	BEYOND A REASONABLE DOUBT	$1.95

Edward Grierson

☐	P 528	THE SECOND MAN	$2.25

Cyril Hare

☐	P 455	AN ENGLISH MURDER	$1.95
☐	P 522	TRAGEDY AT LAW	$2.25
☐	P 514	UNTIMELY DEATH	$2.25
☐	P 523	WITH A BARE BODKIN	$2.25

Robert Harling

☐	P 545	THE ENORMOUS SHADOW	$2.25

Buy them at your local bookstore or use this coupon for ordering:

HARPER & ROW, Mail Order Dept. #PMS, 10 East 53rd St., New York, N.Y. 10022.
Please send me the books I have checked above. I am enclosing $ _____ which includes a postage and handling charge of $1.00 for the first book and 25¢ for each additional book. Send check or money order. No cash or C.O.D.'s please.

Name _____

Address _____

City _____ State _____ Zip _____
Please allow 4 weeks for delivery. USA and Canada only. This offer expires 5/1/82. Please add applicable sales tax.

Matthew Head

☐	P 541	THE CABINDA AFFAIR	$2.25
☐	P 542	MURDER AT THE FLEA CLUB	$2.25

M. V. Heberden

☐	P 533	ENGAGED TO MURDER	$2.25

James Hilton

☐	P 501	WAS IT MURDER?	$1.95

Elspeth Huxley

☐	P 540	THE AFRICAN POISON MURDERS	$2.25

Frances Iles

☐	P 517	BEFORE THE FACT	$1.95
☐	P 532	MALICE AFORETHOUGHT	$1.95

Lange Lewis

☐	P 518	THE BIRTHDAY MURDER	$1.95

Arthur Maling

☐	P 482	LUCKY DEVIL	$1.95
☐	P 483	RIPOFF	$1.95
☐	P 484	SCHROEDER'S GAME	$1.95

Buy them at your local bookstore or use this coupon for ordering:

Austin Ripley

☐ P 387   MINUTE MYSTERIES $1.95

Thomas Sterling

☐ P 529   THE EVIL OF THE DAY $2.25

Julian Symons

☐ P 468   THE BELTING INHERITANCE $1.95
☐ P 469   BLAND BEGINNING $1.95
☐ P 481   BOGUE'S FORTUNE $1.95
☐ P 480   THE BROKEN PENNY $1.95
☐ P 461   THE COLOR OF MURDER $1.95
☐ P 460   THE 31ST OF FEBRUARY $1.95

Dorothy Stockbridge Tillet
(John Stephen Strange)

☐ P 536   THE MAN WHO KILLED FORTESCUE $2.25

Henry Wade

☐ P 543   A DYING FALL $2.25
☐ P 548   THE HANGING CAPTAIN $2.25

Buy them at your local bookstore or use this coupon for ordering:

HARPER & ROW, Mail Order Dept. #PMS, 10 East 53rd St., New York, N.Y. 10022.
Please send me the books I have checked above. I am enclosing $ _____ which includes a postage and handling charge of $1.00 for the first book and 25¢ for each additional book. Send check or money order. No cash or C.O.D.'s please.

Name _____

Address _____

City _____ State _____ Zip _____
Please allow 4 weeks for delivery. USA and Canada only. This offer expires 5/1/82. Please add applicable sales tax.

Henry Kitchell Webster

☐ P 539 WHO IS THE NEXT? $2.25

Anna Mary Wells

☐ P 534 MURDERER'S CHOICE $2.25
☐ P 535 A TALENT FOR MURDER $2.25

Edward Young

☐ P 544 THE FIFTH PASSENGER $2.25